I remember thinking,
I need help, I need . . .

I snagged an outcropping of rock and held on for all I was worth. I watched in horror the spectacle before me, watched as millions were swept down into the yawning pit below me. I gave up any notion of trying to save these poor souls. Instead my full concern was focused on my missing family. I had to get them back, no matter what it took. I was frantic with worry, and that was peculiar, since worry was not usually a part of me.

It was then, by the purest fluke, that I spotted . . . *them.*

Perhaps what caught my eye was that they were still on a boat. Picard, in a dazzling display of single-mindedness, was desperately trying to steer his yacht out of the whirlpool even though it was already heading down into the abyss. Data was there as well, pitching in to the best of his flunky capacity.

The first thought that occurred to me was that I was going to be rid of two irritants. It also happened to be the second thought, as well as the third. But although I lacked the power to control or influence my immediate environment, I was still Q. I reached out, just as Picard and Data's vessel disappeared into the trench, and plucked them back to safety.

Picard immediately demonstrated his gratitude by glaring at me and saying, "Q! So this is *your* doing! I should have *known!*"

STAR TREK
THE NEXT GENERATION®

I, Q

JOHN DE LANCIE
AND PETER DAVID

POCKET BOOKS
New York   London   Toronto   Sydney   Singapore

POCKET BOOKS, a division of Simon & Schuster, Inc.
1230 Avenue of the Americas, New York, NY 10020

Originally published in hardcover in 1999 by Pocket Books

This book is published by Pocket Books, a division of Simon & Schuster, Inc., under exclusive license from Paramount Pictures.

ISBN: 0-671-02444-2

First Pocket Books mass market paperback printing December 2000

10 9 8 7 6 5 4 3 2 1

Printed in the U.S.A.

I, Q

There seemed to be no reason to go on.

The planets . . . the planets had held fascination for her . . . once.

She had contemplated those miracles of natural construction, moving in their relaxed, elliptical paths around their respective suns. They seemed of infinite variety, some huge, some small. Some with rings encircling them, glittering in the rays of starlight that managed to reach and illuminate them. Some were freezing cold, balls of ice in space, while others were volcanic, seething with molten activity, their surfaces in such a constant state of flux that they seemed almost alive. Within these extremes there was a vast spectrum of worlds—temperate, dry, lush and green, flat and dull. An endless assortment of planets from which to choose . . .

But. But, but, but . . .

She was tired of looking. The unending choice had become repetitive. Big worlds, little worlds, inhabitable, uninhabitable . . . what difference did it make? The variety was so endless that, paradoxically, it made them seem very much the same.

Of course there was the multiverse . . . the multiverse had also held fascination for her . . . once.

There was a time when she could have stared *forever* into its mysteries, spent eons contemplating its infinite aspects. She could see endless possibilities, played out simultaneously in a dazzling array, a procession, of realities. In one universe, an action led to war. In another, the same action led to peace, as thousands of events played upon it, one tumbling against another, an array of cosmic dominos. And to shape it all was an activity that was nothing short of amazing.

Oftentimes it had pleased her to study a particular galaxy (chosen at random) in one of the universes that comprised the multiverse.

Since she lived in all times simultaneously, she was able to examine their past, present, and future all at the same time, tracking the delicate fibers of eternity's tapestry. Sometimes she would go backward to discover how a galaxy, or even a world within a galaxy, was progressing in its development. Or she would simply pick a world and watch events unfold. Despite her limitless knowledge, a vision of the future was not always within her purview. She could be as surprised as anyone when things happened a particular way. On occasion she would survey any number of worlds, comparing and contrasting, looking for the similarities and delighting in the differences.

But. But, but, but . . .

She was tired of looking. For she had come to realize that none of it made a difference. Nothing of any consequence would ever truly occur because there were no absolutes, except perhaps that the multiverse had become absolutely, screamingly dull and boring. Because anything could happen, everything seemed pointless.

And of course, there were people. Individuals had fascinated her . . . once.

There were individuals of such vile, irredeemable natures that nothing they ever did was of benefit to the commonweal, and consequently nothing good ever stemmed from their actions. Conversely, there were individuals of such purity that they were incapable of harming anyone or anything.

Of course . . . sometimes the vile individuals inadvertently killed someone who was even more vile than they, so greater suffering was averted. And sometimes those of the purest nature gave succor to someone who wasn't deserving, leaving that individual free to do even greater harm. The same old song that put the "verse" in "multiverse" . . . not to mention "perverse."

But. But, but, but . . .

There was nothing in the multiverse that could really be counted on, nothing that served as a bedrock. The center had not held, and the multiverse, that grand experiment, had become an abysmal failure.

Life. Life had held fascination for her . . . once.

The variety of life that existed was limitless. In one galaxy, there was a race that was so old, it had forgotten it was even alive. In another, a race of beings lived as pure thought. In yet another there was a group that assumed it was the preeminent force, not realizing there was another race far more advanced, albeit microscopic, living out its life as undetectable entities within the minds of the "superior" race, manipulating everything they did. Every war, every discovery, every step forward or back that the "superior" race had taken was, in fact, the collective life of a totally unknown race of beings whose existence hadn't even been thought of and, indeed, never would be discerned by these "oh, so superior" beings.

And yet each life, each race, so different from one another, sought the same things: survival; happiness (although the definitions varied widely), propagation of the species; good food; good companions; good . . . life.

But. But, but, but . . .

3

They were so damned noisy!

When the multiverse began, it wasn't teeming with life. It was gloriously, stupendously quiet. Back then, it was possible to think, to contemplate, to look about and truly appreciate the multiverse for what it was. Unfortunately, it had been impossible to leave well enough alone. More lives had sprung forward, one piling atop another, until the multiverse was a cacophony of voices raised in songs of joy or shouts of protest. It was distracting and annoying; and it made her nostalgic for the way it had been in the beginning. Or at least how it had seemed in the beginning.

She now stood upon the beach and contemplated an end to it all.

She liked the beach. She liked that the water lapped on the shore, caressing the sand like a lover. She liked the horizon: the horizon where the pink sky met the ocean, or the land. This was, of course, a bit fanciful, for they didn't truly meet—it just seemed that way.

Then again, that was the problem, wasn't it? Reality was, after all, remarkably subjective, a term applied by lesser lights who had no real grasp of the Way Things Were. The multiverse provided a dazzling illusion of reality, a thought that only sent her into a deeper spiral of depression on this most fateful of mornings.

The sky was now a dark blue, perhaps mirroring her increasing despair. She allowed the sand to work its way between her toes. She had never really liked her toes. They were too long, not feminine. They were "mannish" toes.

She was more or less satisfied with the rest of her. Her legs were long and lanky, her hips were nicely rounded, and her breasts were just so. She wore no clothing; it was an unnecessary affectation. The breeze caressed her long hair and tickled her shoulders. It felt nice . . . but what was the point of feeling nice? That, too, would pass, as all things did. As all things must. *All* things.

She knelt down and built a sand castle. It was a rather impressive construction. She meticulously designed the turrets, even created a courtyard and a moat. Then she sat back and stared at it, as the sky turned dark.

The water level began to rise, filling the moat, splashing into the channel she had shaped. For a moment, the moat looked as if it would hold and the castle appeared a stout fortress against the rising tide.

But eventually . . . the foundation gave way, as all things eventually give way.

She watched this little drama, seated several yards back with her knees drawn up and her arms wrapped around her legs.

Before too long, the castle had collapsed completely. Its proud turrets were gone, its seemingly unassailable walls a mere memory. And still the water continued to rise.

And still she watched.

The darksome water stopped short of engulfing her, lapping her toes but coming no closer. She simply sat there, immobile as a statue. Finally the tide began to recede, and she couldn't help but stare at the place where the castle had been. There was now only a sinkhole with little bits of flotsam and jetsam swirling about.

It was an image that pleased her, and pleasing images were oh-so-rare.

She looked heavenward, her eyes as dark as the sky itself. Flotsam and jetsam indeed. A sinkhole, all of it, all of it going down the drain. Yes. Yes, she was sure that that was how it was all going to end. She couldn't be absolutely certain, of course. For this was the multiverse, and what occurred was entirely subjective, open to debate every step of the way.

Perhaps that was the most tiresome thing of all. The endless debate, the struggling, the second-guessing. It was more grief than she needed, more than anyone needed. Wouldn't it be nice to have a peaceful end to it all?

She rose and took a step toward the ocean. It was time. On the one hand it seemed as if the ocean took no notice of her. On the other, it appeared to move up toward her, as if begging her to join it. She moved a step closer, and the water showed its excitement. It lapped at her feet. *"Come to me"* it seemed to say. *"Come to me and put an end to it all."*

A third step, a fourth, a fifth . . .

And then . . .

She stepped on something.

She stopped and looked down. It was partially buried in the sand. It appeared to be glass. . . .

A bottle.

"A bottle!?" she said aloud, the first words she could remember uttering in quite some time. She knelt down and picked it up. There was something inside the bottle—a scroll—a message.

Her interest was piqued. The bottle was stoppered, and it took her a few moments to work the cork free. She was surprised to find that the pure action of prying it loose was exciting. She felt a rush of curiosity, of anticipation. Where was this message from? Who had sent it? How had it gotten to this far-flung shore, and what possible significance could it have?

The cork made a most satisfying popping sound when it was finally yanked free. She worked her fingers into the neck; extricating the manuscript was a deliriously prolonged ordeal. Several times, the tips of her fingers grazed the pages, but then the manuscript settled back down into the bottle just out of reach. For a moment she considered breaking the bottle. But she couldn't bring herself to do it. For whatever reason, she felt it was important to keep the bottle intact.

Finally, finally, she snagged the papers securely. Slowly, she slid the sheaf of papers out of the bottle. They were dry, almost brittle to the touch. They didn't unroll easily. It was impossible to tell just how long they'd been in there. She tried to flatten them out on the sand, but they defied her efforts. She finally rolled them in the opposite direction, twisting them delicately back upon themselves, so that at last the pages stayed somewhat flat. The writing was perfectly legible, and after a quick glance she could see that it was a narrative. Yes, a narrative!

And what a truly remarkable narrative it was. There was much within it she already knew, and yet so much that she didn't. To actually discover something outside her knowledge was indeed amazing; it was exhilarating! She read quickly . . . of the great party, and the great pit . . . the amazing descent . . . the trial . . . the riot . . . the terrifying battle atop the train . . . the reunion of father and loved ones . . . the voices crying out . . . the . . .

She stopped for a moment to gather herself. In her nonlinear existence, her perceptions allowing everything to happen all at once, she normally just chose what was of interest to her and never had to worry about missing anything because she could always jump back or speed ahead to see how the matter resolved itself.

And so, for a moment she thought of simply jumping forward and discovering the end of the story. But she resisted the impulse. Instead she sat down on the sand, stacking the pages neatly on her bare thighs. Although the printing was small, there were quite a few pages. Apparently the author had a bit to say.

The blackened sky hung low as if it had business to attend to, but dared not proceed until she gave permission. But at this moment, her attention was most definitely directed elsewhere.

She slid her hands along the manuscript's edge one final time to make sure that the pages were "just so" in their stack, and then she began to concentrate on the narrative while the rest of the universe waited. . . .

The narrative began thus. . . .

I, Q . . . My instinct is to start with me.

It's a natural instinct, I suppose, since I was there at the beginning. I have been around for as long as I can remember, as long as anyone can remember. And until this day—presuming one could call this a day—I had always assumed I would be here forever. Forever, after all, is a very, very long time. One doesn't tend to dwell on the end, because such an event is naturally unthinkable to one such as me.

And if the end ever did come, if we ever did stand on the brink, on the precipice, on the edge (in short) of oblivion, I had always assumed that I and my equally powerful fellows would be able to mount a defense against it. Each of my fellows, even as a lone individual, can do anything. So when you have an entire Continuum of infinitely powerful fellows, it would seem only logical to assume (there's that word again) that there is nothing in the entirety of reality that could possibly stand against our collective will—except a two-year-old who's teething, but that is a nightmare all its own.

Humans, those ever-annoying creatures, have a saying. Actually, they have many sayings. As a race, they're chock-ablock with homilies and aphorisms that cover just about every circumstance that mortal minds can conceive (which, granted, is not saying much). One of those jolly sayings happens to be, "Never 'assume' because it makes an 'ass' of 'u' and 'me.' " It's a fairly tortured dissection of a word simply to make a point, but nonetheless the point is well taken. I assumed, and therefore found myself in deep . . .

Ah, shame on him! I'm sure you're saying to yourself. He shouldn't be starting with himself. How rude, how vainglorious. He should be starting with Jean-Luc Picard and his pocket calculator, Mr. Data. And so I shall.

You see, they were fishing one day when the End of Everything (that's with a big "E") caught their attention. Of course, they had no idea what was really happening because . . .

Oh, to hell with it! They're boring. I'm sorry, but it's true. They have their uses, certainly, and I suppose I have to admit that in our quest to stave off the End (with a big "E") they've been very useful; but the fact is, I'm much more engaging then they are, and if this narrative is going to be even remotely entertaining, I'm going to have to provide that entertainment by talking about myself first.

Me . . . Myself and I. Three of the best pronouns in the language.

It has come to my attention that there have been numerous studies and tomes published about me. Several of them have been circulating on earth, because humans seem to have a fascination with me bordering on the morbidly obsessive.

And I admit I find them rather intriguing, to the point where I lapse into their perspectives and perceptions, using their idioms and metaphors (such as the comment about the two-year-old earlier). One would have hoped I'd have elevated them. Instead, they have dragged me down. Pitiful. There have been publications on other worlds as well, worlds I've visited and where my endeavors and achievements have also been invariably misunderstood. Of course, I sympathize completely. It is as difficult to comprehend a being like me as it is for a paleontologist to understand a dinosaur by looking at a fossilized footprint.

For example, I remember the residents of Kangus IV, an extremely gloomy race who seemed to have an endless fascination with the prospect of their eventual demise. One of their favorite pastimes was to insert their collective consciousness into a great machine that simulated the destruction of their planet. This machine allowed them to safely experience massive quakes, typhoons, starvation, wars, you name it. The machine was so realistic that while they were in the machine, great, gaping fissures would open beneath their feet, giving them a sense of being swallowed whole. What fun! They would then disconnect from the great machine and stumble out into the daylight, only to be drawn back to the extinction simulation over and over again. And for this experience they paid good money, diminishing their incomes as well as placing themselves in a perpetual state of anxiety.

I stumbled upon their rather macabre pastime and took it upon myself to grant their ultimate wish by destroying their world. I thought they would enjoy it! It took no effort at all but, to my surprise, during the actual event there was so much shrieking and crying and gnashing of teeth that I felt compelled to put their world back together again. Apparently, the real-life experience so completely terrified them that they never again had any dealings with the great machine. Which was good, except it caused the financial ruin of the planet and forced the population to actually talk to one another.

Now, I suppose that small digression seems neither here nor there. But then again, at this particular moment in time, neither am I.

In any event . . .

Fascination with me is understandable. I am a fascinating

individual, particularly to the sort of lower life-forms to which Jean-Luc Picard belongs. There have been committees formed specifically to figure out why I do what I do. Come to think of it, on the world of Angus IV, I am considered a force of unrelenting evil, while on Terwil IX, I am called the Laughing God. That's not a nickname I readily understand. I can only assume that they believe I'm off somewhere, doubling over in laughter whenever anything in their little lives goes wrong. I haven't even been around the planet in two thousand of their years, and yet they still fancy that I take an active interest in them. That I'm somehow "watching" and "listening" to their every move and utterance. I don't dare tell them the truth lest they paint themselves blue and jump off the nearest cliff.

Countless books have been written, as I said, about Me . . . Moi . . . Yours truly. In fact, there is an entire division of Starfleet developing contingency plans in case I should happen to show up one day again on earth. Pictures of me, or at least how I am perceived by lesser minds, are circulated like "Most Wanted" leaflets in a galactic post office. There was one individual, a shape-shifter named Zir/xel, who made an extremely comfortable living simply by showing up in various places looking like me. Most of the time he was given whatever he asked until one day he was shot dead—cut down by some desperate individual who actually thought he was shooting Me! As if I could be dispatched in such a manner. The universe is filled with idiots on both sides of the equation.

Of course, "God" affects different people in different ways. Some honor their god with peaceful worship, or by cloistering themselves, or dedicating their lives to helping the less fortunate. Others honor their god by waging war, piling bodies so high that one would think the respective gods in their equally respective heavens would grow sick of the carnage and blast them all to "kingdom come." Life and death, war and peace, all placed at the foot of some supreme being. And since I myself happen to *be* a supreme being, I suppose I can understand why these lesser creatures are so desperate to please those whom they worship. But they seem to feel no compunction in lying, cheating, stealing, or committing the oldest sins in the newest ways as part of the dreary, endless, and pointless endeavor to satisfy their god . . . or is it themselves? I haven't quite figured that out yet. And what's Love got to do with it? Got me! Oh! well . . .

Allow me to introduce myself. . . . I am called "Q." Known to my friends, relatives, and associates as: The Wonderful, The Magnificent, The Living End. I hail from a realm called the Q Continuum, a place that has existed since before time was time. It is our lot to push, to probe, to experiment, and to see the picture within the great tapestry that is the universe. In other words, to boldly go where no one has gone before. At least, that was our mandate when we first started. It has changed somewhat (some would say "mutated," others might say "devolved"), and now my fellow Q specialize in sitting about on the rocking chair of life, watching the universe pass them by.

That has never been an occupation I've found particularly stimulating. So I have taken it upon myself to continue that which I feel is the one true mandate of our Continuum: to question, to stir things up, to make jokes, to "boldly go where . . ." Sorry, I've already said that. . . . I'm repeating myself. How terribly fallible. I told you I've been with humans too long.

I make lesser beings (of which there is a superfluity) feel poorly about their shortcomings—by way of elevating them, of course! Not for a moment do I think they can even approach my level. But sometimes, every so often, they at least get an inkling of just what my level is. It's their opportunity to look up from the pissoir of life and gaze down the boulevard—if only for a moment. Which is why my occasional slippage is so annoying. Ah well. Lay down with pigs, end up a ham. And a one, and a . . .

Another point of useful information: I am omnipotent. Some might think this to be a bad thing. I, of course, do not. It is the state to which I am most accustomed. I am able to accomplish whatever I desire, simply by willing it to be so. There are some who try to moralize about my activities, to act as if what I do is right or wrong. I don't share that point of view. Right? Wrong? Trivial notions, labels applied by those whose expertise is restricted to labeling others. My actions are my own, and I am answerable only to myself. In that respect, I could almost be considered a force of nature. No one questions the ethics of a hurricane, quake, or ion storm. These things simply exist. I am the same way. I am above good and evil. I cannot be measured, judged or assessed, poked or prodded, quantified or qualified, and I'm not the sort you would want to make angry. In other words, don't tread on me.

I travel, I test, and (with any luck) I'm able to raise some species a bit higher than they were before making my acquaintance.

To that end, there is a particular individual to whom I keep finding myself drawn—other than myself, of course. His name is Jean-Luc Picard, and he is a middle-aged, bald, oddly accented man who oversees activities aboard the *Starship Enterprise.* The *Enterprise* is a vessel belonging to an organization called Starfleet, and the *Enterprise* is the flagship of the fleet, which makes it the most advanced ant on the anthill.

When I first met Picard, I thought him an insufferably pretentious man who heartily deserved to be taken down a few pegs. Arrogantly sure of himself, confident in his ability to see all sides of a situation and then arrive at a solution "best for all concerned," Picard epitomized to me everything that was wrong with the human race. Though these aforementioned traits may also be apparent in Me, they are also well justified in Me. There is nothing more galling than some ephemeral little pip-squeak strutting his stuff—but that's a discussion for another time.

Humans. Don't get me started. Damn . . . too late.

A remarkably aggressive and violent race, spreading their barbaric philosophies throughout the galaxy with the same abandon as they spread many a deadly virus, and with about as much concern for the harm they inflict. The fact that humans have survived this long is nothing short of miraculous. We in the Q Continuum have regularly wagered on the likelihood of their demise. I once hazarded a guess that humans would never make it out of the Dark Ages, thinking that I was a lock to win, and was positively shocked when they muddled through. Like cockroaches, humans seem to thrive in nearly impossible circumstances with a determination that borders on supernatural.

Naturally I have endeavored to treat them with the disdain to which their lowly status entitles them.

Yet . . .

As much as I am loath to admit it, one almost has to admire their pluck.

Imagine, if you will, a rather boorish individual who has unknowingly crashed a party, declaring his invitation simply went astray. Despite every exhortation, delivered in tones ranging from the subtle to the blatant, he remains at the party. Of course, he is nothing more than a nuisance, but one

can't help feel a grudging admiration for his determined obtuseness—that, my friends, is a human, in a nutshell. The
equivalent of a clueless partygoer who can't take a hint.

I have tried to explain, on numerous occasions, why humans would be far better off if they stayed put on their pathetic little planet. There are those, such as Picard, who
believe that I am unfairly trying to restrict them. Nothing
could be further from the truth. In point of fact, humans
have the entire concept of exploration backward. They believe that in order to explore, to learn, to grow, to develop,
one must hurl oneself into the void and see "What's Out
There." But they are all in such an infernal hurry! The truth
is, there is an endless amount of self-examination and self-
exploration they could do on their own little world. They
need to turn inward instead of outward, comprehend where
they've been before they can see where they're going. To
hear Picard speak of it, though, one would think they have
left all of their foibles behind them and are, therefore, ready
to take their rightful place in the universe. Yet less than a
millennium ago, they were convinced that the Earth was the
center of the galaxy! In many ways, they're still just as ego-
centric. And while some of them have the good manners to
keep their mouths shut when confronted with more advanced races, they still believe they are wonderfully impressive beings and that the sun rises and sets solely to benefit
them. Yet their own technology constantly outstrips them.
This was particularly a problem in their twentieth century,
when they created an atomic bomb and then had the remarkable lack of foresight actually to detonate it. They invented
the VCR and then couldn't program it! In houses all over
the world, "12:00" blinked on and off in silent mockery of
their "technological advances."

Yet, as I have said, the fact that they are oblivious to these limitations leaves me shaking my head in a sort of grudging admiration. As for Picard, well . . . once he was the target of my unmitigated disdain. Now, however much I hate to admit it, I realize I may very well have misjudged him. He has a dogged habit of not accepting when he is totally outmatched, and he is ingenious enough to find his way out of situations which lesser individuals would dismiss as hopeless. He also displays a stubborn resistance to change, while still tacitly admitting that he has a good deal yet to learn. In many ways, he is a study in contradictions. Then again, so am I. So is any thinking individual, really, because we all must adapt to changing situations. In a universe of free-floating possibilities, a refusal to adapt is about as contrary to nature as one can get.

Yes. Yes, well . . . now that I've waxed on . . . built up a head of steam, I suppose we must reluctantly start with Picard. It makes sense from a narrative point of view. And besides, one always should try to work from the lesser to the greater. In that spirit, we will begin with Picard and work up to Me.

Now, of course, you may be wondering how I know what Picard was up to on *the* morning, that fateful morning that began the last of all days. I suppose you've heard of the literary technique of the omniscient narrator. Well, who is more entitled to assume that title than one who is genuinely omniscient?

So . . . to get back to my story: Picard and Data were fishing.

I suppose I should speak for just a bit about Data. Mr. Calculator Man . . . Ah . . . I just keep interrupting myself, don't I? Well, that's my privilege. But not yours, so don't get any ideas.

Data is conceivably the most pitiable sentient being in all

creation: a gold-skinned android who should have the word "wistful" tattooed on his forehead. I have already explained to you my problem with humans and their various shortcomings. Well, if humans can be considered a laughably pretentious species, what could be worse than a creature whose highest aspiration is to *be* a human? How inconceivably sad is that?

In Data we have a being who is, in most ways, infinitely superior to humans. He does not age, does not require sustenance, and is heir to none of the frailties that plague humans. In terms of intellect, he is light-years beyond even their most brilliant minds. Even his one alleged "failing," a lack of emotion, is compensated for with an implanted chip that gives him the full range of human emotions. Yet he still considers himself inferior. He wishes to be one of them, and would give up all the advantages that his android status bestows upon him if only he could be a human being. To put it delicately, his desire is shortsighted. To put it indelicately, it's bone stupid. The only rationalization I can offer is that he has been hanging around humans for too long. He would truthfully be better served if he got as far away from them as possible. Cozying up to an old Volvo or maybe a pencil sharpener would do him a world of good! But I know that's not going to happen anytime soon, and so I can only sigh and ponder the remarkable waste of material that Data's aspiration represents.

Picard and Data on this particular morning were on the holodeck of the *Enterprise.* They spend a lot of time together, those two: a boy and his computer. The holodeck is, in many ways, the ultimate fantasy fulfillment—an outgrowth of an ancient form of entertainment called the "movies." It gives humans the opportunity to control, completely and utterly, their environment . . . and their fantasies. With a few words, they can shape the holodeck into whatever "reality" they desire. The fact that this reality is, in fact, unreal doesn't matter a whit when you get right down to it. Humans have so little comprehension of the true nature of reality that there might as well be no difference at all between holodecks and the real universe. As long as they can strap on a feedbag of buttered popcorn and guzzle a gallon of sugar water—all's right with the world.

So . . . back to the holodeck. Picard and Data were relaxing on a small yacht, which was named the *Hornblower* for some reason that I'm sure was important to Picard, but makes little difference to this narrative. The sea was quite calm, because Picard, master of all he surveys, wanted it that way: the ultimate indulgence for one who wishes to control all aspects of the world around him . . . a description that certainly fit Picard to a "tee." The sky was a rich blue, and seagulls circled high above. Picard smiled in satisfaction. In fact, all was right with his world.

Picard was seated in a comfortable chair, which was bolted to the deck of the ship. His rod and reel, locked into a stand in front of him, were easily removable should he manage to snare "the big one." Data was similarly positioned, but while Picard was busy gazing at the sky, Data's entire attention was focused on the fishing gear. Picard couldn't help but notice the intensity with which Data was regarding the pole.

"Data," he said with a familiar touch of reproof in his voice, "this is supposed to be a relaxing exercise."

"Oh?" Data ran this casual instruction through his positronic brain. Understand, an instruction from Picard to plot a course to a star cluster at the far end of Federation space would have been carried out without any hesitation. But the simple order to "relax" required the full weight of Data's brain power to come into focus, and even then he was somewhat befuddled. He interlaced his fingers uncertainly and rested them upon his lap in an attempt to "assume the position." When that seemed insufficient, he awkwardly crossed his legs and simultaneously slumped his shoulders, but he merely looked like a marionette with its strings cut. What made it even more ludicrous was that Data was in full uniform. Picard, at least, had the good aesthetic sense to be sporting a polo shirt, a pair of blue shorts, and sandals.

"Is this sufficiently relaxed, Captain?"

Picard seemed about to say something, but instead he shrugged and replied, "If it's good enough for you, Mr. Data, it's good enough for me."

Perhaps sensing that his relaxed posture was not all that his captain had been hoping for, Data said, "My apologies, Captain. I am not adept at relaxation. I have no such needs."

"It's more than just physical relaxation, Data," Picard said, his eye never straying from the ocean. "It's relaxation of the mind as well. In a way, it's a sort of art form, being able to screen out all your concerns. Believe it or not, 'quality' relaxing can take a lot of work. To just lie back and think about nothing . . ."

"That I can do quite easily," said Data.

"Can you?"

"Certainly." Data paused a moment, and then his head tilted slightly to one side. He stared off into nothingness.

"Data . . ." Picard said cautiously.

Nothing.

"Data."

Still nothing.

"*Data!!*" Picard snapped his fingers in front of Data's face. The android appeared startled as he turned and looked at his captain. "Are you all right? Is anything wrong?"

"No, sir. Nothing is wrong. Actually, in this case, I thought 'nothing' was what you ordered."

Picard laughed softly to himself. "Yes, Data. Carry on . . . carry on."

Data was puzzled, but I suppose he felt it was pointless to pursue the conversation in a fruitless quest for clarification. In observing his interactions with humans, I have lost count of the number of times that Data has chosen not to continue a line of inquiry simply because he realized he was not going to get a coherent answer. I believe the old human phrase for it was, "Garbage in, garbage out."

"Fishing used to be one of my favorite pastimes when I was a lad," Picard said, mercifully taking it upon himself to change the subject. "Oh, I didn't have a ship like this, and it wasn't deep-sea fishing. My father and I would fish in a lake near our home. Simple rod and reel, much simpler than this," and he patted the array in front of him. "Fancy equipment takes the sport out of fishing. Sonar locators, ultrasonic lures that the fish can't resist. My father wouldn't have truck with any of that." Picard dropped his voice an octave in what he presumably thought was a reasonable imitation of his father. "'Man vs. fish, the way nature intended it to be, son.' That's what he'd say to me. A rod, a reel, a worm on the line, that was all you needed. And whatever we caught, we'd take home and prepare for dinner. 'If you catch it, you cook it.' Another bit of paternal wisdom; he couldn't abide waste. My father and I would chat about whatever occurred to us. No holds barred, anything could be discussed. *That* was a *relaxing* way to spend a day."

"Not for the fish," said Data.

"No. Not for the fish," agreed Picard. "We didn't dwell much on what the fish thought. I suppose that's the way of the world. Those above don't have as much concern for those below. It's all subjective, I suppose. But now this fish," Picard continued, patting the rod in front of him, "this fish is quite a different story from the fish my father and I pursued. We're going after . . ." and his eyes glittered with anticipation, "Big Arnold."

"Big Arnold, sir?"

Picard nodded. "A massive swordfish. This big . . . no . . . this big," and he readjusted his arms to encompass the entirety of the creature he was describing. "They say he's so big that he can haul your ship halfway to Bermuda before you know what's hit you. Big Arnold has thwarted the dreams of every fisherman in these parts. But today, Data . . . today is definitely the day."

"Did you program it to be the day, sir?"

"I programmed randomness, Mr. Data. We are sportsmen, after all. There's no fun in forcing the fish to come to you through computer imperatives. If we find him, we find him, and if we don't, we don't. But I'm betting," and he rubbed his hands together in anticipation, "that today is our day!"

"You do not appear relaxed, Captain," Data said. "Your body seems tense, actually."

"Anticipation and relaxation aren't mutually exclusive, Data."

"Is this another topic relating to point of view, Captain?"

"I would say that's a fair assessment, Mr. Data, yes. Then again, all topics relate to point of view, don't they? It's all in how we see the universe: You, I, the fish, all of us."

"They are widely disparate viewpoints," Data pointed out. "For example, since you are fond of discussing fish, it should be noted that they possess a memory of approximately 2.93 seconds. Were you aware that if you put two goldfish in a bowl, upon meeting, their dialogue would sound something like this? 'Oh, what a surprise. Nice to meet you.' Then they would swim on. Thirty seconds later, having completely forgotten the previous meeting and finding themselves face to face again, they would say, 'Oh, what a surprise. Nice to meet you!' It seems a rather pointless existence, since all knowledge is transitory and, as a consequence, meaningless."

"Look at it another way," Picard said. "Every minute crammed with discovery! Never a dull moment. One surprise after another."

"But they never learn, sir. A life without acquisition of knowledge is a meaningless life. I am aware of some humans who go through life never learning and never forgetting. It would seem fish go through life never learning and never remembering. I do not think that is good."

"I don't know about that, Data. Who are we to say that the way we go through life is in any way superior to what a fish experiences?"

"As you said, sir, we are the ones on this end of the fishing line."

Picard laughed. "Yes . . . yes . . . quite right . . ."

At that moment, Picard's fishing line snapped taut. There was a high-pitched "whizzing" sound as the line spooled out of the reel. Picard promptly belted himself into his seat and grabbed the rod. "We have a strike, Data!"

"So it would seem, sir. Is there anything I should do?"

"Pray!"

About forty yards away something big broke the surface. "I think it's him! Big Arnold himself!"

"Are you sure, Captain?"

At that moment, the fish leapt high into the air. He was massive, water glistening on his scaly hide. His long snout, like a rapier, pointed skyward before he plunged back into the sea.

"Positive!" crowed Picard.

For long minutes, Picard fought the fish, man against nature in microcosm. Data simply watched. Picard had stopped talking, except for occasionally muttering self-encouragement such as, "Come on, Picard, you can do it. He's yours, he's yours."

Fortunately, no one but Data was there to witness Picard's bizarre murmurings.

Suddenly the good ship *Hornblower* pitched sharply in the direction of the struggling fish. Picard was genuinely surprised that the creature was capable of putting up such a fight.

The ship lurched a second time, then a third. The fourth time, the whole ship began to move backward, jolting Picard from his supreme confidence, ever so slightly.

"Shall I activate the engines, sir?" asked Data.

"No . . . no, it's all right. Let him wear himself out. He can't pull us forever." But there was doubt in Picard's voice, notable in that anything approaching humility was a rarity for Picard.

The ship continued its backward motion, faster and faster. Picard held resolutely to the rod. "Something's wrong," he said. "Something is very wrong. I don't think it's the fish that's pulling us."

"Then what is, sir?"

"I don't know . . ." There was a large knife in a bracket along the nearby wall. "I hope I don't regret this," he said, reaching for the knife to sever the line. But suddenly, the line snapped on its own, and Big Arnold was gone. Fortunately for him, in 2.93 seconds he would forget any contact he'd ever had with Picard. Lucky fish, that one.

However, the *Hornblower* did not slow down. If anything, it sped up. Something was pulling it farther and faster out to sea.

The skies above them began to darken, and a stiff wind

rose. The seas became confused, surging furiously. Anything that wasn't fastened down rolled about the deck. Picard looked at the massive thunderheads rolling in. "What in hell is going on?" he demanded.

"You did indicate random elements in the program, sir," Data pointed out with admirable sangfroid.

"I know, I know, but *this* . . . ?" He waved his arms about like a confused scarecrow. "I didn't program this. . . ."

"Captain, we are no longer moving in full reverse," Data informed him. "We are now angling approximately thirty degrees to port, and our speed is increasing."

"Engines on-line, Mr. Data! Quickly, if you wouldn't mind."

Data fired up the engines, but even at full bore, there was no change in direction. The sound of the engines was now completely lost in the howling of the wind and the rumbling of thunder overhead. The ship's propellers slowed the vessel for only a few moments and then the pull of the sea overwhelmed them again.

"Captain!" Data's voice cut through screaming wind. "Whirlpool, dead ahead!"

"Whirlpool?" Picard glanced over his shoulder in astonishment.

The whirlpool was immense—miles wide. It let out a roar like a million souls howling for redemption. Its interior was the inkiest black. It dragged the *Hornblower*, as well as everything else, toward its maw. The ship had no means of escape.

At this point, Picard clearly had had enough, and decided to play his trump card. "End program!" he shouted above the screeching wind.

Nothing. His instruction to the holodeck didn't register at all. He might as well not have said anything. "End program!" he bellowed, even louder than before.

Still nothing. The holodeck ignored him.

"Captain!" Data called to him. "Permission to be unrelaxed, sir!"

Picard didn't bother to answer; he was trying to think, his thoughts racing, tumbling over one another in a barely controlled torrent. Abandoning ship was not an option. For some reason the holodeck appeared intent on turning what was to be a casual day of fishing into a nightmare, and there wasn't a single thing he could do about it.

The *Hornblower* was now caught on the outer rim of the whirlpool. From that point on, it was only a matter of time before the ship would be swallowed completely. The ship began to spin about in ever-tightening circles.

As he looked into the whirlpool, he could see hundreds, thousands of objects, spiraling down, down. "What in the name of God . . . ?" he shouted, but the rest of his famous last word were lost as he, Data, and his ship plunged into the blackness below.

Fishing on Dante IX is quite different from what Picard and Data had been doing on the Holodeck of the *Enterprise*. As a matter of fact, the term "deep-sea fishing" on Dante IX is so literal, it's downright comical. Let me briefly explain. We of the Q, you see, can go wherever we wish, and whether it's the depths of space or the bottom of an ocean is of no matter one way or the other.

The fish on Dante IX are monstrous compared to the relatively puny creatures Picard was hunting. They make their homes at the bottom of the ocean, never getting near the surface at all. Consequently, not only do the residents of Dante IX never eat fish, but many of them don't even believe that fish exist, having never seen them.

But they do exist. And they make fine eating.

Of course, being a member of the Q Continuum, I don't have the same need for sustenance that Picard and his ilk require. But that doesn't mean I'm incapable of enjoying a fine delicacy when it's available. I could, naturally, just will the creature onto a plate, but where's the sport in that?

So my family and I went "deep-sea fishing" this fine day; and we were doing it while standing at the bottom of the ocean—that's the "deep-sea" part. My family, by the by, consisted of myself, my wife (to whom I shall refer for your convenience as Lady Q, although we tend to address each other simply as Q since we all know who we are), and my son, whom I hereby designate as little "q."

The Lady Q is a rather brassy individual, with a low tolerance for foolishness of any kind—most particularly mine, if truth be told. But although she displays little patience for me, she dotes endlessly (some would say nauseatingly) upon our son, q. I can hardly blame her. Young q maintains a unique position in the universe—to say nothing of history—in that he is the first Q born within the Continuum. The closest before that was Amanda Rogers, and she was conceived and raised on Earth . . . the poor thing.

As a result, Lady Q takes the responsibility of his upbringing most seriously. As for me, my position is that "all work and no play" makes for a dull boy. Needless to say (but I'll say it anyway), harmony is not a constant in our household.

At this particular point in time, q was the equivalent of ten Earth years old. He was, of course, far ahead of that in *actual* development. A young omnipotent being is hardly the same creature as a young mere mortal. Still, he had a good deal of learning to do, and I was doing my level best as his father to instruct him in the many splendors and varieties of experience the universe had to offer. The Lady Q, however, felt obligated to keep a sharp eye on him . . . and, more than likely, on me. Her perpetual suspicion of me is a trait that I have chosen (because I have no other choice, really) to find endearing. There are times she is as cuddly as Lady Macbeth! So when q was intrigued with the idea of deep-sea fishing on Dante IX (I had regaled him with tales of my youth), she chimed in that she was game for fishing as well. Frankly, I'm convinced she was motivated more by the principle of spying on me than by any real interest in fishing.

So there we were, the three of us, comfortably situated on

the ocean floor, rods in our hands, and the fishing lines floating a good two hundred feet or so above us. The Dante IX fish are rather clever, you see . . . at least, clever as far as fish go. So I decided the best plan was to get right down in the goo and let our hooks dangle up from the bottom. They would never expect us coming from that direction. So far none of the fish had gone for the bait, but I was quite certain that they would before long.

"I almost feel sorry for them, Father," said q.

"Why?"

"They don't have a chance against us. We're of the Q Continuum, and they're just fish."

"That's their lot in life, son," I replied. "Just because they're fish doesn't mean that we have to feel sympathy for them."

"It doesn't hurt to do so," Lady Q said blithely. She had a rather offhand way of speaking when she was contradicting me, something she did quite often. "Having sympathy for lower life-forms is a good habit to learn."

"My, aren't we the sentimentalist today?" I said.

"My darling Q," said the Lady, between clenched teeth, "might I remind you that the times in your life you've gotten into the most trouble have been caused precisely by a lack of sympathy for lower life-forms?"

"Your mother is exaggerating."

"Your mother is doing nothing of the kind," said Lady Q.

"What sort of trouble did you get in, Father?" asked q. His eyes were wide with excitement.

"Well . . ." I shifted uncomfortably on the silt of the ocean floor. I didn't like the way the conversation was going. "There was that time when the Continuum . . ."

"Go on," she said.

". . . was miffed . . . and we had a falling out."

"They took away his powers," she said with excessive cheerfulness.

"They did!" He looked amazed, his eyes widening to the point that they threatened to abandon his face. "What was that like?! Were you scared? You must have been scared!"

"I was . . . disconcerted. But not scared. Never scared." I looked at Lady Q, as if daring her to contradict me once more.

Her features softened into a smile. "He was not scared," she agreed, looking at me with—dare I say it—genuine admiration. "I will give him that. I have seen your father in many different situations. I've seen him angry, petulant, upset, arrogant . . . but afraid? Never."

"And you never will," I said, secretly grateful for this ringing, if not entirely candid, endorsement.

Then, to my surprise, q reached over and—still holding on to his line—hugged me impulsively. I wasn't quite sure how to react to it. Physical contact has never been my forte. "What's this about?" I asked.

"For being the bravest father in the universe," he said, and he looked up at me in that trusting manner that only children can muster. The kind of manner that makes you feel as if you're the entirety of their universe. "Promise you'll never leave us."

"I can't promise that, q. There are always matters I have to attend to . . ."

"Promise . . . you'll never leave us alone."

There was an urgency to the request that I could readily understand.

No one should be left alone. The solitude, the emptiness—what it does to the mind and spirit—there is nothing in the universe worse than that. You may think there is . . . but there isn't. Not really.

"I will never leave you alone. Not ever, I promise," I said firmly. "In fact, I . . ."

At that moment, I got a good yank on my fishing line. I looked up and a creature only slightly smaller than your average whale had hooked onto my lure.

"Get him, Father!" crowed my son.

Naturally, I could have reeled him in, but I decided to make a bigger moment of it than it truly had to be. The things we do to amuse our children. And so I allowed the creature to yank me entirely off my feet. He kept on swimming, moving quickly, as if he had a chance in the world of escaping from the hook that had lodged solidly in his mouth. I dangled behind him, waving my hands rather comically and showing off, crying out, "Oooo! Ooo! What*ever* am I going to do?!"

I was rewarded with peals of laughter from my son, and an amused-but-silent shaking of the head by Lady Q. It was all quite comical as I pretended to be terror-stricken and I found, to my surprise, that it was fun. It brought me—dare I say it—pleasure.

Understand, I had never anticipated having any affinity for child rearing. Intellectually, I understood all the reasons it should be done, but I was far more concerned with the impact it would have on the Q Continuum. The Continuum had become far too complacent; indeed, it was positively stodgy. New blood was desperately needed. And when one wants to liven things up, there is nothing quite like the pitter-patter of little feet down the spaceways.

Nevertheless, secretly I had regarded the child as a means to an end. I am not, by nature, an affectionate person. The notion of being a caring father who paid attention to and even doted on a child frankly never occurred to me. It was such an unlikelihood that it never warranted serious consideration.

Yet here we were, or at least here I was. There was something in the way the boy looked at me that stirred something within. Perhaps it was the sheer idolization and awe he radiated. Perhaps it was his unspoken ambition to grow up and be just like his father. Perhaps it was . . .

Perhaps it was . . .

. . . that I had no recollection of any father myself.

Not father nor mother.

It is not a subject upon which I choose to dwell, at least not at this time.

In any event, I had come to realize that there was a void within me that I did not know existed. I would not have let someone like Picard, for instance, know of such a thing. He would be entirely too smug, or would make cloying and overly cute comments about my displaying a "human side." I suppose it's simply part of the overwhelming human need to see aspects of humanity no matter where it looks, as if the universe were humanity's mirror and humanity had an urge to admire itself and preen in front of it.

At least we members of the Q Continuum have reason to be arrogant and self-satisfied; we have reason to preen. We really *are* superior, as opposed to humans, who simply *think* they are.

All in all, it was best if Picard and his emotional brethren remained eternally unaware that their "nemesis," their "trickster god," their "own personal demon" had a disgustingly soft spot that could only be described as humanesque in its makeup. No, I certainly didn't need the aggravation of smarmy comments rolling off Picard's lips. Granted, Janeway of the *Voyager* had an inkling, but they were sufficiently isolated so that my reputation would remain untarnished.

So there I was, being "dragged" by the fish. The great

beast swam this way and that, doing everything he could to shake me loose. Naturally, since he was dealing with something beyond his extraordinarily limited experience, disengaging from me was simply not an option. The sounds of my son's laughter, and the amused chuckles from my spouse, followed me as the creature thrashed about more and more. I willed my weight to treble, and then to increase exponentially, and slowly my vastly increased mass brought the exertions of the wayward fish to a halt.

I was about to reel in the leviathan when I noticed that the water was flowing against me—quickly. I, all of a sudden, had the feeling of being in a river, a very swiftly moving river.

This was nothing short of astounding. Dante IX only had one small moon. Certainly whatever effect it had on the planet's ocean wasn't sufficient to cause this sort of tidal action. No, it most definitely was not the moon that was causing this anomaly. And there were no storms on the surface . . . so, what could it be?

It was then I heard the first small buzz of alarm at the back of my neck, my first inkling that something was indeed wrong. I immediately tried to stop the movement of the water. This endeavor should have required no great effort. A simple willed command from me should have been enough to bring the water to a halt. I am Q, after all. If I couldn't calm the waters, I wouldn't have been worthy of the letter. I would have been a P or an R. But I was a Q, and how could the water simply ignore my desires?

And yet that was exactly what it was doing! What began as a casual command developed into a contest of wills. I ordered the water to stop, and when that didn't work, I alternately commanded, begged, sobbed, howled, and an assortment of other stratagems that I can't now bring myself to admit. And all of this happened, you should understand, within the space of a few seconds.

Nothing helped. Nothing slowed the water, or even came close to slowing it. The ocean around me had simply gone berserk, and nothing I could do seemed to persuade it to act in a manner that was remotely sensible.

That was when I heard a scream.

It was the Lady Q. My "antics" with the fish had dragged me out of their sight, but I heard the cry of alarm distinctly. There was an accompanying shout from my son as well, and in those two screams I heard something that was utterly unthinkable as far as the Q Continuum is concerned: fear. Pure, stomach-wrenching, gut-twisting fear.

My immediate instinct was simply to rematerialize myself at their sides, but I resisted the impulse. Whatever they were facing, I didn't want to appear right in the middle of it, thereby leaving myself open to ambush. Besides, I would get there fast enough by simply allowing nature to take its course. The current of the water was a fearful thing, and it sent me spiraling straight back toward where I had left my family. The fish I had been trying to haul in was long forgotten. Indeed, for a moment I thought I saw him some yards away being pulled along with me, but this was no time to dwell on the fate of sea creatures.

The water was dark ahead of me, forming itself into a huge black funnel. Down, down, the water swirled . . . into an enormous crevice—and my family with it. Even though I no longer heard their screams and cries, even though I couldn't see them, I knew that they had been swept into the void. My every instinct told me so, and my instincts were never wrong.

They must have been standing near the fissure when it opened. Under ordinary circumstances, the Lady Q would have been able to propel both of them to safety, but this had all happened much too quickly, and the circumstances were far from ordinary.

I reached out with my mind to communicate with my missing mate and son.

Nothing. Nothing at all. They were gone, swallowed up.

I was alone. The concept was even worse in the reality than it was in the abstract.

I remember thinking, *I need help, I need . . .*

That was when I started to hear other screams. For a moment, I imagined that the yawning pit below me was the gateway to an afterlife of eternal punishment which I had always believed did not exist.

Upon closer examination I now saw creatures, thousands, perhaps millions, caught up in the whirlpool like ants circling a drain. I looked in vain for any trace of my family, but the Lady Q and q were not among them. They had already disappeared into the pit.

I snagged an outcropping of rock and held on for all I was worth. I watched in horror the spectacle before me, watched as millions were swept down. I gave up any notion of trying to save these poor souls. Instead my full concern was focused on my missing family. I had to get them back, no matter what it took. I was frantic with worry, and that was peculiar, since worry was not usually a part of me.

It was then, by the purest fluke, that I spotted . . . *them.*

Perhaps what caught my eye was that they were still on a boat. Picard, in a dazzling display of single-mindedness, was desperately trying to steer his yacht out of the whirlpool even though it was already heading down into the abyss. Data was there as well, pitching in to the best of his flunky capacity.

The first thought that occurred to me was that I was going to be rid of two irritants. It also happened to be the second thought, as well as the third.

The fourth thought brought with it a tired and frustrated sigh, because I knew precisely what track this train of thought was roaring down.

Perhaps I lacked the power to control or influence my immediate environment, but I was still Q. I shut from my mind the image of the Lady Q and q vanishing into the abyss, their cries for help that went unanswered, their outstretched arms . . . such images would only impede what I now had to accomplish. I reached out, just as Picard and Data's vessel disappeared into the trench, and plucked them back to safety. I suppose the move served my ego as much as any interest in their well-being because at least I got to feel that I'd accomplished *some*thing. They now crouched next to me, balanced precariously on a cliff overlooking the maelstrom below.

Picard immediately demonstrated his complete ignorance and ingratitude by glaring at me and saying, "Q! So this is *your* doing! I should have *known!*"

Some humans are so naturally boorish, they don't even have to work at it. I was in no mood. "Shut up, Picard!" I shot back at him. "My wife and son just disappeared into that thing, and if I hear one more word out of you, *one more word,* you're going to be next! Do I make myself clear!"

Picard had never seen me angry, not . . . really angry. Truth to tell, he didn't see me really angry at that moment either. If he ever did witness such a spectacle, it would most likely sear his retinas. He was clearly taken aback, and I heard Data say to him in a low voice, "It would seem that Q is as powerless in this situation as we."

"Don't flatter yourself, Data," I retorted. "If I were as powerless as you, you would be down there!" And I pointed to the abyss.

"What's causing this, then?" Picard said, a touch less arrogant than before. "Someone, something, must be behind it. Is it a natural phenomenon? What is it? Do you have any idea, Q?"

A half a dozen answers immediately came to mind. But I said "No," which was extremely bothersome. The notion of being as much in the dark was odious to me. "No, I don't know." I waited while Picard coughed up water from his lungs. "It just started . . . happening . . . while I was fishing."

"But where are we?"

"Well, I was on Dante IX. You were on the holodeck. . . ."

Picard looked dumbfounded. "How did you know?"

"Because I'm Q, that's how. What part of 'omniscient' is unclear to you?"

"Save the attitude, Q. Now is not the time."

That was true enough. I had slipped automatically into old habits. We stood there, the three of us, in silence, my power still maintaining our safety zone. I was becoming truly apprehensive. I didn't know how long I would be able to sustain the protection, but I was already tired from doing so. I wracked my brain for alternatives, and that was the moment Picard decided to become compassionate. "I'm sorry," he said softly.

"Sorry? For what?"

"I had no idea that you had either a wife or a son. This must be . . . very painful. . . ."

"Picard, you've no idea what I'm experi . . ."

It was Data who interrupted us. "Sir," he said, pointing upward, "it appears the whirlpool is . . . draining the ocean dry."

"Impossible," said Picard, but he didn't sound completely certain.

"Not only is it not impossible, sir, but it is occurring at an accelerated pace."

That last comment was obvious, as the water that threatened to suck us down like so much debris was now moving ever faster. I strained myself to the utmost, Picard and Data clutching the rocks just in case my "comfort zone" evaporated and we found ourselves exposed to the ravages of the sea. Water swirled around us, faster and faster . . .

. . . and then it was gone.

It vanished with a loud popping sound, as if someone had just released the cork from a bottle. A few stray puddles of water remained . . . but all around us was land— land that until a few moments ago had been covered by the ocean. Mountain ranges, and wide plains as far as the eye could see, thick with marine vegetation and very much exposed.

The sky was dark, the sun just barely peeking through. Even so, it was certainly the first time the sun of Dante IX had ever shone upon that world's seabed.

The water was gone, and what lay beneath us, in full view, was a huge trench. It stretched as far as the eye could see, and its depth was unknowable. What I did know was that I had witnessed countless poor devils from a variety of dimensions being hauled into that abyss. Picard and Data had seen it too. They had been, after all, in the midst of it.

And the victims were hardly local, or even limited to a couple of races. I'd seen humans, Andorians, Vulcans, Tellarites, Klingons, Cardassians, Borg, on and on, with the maelstrom giving no preference, making no distinction between peace-loving and warmongering. All were equal, all were helpless, and all were gone . . .

. . . except us.

What seemed an eternity passed before I rose unsteadily to my feet and said, "All right . . . now . . . I'm going in after them."

"What?" Picard said.

"I'm going in. Understand me, Picard," I said and turned to face him, "you and your entire species can go hang, along with the rest of the universe. But someone took my wife and my son, and I'm going in there to get them!"

"It's foolishness."

He said it with such deathly calm that I couldn't quite believe it. "Did you hear what I said? My family"—I pointed at the abyss—"is down there!"

"Look at your hand," Picard said quietly. "The one you're pointing with. Look at it."

Despite my better judgment, I did as he instructed. I noticed that it was trembling. I tried to steady it. I couldn't. A hand that could collapse a planet with a gesture, and I was unable to keep it still.

Picard, however, was the picture of cool.

"Before you embark on any sort of rescue mission, you have to calm yourself. If you do not, you will rush headlong into a situation that could prove fatal to you, and then of what benefit will you be to your family?"

"But . . . but . . ." The "but" came easily; everything after that simply hung there, unspoken.

"I know you're frustrated," Picard continued. "I know that you want to charge to the rescue. But you'll be serving yourself, your wife, and your son far better if you take some time to investigate the situation."

"I can conduct a full scientific analysis," Data offered. "Certainly by computing the events and studying samples of the—"

I gestured impatiently for him to be quiet. "That's going to take too long!"

As much as it galled me, however, Picard was right. I needed to find out what was going on before jumping to conclusions. I turned away from the abyss. "And what of you?" I asked after a moment. "Do you want to come along? Or shall I find a way to get you back to your starship?"

Picard looked up at the sky, and then once more at the trench. "If something this widespread is happening, it's only a matter of time before the *Enterprise* is affected . . . before everything in existence is affected. If it's possible to head it off now, so much the better. Besides," he said smugly, "I'm getting the impression that you need us."

"Keep telling yourself that, Picard." I clapped my hands and rubbed them briskly. "So . . . the way I see it, there's only one sensible place for us to go."

"Where would that be . . . ?" Data asked. He actually seemed interested. Perhaps androids are programmed to enjoy going to new places.

"The Q Continuum," I said. "They would know what's going on."

"But . . . but how do we get to—?"

"Leave it to me," I said, snapping my fingers for dramatic effect. We vanished in a flash of light.

I have an intense dislike of crowds. The reason is quite simple: one tends to get lost in crowds, and I find that notion deplorable. I don't like blending in. I prefer to let the universe know that I'm "on deck" and "ready for action!"

Occasionally, I find myself in crowds, nonetheless. So I turn it into an opportunity to study what happens when a large number of sentient beings gather and try to engage in some sort of celebration or ritual.

I remember one occasion on a Rigel colony composed largely of humans. They were in the midst of celebrating a holiday, which had its origins on Earth, called "Fat Tuesday." It seemed an odd choice of name. I've never thought of the days of the week as being either fat or thin, but I have long ago learned that trying to discern coherent or rational thinking in humans is an utter waste of time.

By the way, this particular event took place right on the heels of my very first encounter with Picard at Farpoint. Between you (whoever that may be) and me, I found everyone on the *Enterprise* remarkably stuck-up and completely incapable of having anything approaching a good time . . . with the possible exception of the security chief, Tasha Yar, who I thought had real potential. Unfortunately that potential was never as fully developed as Yar herself. More's the pity. Of course, I didn't let on for a moment that I was in any way disapproving of Picard and his crew—quite the contrary. I worked "overtime" to elicit a smile, to infuse a sense of fun. But there's just so much you can do before that kind of "poopiness" drags even the most devout partygoer into the toilet. After a valiant effort on my part to "put a good face" on the occasion, it became painfully evident to me that it was time to leave the good ship *Enterprise* and find another party if I had any hopes of retrieving the evening.

In any event, that's how I wound up on the Rigel colony on Fat Tuesday.

I chose not to let the colonists know that a being of infinite power was walking in their midst. Why? Because the recent experience with Picard was fresh in my mind—two nanoseconds fresh, to be precise. How depressing the whole episode had been. One would have thought that Picard, when confronted by a superior creature such as myself, would have had the common decency to at least genuflect. But no. No laughs, no genuflections. Naturally, I was now leery of the entire human race. So, when I popped in on the Rigel colony to observe their Fat Tuesday revelries, I did so incognito.

The colony was packed. There were people lining the streets, laughing, singing, drinking—it was so refreshing! Although, when two besotted humans had the temerity to elbow me in the ribs, I indulged in some harmless gene rearrangement. I assure you that a few hours spent as lice on a chimp's back did them no end of good, doubtlessly improving their appreciation of lower species (presuming that there are species lower than humans) and encouraging them to watch where they were going in the future.

As I made my way through the overcrowded avenues, I observed humans in their element. This holiday, apparently, gave them license to engage in activities that would have made a merchant mariner blush. There were times I actually averted my gaze lest my delicate nature be too offended. Of course, these humans showed no hint of shame. Quite the contrary, they looked upon the celebration as an opportunity to revert to their true natures, on the assumption that the holiday absolved them of the most lascivious indiscretions. Debauchery by an individual is deplorable. Debauchery en masse is a party.

During the drunken revelries a crone of a woman approached me with what could only be considered, even by human standards, a rather demented gleam in her eye. "There's a red dot patrol at the end of the street," she said, her back a bit stooped and her face tilted to look up at mine.

I cocked an eyebrow and decided, out of a sense of scientific curiosity, to engage the crone for a moment. "Indeed?"

She had a sheet of round red stickers in her hand, and she bobbed her head as she said, "Oh yes, yes indeed. They're checking to make sure that you're wearing a red dot. But don't worry. I'll take care of you."

I began to ask just how she intended to do that when, to my astonishment, she peeled one of the dots from the sheet of paper and slapped the absurd little thing on my groin. I stared at her. "Are you insane?"

"Gives you protection. Here, let me make sure it's on right." Her companions, an array of elderly buffoons, were standing a few paces away, guffawing loudly. I, however, did not appreciate being the butt of their joke and decided to show these humans the secrets of the universe. Ironic, really. Some humans spend their entire lives searching for the smallest glimmer of those secrets. I, as punishment, showed them the whole ball of wax. They promptly melted, as I knew they would.

After an instant of seeing "nirvana," these idiots (and I now use the word advisedly) spent the rest of the evening on a street corner blabbering some nonsense that was interpreted by the passersby as "speaking in tongues." Medics were summoned but were at a complete loss to explain why four previously healthy humans were suddenly reduced to singing over and over again:

"I was sitting on the pot with my hands on my knees;
When lo and behold I felt a cosmic breeze."

I won't bore you with the rest of the lyrics; suffice it to say a record producer showed up on the scene and turned this drivel into a huge hit that played for the better part of a year.

How dared these humans treat me in such a cavalier fashion? Red dot my omnipotent ass!

Of course that was not the end of it. Doctors subjected these four humans (who had now gained great popularity as a singing group) to a battery of psychological and psychiatric tests. (The aforementioned record producer was delighted. The last time he had benefited from this level of notoriety was when he had released the "single" of a would-be troubadour on death row. The convict was executed, as he rightfully deserved, if for no other reason than to stop his detestable singing. However, the song was released immediately upon his death, accompanied by a press release claiming that the state had killed a budding "Pavarotti," no less.) The simple truth, which eluded every doctor in the realm, was that I had forced those four ingrates to take a good look at the cosmic "hole in the donut," which understandably had the effect of splattering their brains across the universe.

As I said, I dislike crowds.

Which reminds me of another story. It took place on Earth during one of their end-of-the-year celebrations.

Once upon a time, thousands upon thousands of humans

congregated in a place called Times Square in a town called New York City in a state called New York (thus demonstrating the remarkable lack of human imagination in coming up with two different names). At the end of each Earth year, Times Square is packed with humans quivering in anticipation as they fixate on a ball (which signifies the passing of time) that drops from a tower at the stroke of midnight. Imagine their state of mind when that yearly ritual closed out a century. Of course most of them were so cockeyed drunk when the hour approached that they didn't see just one ball drop but rather two, or four.

It was such a bizarre event to get worked up about that I wanted to observe the phenomenon at close range. I stood in the middle of Times Square in the midst of the surging mass of humanity. They were crushing in from all directions—it was indeed a most disconcerting sensation. Nonetheless, I took it in stride. They were, after all, only humans, and certainly no threat to me.

It was interesting to watch the humans up close and personal. There were so many expressions on their faces—hope, fear, excitement, even boredom—the entire gamut of human emotions. It was as if humanity realized that it was standing on the precipice of something . . . remarkable. As if they knew, as I did, that the next century could be a time of great achievement—unparalleled in human history.

So, there I was in Times Square fending off the pickpockets when I noticed a young lady across the square. In this crowd of thousands, she was alone. All alone. She had long black hair, and she was rather pale, but her eyes were a remarkable cobalt blue. There was something about her, something special I couldn't quite put my finger on, so I moved toward her. It was no great trick. There was no reason for me to wend my way through the crowd. I simply willed myself to be next to her, and I was. She looked startled when she saw me.

"You appear perplexed," I said.

"Not really," she said. "Just a little afraid."

"Why?"

"Because . . ." Clearly she was about to toss off an answer, but then she stopped and considered a moment before she responded. "Because, if you really want to know, I'm thinking about everything that we've done so far . . . and everything we can be . . . and I see tremendous opportunities. I see what we can achieve. I see . . ." She looked to the night sky, which was devoid of clouds. The stars glittered in a manner that was doubtless impressive to someone who has never walked among them. "I see great ships, cruising the spaceways. I see species—all sorts of species—from different worlds, coming together. I see a new era of harmony, a new golden age for mankind—for universal kind. I see so many possibilities."

"Why would that make you afraid?"

"Because I'm afraid that we'll blow it."

"Blow it?" I had no idea what she was talking about. Even when you're omniscient it's hard to be current with the myriad ways humans mangle their language. "Blow what?" I said.

"It," she said. "We might not make *it*. We might annihilate ourselves before that vision can ever be realized. And that would be just the most incredible waste. We're at a crossroads, and I hope we're able to take the right one. As the poet said: 'Of all sad words of tongue or pen, the saddest are these: 'It might have been.' "

I wanted to share my latest poem with her, "On the road to Alpha Centauri, I stopped for a pint at the brewery" . . . but, somehow, I didn't think the mood was right.

She continued, "I can't wait to find out what happens. The

suspense is killing me. I wish I could live forever just to see how it all turns out."

I was impressed. I was *very* impressed. Something about the way she spoke, something in her quiet conviction that humankind had all sorts of possibilities which might be realized if only humanity were up to the challenge . . . very interesting . . . very uplifting.

Okay, I liked her. She was possibly the first human I ever actually liked. Perhaps it was because our meeting was so brief. For all I know, if I had continued to spend time with her, she might well have turned out to be as dreary as the rest of her race.

"What is your name?" I asked.

She looked up at me, a hank of hair covering part of her face. She brushed it back in a casual manner and said, "Melony."

"Happy New Year, Melony," I said.

Impulsively, she stood on her toes, for she was half a head shorter than I, and kissed me on the cheek. She gasped the moment her lips pressed against my face. Something in that contact had jolted her. Perhaps I had let my guard down ever so slightly, and she had gotten just an inkling of who I was, although she wouldn't have been able to explain it to anyone, including herself. She tilted her head slightly, and it seemed to me as if those blue eyes pierced to the back of my head. There was definitely something about her!

I turned away and slipped back into the crowd. I glanced behind and saw her trying to follow me, but the people were packed in so tightly that she couldn't make headway.

"Possibilities," I murmured to myself. "They have definite . . . possibilities."

My thoughts were suddenly interrupted by a great roar from the crowd. They were watching a gigantic electric ball sliding down a pole in Times Square. It was already on its way down, and the crowd was chanting, "Ten . . . nine . . . eight . . . seven . . ."

Melony had completely lost sight of me. I saw her give a little shrug, and then join in the counting. "Six . . . five . . . four . . ."

One step and then another, and I was at the far end of Times Square. It made it easier for me to observe them all as they stood shoulder to shoulder, packed in like so many stuffed olives. As the countdown continued, I was surprised to hear myself mutter, "Good luck, humans."

". . . two . . . one . . ."

The shouts of "Happy New Year!" however, were drowned out by a massive explosion.

The first of the explosive charges was set off as the huge ball made contact. People stared in disbelief, unable to process what they were seeing. Then the second explosion went off, and then the third, and by that point even the dullest humans had come to the realization that their celebration had gone very much awry.

Huge, flaming pieces of the erstwhile ball tumbled toward the crowd in what seemed like slow motion, while chunks of the building followed close behind. And still the explosions continued, one explosion for each century, it would later be announced by the terrorist organization that set them. There would be governmental investigations, and finger-pointing, and accusations of slipshod security procedures, and an entire presidential administration would collapse when attempts at retaliation were deemed by the public not vengeful enough.

Times Square was a ring of fire. Everywhere, buildings were collapsing. From beneath the streets there were even more explosions, as gas mains erupted with volcanic force.

People tried to run, of course, but there was nowhere for them to go. They were packed in too tightly, you see. They screamed and cried out, begging for their maker, their creator, to intervene, but their god simply looked down, shrugged, and said, "Sorry. Free will. Better luck next time," then rolled over and went back to sleep.

I watched it all. I had an excellent view.

The explosions seemed to stretch on forever.

Finally, even I couldn't stand it any longer. The entire display was so distasteful. I stepped forward. "All right, that's enough of that. Whichever of you sadistic scum was trying to make a point, I trust that it's been made." And so, intervening where their god showed no inclination to do so, I snuffed out the flames. Then I waited a few moments for things to calm down, and began to look around.

It was a pathetic sight, truly pathetic. Humanity had been poised to celebrate its aspirations for the future, and some vomitous little psychopath had chosen that very moment to make a political statement that necessitated the slaughter of thousands. And all for what? "See the world the way I do or die"?

I shook my head in disgust. I had totally underestimated the human capacity for carnage.

It was some minutes before I spotted Melony's body, or at least what was left of it. A chunk of the demolished ball had fallen on her and others nearby. Only her head and left arm were visible. For all I knew, the rest of her wasn't attached, but I didn't feel inclined to check. Her hair was thick with blood, her arm was at an odd angle, and her eyes . . .

Those glorious cobalt blue eyes that had possessed such an intriguing mix of fear and anticipation stared at . . . nothing.

I crouched next to her and closed her eyelids with my

hand. "At least it wasn't the suspense that killed you," I said. It was a morbid attempt at humor. She didn't laugh.

I walked away shaking my head, thinking that for every thoughtful, contemplative specimen such as Melony, there was an overabundance of beasts on this planet ready to brutalize their fellows for whatever reason caught their fancy and in whatever way seemed the most expedient.

"Foolish race," I said to myself. "Foolish, foolish race."

I took one final look at the carnage and, as sirens sounded in the distance and the looters began making their rounds, I vanished.

So you see, I come by my antipathy of crowds rather honestly.

This is all by way of explaining how "put off" I was when, arriving at the Q Continuum, I was met with a mob of "well-oiled" Qs. I couldn't help but wonder where this group of devout teetotalers had been hiding the stuff all these years.

Picard, Data, and I had materialized in a burst of golden haze. (I like "golden," it has a celestial feel about it—very dramatic.) What I beheld when I landed was barely controlled chaos.

Everywhere, my fellow members of the Q were in a state of physical refraction, indicating their high level of excitement. The subether was in massive quantum flux as it responded to both the conscious and subconscious overstimulation of the eternal beings collectively referred to as the Continuum. This must sound like a lot of technobabble to you. In layman's terms: The shit had hit the fan. It was difficult for me to know where to look first. Below me, eternity stretched out; above me, infinity yawned. To the right of me was endlessness; to the left of me was pointlessness; and it was all shimmering and throbbing with an intensity all its own. Usually the Continuum was regulated by the combined will of the Q, but in this case, there seemed to be nothing coherent holding it together . . . and yet, I was seeing more enthusiasm, more spontaneity than I had in eons. I tried to catch the attention of one of the passing Q, but was unable to do so—so great was his excitement. "Hey, you!" I shouted, but still got no reaction.

That was when I heard a rather loud thud. I turned and saw that Data had passed out.

"Passed out" is actually a depressingly human term, and I should know better than to use it. "Shut down" is more like it. "Crashed" might be an even better word. Picard knelt next to him, calling out his name. It struck me as a little ridiculous, kind of like addressing a broken platter after it's hit the floor. Data's golden eyes remained open and unblinking, as if he were going to snap back into active mode at any moment.

"What's happened to him?" said Picard.

"I should have known," I said.

Picard looked up at me, still not comprehending. "What? What should you have known?"

"Data has no human perceptions. His positronic brain tried to process the Q Continuum as it truly is, rather than filtering it through some reference he could grasp." I stood over Data, arms folded, making no attempt to hide my annoyance with the situation. "It was too much for him."

"What?" Picard stared around himself.

It was at that point I remembered what should have been painfully obvious, and indeed would have been if I hadn't been so distracted by the dire situation facing my family. The simple fact was that Picard also wasn't seeing the Q Continuum in the way that it actually existed. This was, of course, fortunate, for if he had, he would have suffered the same fate as Data. Data, aside from his occasional dabbling with dreams, was still a stranger to the concept of imagination. He was far too literal-minded. Picard's mind, however, was fully capable of automatically guarding his sanity by the simple expedient of preventing him from truly seeing what surrounded him. It was a bit impressive; other humans would have needed my help in shifting perceptions. It was an indicator of the strength of Picard's brain.

It was no more than a simple mental adjustment, really, for me to see the Continuum in the same way Picard was seeing it. By giving us a common frame of reference, I hoped to simplify further communication between us. And since bringing him up to my level was clearly impossible, the only other choice was to bring myself down to his. I stooped to conquer.

In an instant, Picard had on a trench coat, black slacks, and polished shoes. He sported an old-style fedora on his head, tilted rakishly. Some people's delusions about themselves are boundless, and at this moment I was happy to support that delusion. As for Data, although he was still in "crash mode," he was attired in a pin-stripe suit with a pale blue tie knotted nattily around his throat. Picard crouched at his side, waving his fedora in Data's face as if hoping the breeze would somehow revive him. A twelve-volt battery and a good set of jumper cables would have been more effective.

Not wanting these two gallants to think that they were the only "trick-or-treaters" dressed up for the occasion, I too wore a trench coat, with what appeared to be some sort of gold badge attached to the outer lapel. I was standing in what was clearly a street, and the rude honking of an automobile horn prompted me to step onto the curb and out of the way. Another Q hurtled past in a car, waving to me and whooping his joy. What he was joyful over, I couldn't say.

The car was a roadster, circa Earth's early twentieth century.

We were in Times Square again, but it was a different era. The women wore thick fur coats over long, elegant shimmering gowns cut high on the leg, in some cases almost to the hip. Invariably, they walked past on the arm of large bruiser-types, although naturally I recognized all of them as my fellow Q.

"This is . . ." Picard began to say, and then hesitated as he took a moment to try to understand what he was witnessing. "This is . . . this is a Dixon Hill environment. I recognize it. It has to be . . ." He looked around. "It has to be from the fourth novel—the one about the serial killer who strangles a beautiful woman every December 31. It's called *Wringing in the New Year.* But what are we doing here? Is there going to be a murder . . . ?"

"I doubt it," I told him. "It simply looks this way because it's an environment you're familiar with . . . and a state of mindality that is at least somewhat akin to what's really happening."

"Of . . . mindality? I don't understand."

I blew air impatiently between my lips. "Mindality. The combination of mind and reality. Like Clamato—clam juice and tomato. Reality is an illusion, as subjective as anything else. You should know that by now, Picard. That's how the universe works. You've certainly seen it enough on your own world. Your personal universe remains immutable, until someone with sufficient power and imagination decides to change it. The people you call inventors think they're delving into some great font of knowledge from their own heads. Not at all. They simply tap into mindality with sufficient strength and force to make the reality of their world match the one they've conjured in their heads."

Picard nodded in what actually seemed to be understanding. "We are such stuff as dreams are made of," he intoned, and then looked at me and said, "Shakespeare."

"Yeah, whatever," I said. "Let's try and keep our eye on the ball. You may have forgotten that we have a dire situation on our hands, Picard, but I have not."

I had to admit, however, that the situation around us looked far from dire. Car horns were blaring, couples were kissing, and everywhere there was a sense of celebration. And just as I had witnessed all those centuries before, people were crowding into Times Square, looking up at something.

It was not, however, a glowing electronic ball festooned with thousands of lights. There was nothing festive about it. Don't get me wrong, it was a "New Year's Ball"; but this ball was solid black. It reminded me of a black hole—it reminded me of a funeral.

I realized that I had stopped talking out loud, and Picard was now staring at me. I picked up where I thought I had left off. . . . "A new year," I told him, "is a time not only of new beginnings . . . but an end to what was."

"Out with the old, in with the new," Picard nodded. And then he looked at me gravely and said, "And if there is no new? Then what?"

One has to say this much for Picard: not very much slips past him.

"All right," I said after a moment's consideration. "This is the situation, Picard. I hope you're listening closely, because I don't want to have to repeat it. . . ."

To my astonishment, his voice hardened. "Stop it, Q. Stop it right now."

"Stop—?"

"The arrogance. The condescension." He walked toward

me, shaking a finger angrily. "I'm used to it under ordinary circumstances. I—" He stepped quickly to one side as a Q on a bicycle nearly ran him down. Picard didn't even bother to glance after him. "I've even grown to tolerate it, although I probably shouldn't have. But what we have here is far from an ordinary circumstance. Your wife and child are gone, the very fabric of reality is undergoing some sort of massive shake-up, and—admit it—you don't know why. You're confused and probably even a bit scared. We're on equal footing here for once, Q, and if you have any interest in my working with you to sort this out, you'd be well advised to toss aside your attitude before it truly gets in the way. Have I made myself clear?"

He was right, of course. Right about everything. I really didn't have any idea what was going on, and not only that, but there was a most distressing sensation of fear gnawing at my gut. This entire business was something I had never seen before.

You have to understand just how alarming that can be for someone like me. When you have existed as long as I have, there is a tendency to feel that everything that can be seen, has been seen. The truth is that history repeats itself constantly, and whatever activities and behaviors I might witness, whatever phenomena may unfold before my eyes, at some point I've seen it all before. In fact, based upon previous observation, I'm usually able to predict just how the situation will turn out.

Perhaps it's that very repetition that leads to the sort of ennui and boredom that had settled upon the Q Continuum eons earlier. The sense of "been there, done that—got the T-shirt." It can all be rather suffocating. But boredom is comforting—to some. No worries or problems present themselves because everything is preordained. It's impossible to be surprised by anything . . . and that prevents one from getting too discombobulated.

But now, I was faced with something unlike anything I'd ever experienced—and I didn't like it! I've been powerless before, and I can assure you that it's probably my least favorite thing in the universe, being powerless. But even then, when I wasn't omnipotent, I at least knew where I stood. This time . . .

This time I didn't. And it bothered the hell out of me.

Naturally I could not, would not, say any of this to Picard. "You are right, Picard" were the four words I should have said, but unfortunately, my baser instincts took hold. "You. Are. Right. Picard." are simply four words that don't string together no matter how sincerely I try to get my lips around them, so . . .

So instead I simply glowered at him.

"All right . . . this is the situation," I began again, acting as if he hadn't spoken. "Something is happening in the so-called real world. As a consequence, there's a ripple effect that is sweeping through every realm. This New Year's scenario you see is your way of processing some important information, information that the Continuum knows as well . . . that something is ending."

"And that black ball up there," Picard pointed, "is a way of letting me know that there is nothing to come afterwards but oblivion?"

"Yes," I said, nodding. "That is precisely right."

"And what do we do about it? And about Data?" he added after a moment, looking down upon his fallen Tinkertoy.

"We leave him," I said. "He always irritated me with his endless yammering about wanting to be human. In a perfect imitation of Data's mechanical whine, I said, 'Oh, I wish I weren't a poor, helpless android who is stronger than ten combined humans, and can think faster and know more than any creature that has ever walked on two legs upon the dreary earth. Oh, beat me with a stick, I wish I were human.' " I shook my head and, returning to my own voice, I said, "He could be running your planet, your entire Federation if he chose. But instead all this android wants is to be less than he is. What a tremendous waste of material."

"He doesn't want to be less than he is. He wants to be different," Picard said sharply. "You, of all individuals, should understand that. Look at you! A self-proclaimed omnipotent being, who needn't worry about anyone or anything. Your fellow Q keep to themselves, leave all of us 'lesser' beings alone. But not you, oh no." He advanced on me. I could always tell when Picard was upset; his head tended to look pointier. "You have to meddle with humanity, get involved, get your hands dirty, like a child neatly dressed for Sunday school who sees an absolutely irresistible mud puddle."

"Picard," I said, making no effort to keep the edge of danger from my voice, "you are starting to annoy me. First you scold me about the manner in which I address you. And now you seem to be put out because I'm expressing my opinions about Data and his endless pining for the dubious gift of humanity. Sitting in judgment of me can be hazardous to your long-term health."

He didn't appear to be the least bit daunted at what I said. He actually continued to glare at me.

"Picard," I said slowly, exhibiting as much patience as I could muster. "We are accomplishing nothing. I want to find out what's going on. So do you. We can do this together or not . . ."

"You want me with you." Picard suddenly regarded me with amazement. "Why?"

"Don't flatter yourself. Whether you're with me or not, I don't really care."

"I think you do," he said, eyes narrowed. "And I think there's an assortment of reasons. Perhaps you simply want someone to lord it over. Perhaps you want to avail yourself of Data's scientific acumen or my strategic viewpoints. Or maybe it's something else. Perhaps it's—"

"Masochism?" I suggested. "Maybe I'm a masochist. Have you ever thought of that?"

"No."

"Picard, truly, what does it matter? We're faced with some sort of cataclysmic situation that may have already claimed my wife and my son . . . and . . ."—I looked around at the pandemonium that surrounded us—". . . the collective sanity of the Q Continuum. Is there really anything to be gained by standing around and trying to sort out exactly why I feel your presence is required . . . ?"

"So! You do feel it's necessary to have Data and me along." He spoke as if he had just had some sort of cosmic revelation.

"If that will shut you up, then yes, fine. You're necessary. Does that make you feel better, Picard? Does that appeal to that aspect of humanity which dictates that, first and foremost, your pathetic little species has to be at the center of everything having to do with the unfolding of the universe's destiny?" I shook my head, amazed. "Picard, the self-obsession of your entire race in general, and you in particular, is absolutely beyond the pale. What does it matter why you're here? You are here!"

"It matters to me," he said very quietly. In all the time that I had interacted with him, I had never heard him quite so serious or sober as he was at that particular moment. "Because I think that, despite all that you and I have been through from time to time in our . . . 'association,' " he said, for lack of a better word, "what we are about to encounter is beyond anything that either of us has experienced. And I simply think it will be healthier for our continued interaction if we know where each of us stands from the very beginning."

"Picard, what would you have me say? What possible explanation for my decision to bring you along—aside from pure stupidity—would you accept?"

"Perhaps . . . that you would be lost without your Boswell."

It was neither Picard nor I who had spoken. Data was still on the ground, lying flat on his back, but his golden eyes had refocused. His brain, such as it was, was back in charge. His gaze flickered from Picard to me and back.

Picard knelt down next to Data, overjoyed that his personal computer had apparently rebooted. "Data . . . are you all right?"

"My circuits appear to be back on-line and functioning in a reliable and standard manner," Data told him. "I am not entirely certain why, however. Nor do I comprehend," and he glanced around himself, "why we appear to be in early twentieth-century Times Square."

"You . . . see it as I do?"

"Is there any reason it would be seen in some other way?"

Instead of answering Data's question, Picard looked to me. "Did you do this?"

"I may have done," I replied casually. "I don't necessarily remember." Then I looked at him scornfully, an expression I had mastered through many years of practice. "Of course I did it. You seemed paralyzed at the thought of leaving the walking toaster behind, so I brought him around by altering his mind to perceive the Q Continuum in a way that wouldn't be too much of a strain. Is that satisfactory to you, Picard, or are you going to find some aspect of my good deed to complain about?"

I could tell that Picard wanted to snap back a defiant response, but obviously he thought better of it. "Your . . . aid . . . is appreciated. Data, what was that you said earlier? About Boswell?"

"Ah. From the chronicles of Sherlock Holmes. Holmes at one point implores the then-married Doctor Watson to accompany him on a case, stating that he would be lost without his Boswell. That is to say, he required the presence of his chronicler in order to function. Q finds himself in a situation that is rife with uncertainty. Perhaps, in order for him to function at his best, it is necessary that he bring a familiar aspect of his life with him. In this instance, that familiar aspect would be you. Q is accustomed to feeling superior to you, sir, and not without cause. . . ." At Picard's priceless expression, Data promptly amended, "No offense intended, sir."

"None taken," Picard said, but he still looked a bit put out.

"In any event," he continued, "since Q may find himself facing a power that is even greater than his, he might well feel the need to have someone at his side to whom he can feel superior. To provide balance, as it were."

"As it were," commented Picard dryly. He turned to face me. "Is that the case, Q? You want me around so that you can have someone to lord it over in the face of adversity?"

"Truth to tell . . . I'm not sure. I suppose I could have just let you and Data disappear down the sinkhole with the rest of the flotsam and jetsam. And perhaps I should have, because then I could have been about my business far sooner, and not wasted valuable minutes catering to your inflated ego, and your overwhelming need to precisely determine your position in the universe. That said, as far as I'm concerned, you're here because . . . you're supposed to be here. I don't quite know why. I just have the sense that you are. And when one is as attuned to the universe as I, one tends to go with his instincts." My face darkened as I added, "That's the final answer you're going to get from me. And if it isn't satisfactory, there's a gigantic hole with your name on it into which I will be more than happy to toss you. Are we clear with each other?"

Picard must have realized that he'd pushed matters as far as he could. So he nodded. "Crystal clear. So, Q, if you're that attuned to the universe . . . tell me what's happening to it. What is all this?" He gestured to the pandemonium that was the Q Continuum.

"That is what we're here to find out. And there's only one place I can think of where we might get an answer.

"And that would be . . . ?"

"HQ," I said.

Picard looked slightly pained. "I might have known."

"I'll take us there immediately," I said, and—with my customary nonchalance—envisioned us being at HQ.

Nothing happened.

Picard seemed politely confused. "How are you taking us there?" he inquired.

"Be quiet." I pictured HQ, this time putting more than casual effort into it. Still nothing. "Something is wrong," I said.

"Are you losing your powers?"

"I . . . don't think so." I tried to keep the worry out of my voice. "After all, I brought Data back easily enough. But something is definitely up. Perhaps HQ isn't inclined to talk to me. Well, I'm not going to let a little thing like not being wanted slow me down."

"You never have before," Data observed.

Fortunately for his continued android existence, I let the comment pass. Instead I hailed a cab.

None of the cabs even slowed down. Indeed, several of them snapped on their off-duty lights as soon as they saw me. I noticed the Q cab drivers averting their eyes as they passed by, as if they were afraid to acknowledge my very existence.

"What did you call it again . . . 'mindality'?" Picard asked after the tenth or so cab had sped past us. "Influencing one's environment or causing it to conform to one's worldview through sheer force of will?"

"An oversimplification, but the easiest way I could think of to explain it to you," I said.

"All right. This is a Dixon Hill environment. Let's see just how much I can influence it."

Before I could say anything, Picard had stepped into the middle of the street. A cab was bearing down on him and didn't appear to have any inclination to slow down. Picard reached into his coat as if he knew just what he would find there and pulled out a revolver. It was sleek and black and had the initials "DH" engraved on the handle. He aimed it squarely at the windshield of the oncoming cab.

I knew the Q who was driving it all too well. He was the one who had restored my powers after the Continuum had annoyingly seen fit to strip me of them. He certainly had a knack for showing up at difficult times. He slowed down, cast an uncertain glance at me, and then brought the cab to a halt. The "off-duty" sign atop the cab glowed pale yellow.

"Take us to HQ," said Picard. The gun didn't waver as he held it steady.

Q pointed toward the top of the cab. "I'm off duty," he said.

Picard angled the gun slightly and fired off a round. The bullet shattered the off-duty sign. Q jumped, a bit startled at the abrupt noise.

"Your shift was just extended," Picard told him.

All around us, everything came to a momentary halt as the blast of the gun cut through the hubbub and commotion. Everyone was staring at us. I, for one, didn't mind a bit. It was always nice to shake things up in the excessively complacent Q Continuum. The fact that the place was a hive of industry for the first time in eons didn't make it any less satisfying.

Q hesitated and then shrugged. "Get in."

We quickly did so, and the cab roared off. Picard and Data were in the backseat, while I took up residence in the passenger seat. I turned to Q and said, "You want to tell me what's going on?"

"I don't have to," he said and kept his eye on the road. We sailed through traffic lights with little regard to whether they were red or green. Every so often, cars would screech to a halt to avoid slamming into us. "You'll find out at HQ," he replied.

"But perhaps you can save me a trip."

"Why should I? I can use the fare."

I glanced at the meter. We had gone five blocks. The fare was up to eighty-seven dollars. "I think you've got the meter slightly rigged."

He shrugged noncommittally.

"Look . . . Q," I said, leaning over and lowering my voice. "Playing along with Picard's vision of the Continuum is all well and good, and can certainly provide a few giggles. Under ordinary circumstances, I'd find it heartening, because I wouldn't have thought you or any other Q capable of amusement. But we both know that something very ugly is happening, and I want to get to the bottom of it."

He looked at me with a strange grin. "Perhaps it's not as

ugly as you think. Perhaps it's glorious. Perhaps it's everything we could have hoped for."

"What is this 'it'? What are you talking about? Why don't I know about it?"

"Why would you?" He allowed annoyance to creep into his voice. "You're never here, Q. You're always somewhere else, exploring this thing or getting involved with that thing. As skittish as we felt about the entire matter, some of us hoped that your union with Lady Q and the birth of your son might serve at least one useful purpose: to ground you. However, not only has that not been the case, it appears to have had a negative effect on them as well. The fact that you've lost them may in fact be the best thing for them. You certainly haven't been a positive influence."

"So you know they're gone," I said intently.

"Know? Of course I know. What part of—"

"—omniscient don't I get. Yes, I know. Then you must know where they are. Know whether they're all right or not."

He said nothing. The numbers on the meter kept climbing.

I suddenly realized I wasn't in the mood for fooling around. I grabbed him firmly by the shoulder, so firmly that he winced in pain. "Tell me," I said. "Tell me where they are, and tell me what's going on."

Instead of replying, he angled the cab over to the curb and flipped the flag up on the meter. "You're here," he said flatly.

I looked out the window. We were next to a large, gleaming white building with stone columns that seemed to stretch upward to infinity. The words "CITY HALL" were carved into the upper section.

"That'll be $926 and twenty cents," Q said, tapping the meter.

Picard leaned forward from the back seat and handed him a thousand-dollar bill. "Keep the change."

"Thanks. Baby needs a new pair of shoes," Q told him, taking the proffered bill.

We climbed out of the cab and stood on the curb. The noise of Times Square in the distance was still audible. "Q," I said, leaning on the open passenger door. "Q . . . please . . . tell me what's happening."

Q smiled and said, "It's a wonderful moment, Q. I almost envy you, your not knowing. Because you will have the chance to experience firsthand the excitement and glory of the Great Discovery. And I suspect that even you will find fulfillment, Q. Even you."

"Don't bet on it," I told him as the cab pulled away. As we turned and headed into City Hall, Picard mentioned something about hoping he didn't have to fight it. It was a joke, but I wasn't laughing.

"Picard, that's been a new pin on them." Q told him, giving the profound rill.

We glanced out of the dale and ahead on the cable. The voice or three figures in the Guinare was still another. "Q" began rearing on the open passenger door. "I... please . . . where what a happen to...

Q rushed and said, "It's wonderfully mounded of? I sudden convened with new begation. Because you tell the...

Once we were inside City Hall and the great door swung shut behind us, all was fearfully silent. Our heels click-clacked loudly on the gleaming floors and the lights were dimmed; there didn't seem to be anyone about.

Not that I was fearful, you understand. It was, after all, my own familiar Continuum, no matter what the current visual images were telling us. But I was nonetheless concerned. I was all too aware that I was witnessing something far outside the norm, and I still had no solid information about what precisely was happening. But I was beginning to have some vague and frankly disturbing inklings. I was not going to share them with Picard and Data, though. Better to know for sure first.

"This way!" a voice suddenly boomed. The floor reverberated under my feet in conjunction. "I've been waiting for you."

"Let me guess," Picard said to me. "It's . . . Q."

"That's right," I said.

"You know, Q . . . there are twenty-five other letters in the alphabet. Certainly you and your associates could have used at least a few of them, just for clarity's sake."

"You mean for your sake. Picard, you can be quite tiresome. Has anyone ever told you that?"

"I'll answer that question honestly if you'll answer mine."

I didn't see fit to dignify the comment with a response.

We went up a curving set of marble stairs. At the top of the stairs was a large set of double doors that stood partly open. Light cascaded from within. "This way. Keep coming," came the voice. I pushed the door open.

We were in a large office, with mahogany furniture polished to such a rich and reflective sheen that I could see myself in it. At the far end was a wide desk, with—conveniently—three chairs lined up facing it. Behind the desk was, of course, Q.

He came across as very much the avuncular sort, this Q did. A bit rotund, with patches of white hair clinging to either side of his otherwise bald head. He had a salt-and-pepper beard that he was scratching distractedly. However, these aspects of his outward appearance were merely a façade. I had known him for . . . well, always, of course. He was, in fact, a fairly nasty customer. He was superb at putting forward a disarming attitude, convincing everyone around that he was a pleasant sort with not an enemy in the universe. But in reality he was a ruthless maintainer of the status quo, and a formidable enemy. He and I had not seen eye to eye since before Picard's ancestors hauled themselves out of the primordial ooze. Whatever actions had been taken against me by the Continuum as a consequence of my perceived "indiscretions," it had been this Q who had been one of the loudest advocates, if not the prime mover.

Picard and Data knew none of that, of course. All they knew was that this was easily the most pleasant and welcoming member of the Continuum they'd yet encountered. "Come in, come in," he said, getting to his feet and extending a big hand toward Picard. "Captain Picard, I've heard a great deal about you. Never actually had the honor, though."

"Honor." The word seemed to amuse Picard. "From what

Q has said, I wouldn't have thought that you would hold me or my species in any particular esteem."

"Oh, quite the contrary," replied Q. "Anyone whom Q finds so endlessly fascinating and needs to visit time and again certainly must have something going for him. And you, Mr. Data." He shook Data's hand firmly as well. "Quite a remarkable achievement, you are."

"I am something of an advancement in artificial intelligence, yes, thank you," Data said.

"Artificial intelligence? Nonsense. No such thing," said Q. "The human brain is a machine, nothing more. An organic machine, but what of that? Organics are given far too much credit. The function remains the same, even though the manufacturer might change, and what should be considered above all else is efficiency and quality of performance. So . . ." and he sat once more behind the desk, gesturing for us to follow suit. Picard and I sat. Data remained standing. "I know why you're here, of course. You want to know what's going on."

"That would be preferable to ignorance," said Picard.

"Don't be so quick to dismiss the joys of ignorance," Q said, waggling a meaty finger. "It is, after all, bliss."

"Q," I said after a moment of silence, leaning back in the chair and trying to look as casual as possible. I interlaced my fingers and crossed my legs. For me to look any more snug, someone would have had to toss a blanket over me and serve me some hot cocoa. "All of this we're witnessing . . . the great sinkhole that swallowed my family, this excitement in the Continuum . . . is it what I think it is?"

There was no need for dissembling, of course. We were, after all, Q. On the cab ride over, Q had deliberately blocked his thoughts. But here in this office, this Q was making no effort whatsoever. I knew in an instant the answer to my question, almost before I'd even framed it.

Yet Q didn't reply immediately. Instead he leaned back, steepling his fingers and regarding me almost with amusement. Knowing the answer to the question was a given, he instead said, "Do you understand why we are reacting the way we are?"

"Of course," I said. "Who, better than I, knows the insufferable ennui that has settled over this entire Continuum? We've seen it all, we know it all, we've done it all. And for uncounted millennia we've just been sitting about, contemplating our collective navels and wondering when something, anything, was going to occur that would terminate this endless boredom. So it doesn't surprise me the Continuum is ecstatic about it."

He smiled. For a moment there was a hint of the wolfishness behind his smile which I knew was ever-present. "Naturally."

"Q . . ." Picard began.

"Yes?" we both replied.

"Well, that was inevitable," he muttered before starting again. "Q . . . either of you . . ." he added quickly, "it's fairly evident that the two of you fully understand what you're discussing. Unfortunately, Data and I do not. Perhaps if you elaborate or clarify our situation, we can provide some sort of help. . . ."

"Help?" Q said to them, his eyes twinkling as if he'd just heard the greatest joke ever told.

(The greatest joke ever told, it should be noted, was developed in a monastery in the upper mountain regions on the larger moon of Sicila IV. What made it so great was this: with most other jokes, repeated tellings only diminish their effectiveness—but not this one. The joke of the Sicila monks was so multilayered, so comically hilarious, that it became funnier upon repeated tellings. In fact, it was so funny that it was addictive. Hearing it once was insufficient. One had to hear it repeatedly. It was like a narcotic. Indeed, to hear the joke once was to have your life ruined, because then you had to hear it again and again and again. It became impossible to get on with anything else. You lived for the joke. You died for the joke. The only ones who were immune to the joke were the monks themselves, since, by a strange twist of fate, they had no sense of humor whatsoever. Casual telling of the joke to groundskeepers or the occasional odd visitor to the monastery was enough for the monks to realize what a horrific weapon had been handed to them. So naturally the entire order committed suicide rather than take a chance of the joke spreading further and more damage being done. Thus was the greatest joke ever told brought to a tragic and untimely end. I know it, of course. But to be honest, I don't think it's all that funny. Something about sentient potato salad. Perhaps I'll tell it later.)

"Help?" Q said again. He turned and looked at me, his ample stomach shaking from mirth. "They want to help? Heavens, Q, I begin to understand why you find them so entertaining."

"I'm ecstatic that we can be a source for such merriment," said Picard in his trademark "we are not amused" manner. "But would you be kind enough to at least give us some inkling about what is going on?"

"Captain, I believe what is being discussed is . . . the End."

"The end?" Picard looked at us in confusion. "The End . . . of the Q Continuum?"

"Among other things," said Q. He leaned back once more, having composed himself. "Your machine is correct, Captain Picard. What is being discussed is the End of . . . Everything. The expansion is over, the final contraction has begun. The universe has run its course. The End is nigh."

Picard stared at him. It was such an impossible concept that he clearly couldn't wrap his mind around it. "The End of . . . Everything? Of the universe? That's impossible. The universe is infinite. You can't terminate infinity."

"And you are speaking from personal experience, are you, in regard to what can and can't be done on a cosmic scale?" Q asked quietly. There was a faintly mocking tone to his voice.

"Is there some enemy? Some great—?"

"No, Picard," said Q. "It was inevitable. It had to happen sooner or later. In this instance, it is later."

"Later? You're saying it's happening now!"

"Now is late enough. You have no idea, Picard, what it's been like for us," he sighed. "Eons of sitting about, unable to find anything sufficiently worthy of our interest. The Continuum has been waiting for this moment longer than you can possibly conceive. It may seem too soon to you, and I understand why; your species has been around for barely an eye blink, and now you're being flushed away. It must seem dreadfully unfair. Perhaps it is. But there were many, uncounted billions of races, before the human race came onto the scene. Or, to put it in the vernacular: the previous customers have left the eatery. You, I'm afraid, are stuck with the check."

"Are you speaking of entropy?" said Data. "The gradual erosion of the very fabric of the universe?"

"It's absurd." Picard seemed determined to regard this as some sort of cosmic hoax. "The Federation has instrumentation . . . starships, research teams . . . we study the galaxy, the universe around us, constantly, down to its very molecular structure. Are you trying to tell me that the universe is approaching its natural conclusion . . . winding down . . . and *no one noticed it?* That's ludicrous!"

"There's an axiom, Picard, that I'm sure you're familiar

with," he said. "If the universe were shrinking at the steady rate of one inch a day, and all means of measurement were shrinking at a proportionate rate, then there would be no way for anyone to know . . . and that includes all the mighty minds of the Federation combined."

Picard looked at me, and there was incredulity on his face. "And you agree with this?" he said. "This . . . person . . . sitting here . . . tells you that there's nothing to be done. That we are to acknowledge the End of the universe . . . and that is perfectly acceptable to you?" I didn't respond. He rose from his chair. "Well, it's not acceptable to me! It makes no sense! It can't be natural! You saw that . . . thing! That sinkhole! There's some intelligence behind all of this! An entity, a creature that exists. And if something exists, it can be reasoned with . . . or stopped. Anything can be stopped if there are a few beings who are stubborn enough or determined enough to stop it!"

"You're wrong, Picard," said Q, and bit by bit any last hint of his pleasant manner was evaporating. The room suddenly seemed colder, his face darker. "You are in no position to say what form the End will take. Your own people cannot agree on the matter, even though end-of-the-world scenarios abound in your culture. In one scenario, there is a fanfare of trumpets, four horsemen, and an ultimate judgment. In another, a gigantic wolf devours your system's sun while a fire demon sweeps your world clean with his flaming sword. If the true End of the universe involves all of creation being sucked down a gigantic crevice into oblivion . . . who are you to dismiss that scenario out of hand?" He rested his elbows on the desk. Perhaps it was a trick of lighting in the room, but suddenly it was nearly impossible to see his eyes. "A wise human—and there are such things—once said that a little learning is a dangerous thing. You may be quite wise for one of your kind, Captain Picard, but in truth, you have very little learning. Be content to know that the universe is more complex than you could ever imagine."

"But you have unbounded power," Picard said tightly. "I've seen the things that Q here can accomplish . . . and he's just one of your race. When I think of the power at the collective command of the Q Continuum . . . and you aren't even trying to use . . ."

"*Why would we want to?* The final termination of our existence is a consummation devoutly to be wished. We embrace it with open arms. Obviously, you don't understand that. But Q does." He gestured to me. "Even he, who is arguably the biggest maverick of all of us, understands that an end comes to all things. It is the collective desire of the Q Continuum not to combat this event. It would be interference with the natural order of things. Tell him, Q." Picard turned and looked at me.

But I was thinking of my son and my mate. They had not considered this event as a "consummation devoutly to be wished." They had not gone quietly into that good night, no. They had gone down screaming, calling for my aid. Was I to take their death in stride? Nod obediently, accept the collective ruling of the Continuum, and wait for everything to grind to a halt?

Well, that was the natural thing to do, wasn't it?

". . . It's the natural thing to do," I said, giving voice to my inner monologue.

"Exactly!" Q said. "So you see, Picard—"

"I'm not finished."

"What do you mean?" he said, very slowly, very dangerously. It wasn't so much a question as it was a dare to speak my mind.

I rose from my chair. Something about the dynamics of

the moment called for me to be a bit taller. "If we are agreed that all things must follow their nature . . . then it is against my nature to follow. I owe my wife and my son more than that. I owe it to myself. Picard has a point. We are making an assumption that there isn't an entity behind this. Perhaps you of the Continuum are too eager to . . ."

"*We,* Q. We of the Continuum," he said. "You speak as if you are not one of us. But you are, and that membership carries with it certain responsibilities. They are responsibilities you have shirked in the past, but not this time. This time you will abide by our decision."

"Why?" I demanded. "If you truly believe that this is an act of nature—that the universe's time has come—then absolutely nothing I could do could possibly stop it." I was leaning forward on the desk, resting my knuckles on it so that Q and I were only inches apart. "But if you're trying to rein me in, then that implies you're concerned about something. Perhaps . . . you're worried that I can stop this. Is that the case, Q?"

"No. You give yourself entirely too much credit, Q," he said. "And you give us too little. We are certain of the reality of the situation. We would not be reacting this way otherwise."

"Then you won't have any problem if I investigate this myself," I said. I turned to face Picard and Data. "Come, gentlemen. We will away!"

"You will do nothing of the kind."

I turned to face Q once more . . . but he was gone. The jolly white-haired man had vanished from behind his desk. But his presence was most certainly still there. It filled the room, it filled my very essence. Picard suddenly flinched in his chair, covering his ears. Data sat there.

The voice came from everywhere. *"I have never liked you,*

Q. None of us has. And many is the time I've said that I will bring you into line with the rest of the Continuum if it is the last thing I ever do. Well, Q . . . I am rapidly running out of opportunities. Time is growing short, and even I, with all my ennui, have a few goals I would still like to accomplish. You are among them. You will not leave the Continuum. You will remain here, of your own accord or not, that is your choice. But remain you will. Do you understand me, Q?"

I did not hesitate. I grabbed Picard by one wrist, Data by the other, and yanked them both to their feet. Suddenly all of reality seemed to explode around me. For a moment, just a moment, I was certain that I had waited too long, that the End had actually come. I imagined that I heard my son and wife calling to me, except they were speaking not in fear, but in anger. "You've failed us! You've failed us! You, with all your power and pride and arrogance . . . you could have, should have, done so much more! Instead you let us down! When all was said and done . . . you weren't omnipotent! You weren't all-powerful. You weren't ever around! You are the weakest of the weak!"

I tried to speak, but I was unable to, because I knew they were right.

And then everything went mercifully black.

There are certain occasions—we need not be specific at this time, but we all know to what I'm alluding—when one wishes, upon regaining consciousness, that one hadn't, because oblivion was far better than discovering the truth. I can tell you, categorically, that this happened to be one of those times.

I opened my eyes and felt a great heaviness, as if my eyelids weighed several pounds each. Picard was standing a few feet away, looking concerned. Data was next to him, with that annoying deadpan look he so often exhibited. I realized they were looking up at me, and drew from that the logical conclusion that I must be looking down at them. I was elevated for some reason, but I had no idea why. I tried to move my head, to glance around and get an assessment of the situation, but I found I was totally paralyzed. I couldn't move my head so much as an inch. I tried to move my mouth and, lo and behold, I could speak. "What are you gawking at, Picard?"

He appeared visibly relieved, if for no other reason than that I was yelling at him. I found I could turn my eyes around a bit and so I got just a little sense of where we were. It was a park, with trees and walking paths all around.

"What is that annoying sound right next to my ear?"

"Would you be referring to a sort of 'cooing' sound?" Data inquired.

"Yes.

76

"Ah. That would be the pigeon on your head."

"Pigeon!"

"Yes. A large white and gray specimen."

"Get it off me!" I said in no uncertain terms. "Before it . . ."

Data, unfortunately, did not move quickly enough. Considering that the android prided himself on the speed with which he processed information, I have to say that he was very slow on the uptake in this instance. The pigeon cooed once more, left a second little gift on my head, and then fluttered away. "New York," I muttered, "is becoming tiresome."

Picard pulled a handkerchief from the inside pocket of his jacket and handed it to Data. Interesting that he would have Data clean me off. Just goes to show that they may be friends, but they're not equals. While Data was attending to business, Picard asked me, "Q . . . can you move?"

"Oh sure, Picard. I'm just practicing pantomime. Better yet, I've decided birds need more statues to poop on, so I'm obliging them. No, of course I can't move!" I said in exasperation. "Do you seriously think I'd be posed like this . . . how am I posed, anyway?"

"Your arms are outstretched, and your right leg is forward of your left and slightly bent."

"Wonderful. I look like an Irish step dancer."

"May we safely assume," asked Data, "that you have been frozen in place by your fellow Q, so that you cannot in any way interfere with the impending End of the universe?"

"That is a safe assumption, yes." Outwardly, I maintained my normal air of sangfroid. Inwardly, I raged. Were I to voice the fury that was roiling within me, however, it might have come across in an extremely un-Q-like manner. Perhaps, in the final analysis, that was why I had wanted Picard with me in this adventure. As long as he was around, I would be disinclined to give in to the despair that threatened to overwhelm me. Stiff upper lip and all that good stuff.

"They appear to have put you on a pedestal, Q," Picard observed. "Even in the face of oblivion, your fellow Q retain a sense of irony."

"They can retain *this!*" I said, and I tried to make a lewd gesture but was unsuccessful.

"Can you break free?"

"If I could, do you think I would be standing here? Picard, this is getting us nowhere. This is just like that time with the fire," I said.

Picard stared up at me in confusion. "Fire? What are you talking about?"

I hesitated at first, but then realized that with the End of Everything looming just over the horizon, there was no need for reticence. I was about to tell him the story when I heard a burst of laughter coming from the direction of Times Square. I wondered how many of my fellow Q knew that I was here. All of them, most likely. And how many of them cared? None of them, most likely. Well . . . perhaps one. But I knew I couldn't count on his help.

"What were you going to tell me?" asked Picard.

"It really isn't of much relevance to the situation, Picard."

"Who knows what is and isn't relevant, Q?" he replied.

"The important thing is getting me out of this . . . this situation."

"Very well, Q." He folded his arms and waited for a suggestion. Finally, he asked, "How shall we go about accomplishing that?"

"Nothing comes to mind," I admitted.

"All right then. So . . . fire?"

"Yes, well . . ." and I let out a sigh. "You know the Greek legend about Prometheus?"

"The Titan. Yes, of course," said Picard. "He brought fire to mankind, and for his transgression, the angered gods chained him to a rock and left him there for birds to eat his innards. Why?"

"Well . . . if you must know . . . I was Prometheus."

Picard stared at me as if I had just admitted to bedding down his mother. "What do you mean, you were Prometheus? How could there be a—?"

"I assume you've heard of racial memory, Picard. Events so cataclysmic, so monumental that they inform us as to 'who' and 'what' we are. Fear of the dark: the first murder was committed in the dark, did you know that?"

"Did you commit it?" Picard asked stiffly.

"No, Picard, I didn't. I had better things to do than club one of your prehistoric ancestors senseless for the privilege of sitting a hair closer to the fire. You humans invented murder all by yourselves. But fire, well . . ." I shrugged. Inwardly. Outwardly, of course, I didn't move an inch. "You were such a pathetic little race when you first started out . . . not that you're much better now, you understand. And there was a group of you, barely recognizable as human, sitting about and staring forlornly at the forest primeval where eyes stared back at you and prehistoric bestial lips smacked, anxious to dine on a late-evening snack of cold human. You seemed ready for a little 'pick-me-up.' So I gave you fire. I wanted to see what you'd do with it. Not surprisingly, the first human to see fire thought it was something to put on his head. It was hilarious to watch. With that inauspicious beginning, I wasn't sure if you people would ever manage to harness its power.

"Of course, the other Q weren't happy with me. I was supposed to have observed your race from a purely scientific point of view, and they felt I had gone too far. It was their belief that humans would have died off without my interference, and the planet Earth would have had cockroaches as its dominant species, as it was supposed to. They were very disappointed with me. So, to show their displeasure, they chained me to the side of a mountain, and assorted beasts of the wild came along and chewed on me. My body regenerated itself, of course, because this isn't really a body so much as it is a conceptualization for the convenience of whoever's looking at me. Every so often, some daring human would climb up to where I was chained, poke a stick at my liver, and run off, squealing with delight. I can't begin to tell you how thrilled I was to provide entertainment for the first generations of humanity. There was one channel and I was the only thing on. That's one of the reasons I find you such an annoying race. You have this disconcerting habit of reveling in other people's pain. Someone hits his head—you laugh; slips on a banana and breaks his back—you guffaw. Come to think of it, not one of your mangy ancestors tried to free me. . . ."

Picard still seemed incredulous. "So am I to believe . . . that you were the basis of the myth of Prometheus?"

"In short, yes. Norsemen, on the other hand, embellished the incident in other directions and called me Loki, claiming I was chained to a rock with a snake dripping acid on me. Loki, the son of giants; Prometheus, the Titan. I suppose I seemed big to your ancestors. Then again, people were shorter back then."

"Loki, the trickster god. Perhaps the Norse knew you better than you suspected," said Picard. "Q, do you really expect me to believe your . . . outlandish tales?"

"You know, Picard, that's the joy of being held in immovable stasis while the universe teeters on the edge of annihilation. With stakes like those, it doesn't really matter all that much whether you believe me or not, does it? On a scale of one to ten, the importance of my credibility in the eyes of Jean-Luc Picard ranks somewhere in the negative billions."

Data had been watching the entire exchange with nary a flicker of cognizance in his gold eyes, and then, all of a sudden, he came out of "sleep mode."

"Let us assume, for a moment, that your description of history has some measure of truth to it," he said.

"Oh yes, let's," I said sarcastically.

"It is clear that you are not at present still chained to a rock. Obviously you were released. Was that a collective decision of the Q Continuum, to release you?"

I cast my memory back to a time long ago, "No," I said finally. "It was the actions of one Q who unilaterally decided he did not wish to see me continue suffering. He freed me and brought me back to the Continuum."

Picard began to look hopeful. "Which Q? Do you remember? Could he free you now? Can we find him?"

"We already found him," I replied. "He was driving the cab."

Picard began to circle me thoughtfully. "Well, now, that is a bit of a coincidence, don't you think? Of all Qs, the one that was sympathetic to you happened to be the one who picked you up in the cab. . . ."

"He has not been sympathetic to me, Picard," I corrected him. "Believe me, no one in the Q Continuum cares about anyone else. We're a rather self-centered lot, truth be told. And besides . . . if you're implying that somehow that Q would be interested in helping me now, then you obviously weren't listening. Didn't you hear him waxing rhapsodically about the End of Everything? He's obviously as enamored of the idea as everyone else." I was getting very frustrated. When I was chained to the rock, or locked in Pandora's box, I had been able to tell myself that this, too, would pass, because time was on my side. But now, time was not on my side.

And Picard was really beginning to irritate me. "Perhaps not, Q," he continued. "Perhaps he was not embracing the End . . . so much as he was warning you. He may have been trying to let you know that he was no happier about it than you are. But he also knew to openly advocate doing something about it—to suggest something should actually be done to stop it—would result in disaster."

There was something in what Picard was claiming that had possibilities.

He continued, "Think about what he was saying. Think about the qualifiers he used. He said things like, 'Perhaps it's glorious. Perhaps it's everything we could have hoped for.' Perhaps he's anxious to see something done. And he also said that he 'almost' envied your not knowing what was happening. We may have misunderstood what he meant. He may have been trying to let you know that he was on your side."

"It's a reach, Picard. A desperate reach. But if what you're saying is true . . . then why isn't he here? Why is he off with the other celebrants? Why isn't he . . ."

My voice trailed off and, just on a hunch, I reached out. (Not physically! Thought you'd catch me, didn't you?) For we Q do remain sensitive to each other's whereabouts, and even though we are capable of masking our presence, such a deception is virtually impossible if one Q thinks that the other is there. So as an experiment—and I do so love experiments—I reached out and probed, allowing myself to believe beyond all doubt that he was there, that he was right nearby, observing the entire discussion. . . .

He knew I'd found him. He was hiding behind the big chestnut tree. He had, at least, the good grace to emerge before I called out to him. What Picard and Data saw was the pigeon who had treated me in such disgraceful fashion before, fluttering down from overhead and settling on my shoulder. He regarded me with bland curiosity. And then the pigeon opened his beak and said, "I was wondering if you were going to start listening to the human. It seems you listen to everyone else's advice except mine. You have a very odd sense of priorities."

"Not as misplaced as yours," I retorted. "Do I have to talk to a bird!?"

The pigeon vanished in a burst of light, to be replaced by the smirking Q, still in his cabby outfit. "You look quite . . . statuesque," he said.

"Now is not the time for levity, Q," I shot back. A pathetic joke called for a pathetic response.

He shrugged. "There's no time like the present, especially when the future seems doubtful."

"Is what Picard said true?" I demanded. "Are you sympathetic to my cause?"

"Sympathetic? That time the Calamarain almost killed you, I advocated your losing your powers, remember. As for your cause . . . What cause? From where I stand, all I see is you up to your same old stubbornness. Refusing to believe that the Continuum's philosophies and decisions apply to you."

But even as he spoke, I saw something else in his eyes. Doubt, uncertainty . . . and more than that. It was almost as if he were faced with a decision so brutal, so overwhelming, that he had no desire to make it. So instead, he was hoping and praying that I would make it for him.

"All right," I said evenly. "I suppose that's it. "

And then I clammed up.

It was, of course, the perfect angle to take. He stood there, waiting for me to pick a fight, to challenge him. Instead I said nothing. Finally he was forced to say, "So you're prepared to accept the decision of the Continuum, is that it?"

Picard—as much as I hate to admit it—became something of a mind reader at that moment. "Silence implies consent," said Picard. "If he voices no objection, then obviously he accepts it." Q regarded him with a piercing stare, looking something like a bird of prey as he did so, as if he were planning to bore deeply into Picard's bald pate. "That doesn't bother you, does it?" Picard continued.

"Not at all." Q shifted uncomfortably in place.

"Because, frankly, you seem rather bothered. . . ."

"Hey!" He stabbed a finger at Picard. "Don't you presume to judge me. You don't know what's going through my mind. You don't know . . ."

"No. He doesn't know. But he has a sense of it," I said. "It's true, isn't it, Q? You don't want to see this happen. Do you?"

"It's not up to me, Q. Nor is it up to you. It's up to the universe," said Q. His hands were moving in vague, fluttering patterns reminiscent of the bird's wings he'd been sporting earlier. "For all our power and all our omniscience . . . we can't second-guess that." Then, after a moment's hesitation, he added, "She would tell you that if she were here."

"She. The Lady Q."

"Of course."

"You think that she would agree with the Continuum's viewpoint?"

"Absolutely."

"I think you're wrong," I said immediately. "I think she was happier about the birth of our child than she had been about anything in her existence. I think she wanted to see him grow up and claim his heritage. I think, if for no reason other than our son, she would want me to do everything within my power to stop this disaster. But you don't really care about her. She's gone, vanished into a pit, and you haven't done a thing to rescue her or even find out where she is. You have no idea what my feelings are toward her, how could you . . . ?"

"Shut up! Do you think you're the only one who had feelings for her?"

There was dead silence for a moment. But just to show you how obvious Q's emotional state was, how raw, how utterly lacking in subtext . . . it was Data—*Data*—who made the next deduction. Data, who got his emotions through a chip, who only recently had begun to try to incorporate emotional thinking into his hardwiring.

"You are in love with her . . . are you not?"

The statement hung there, daring refutation. I couldn't think of anything to say. Instead I simply stared at Q in mute astonishment. Q, for his part, smiled ruefully.

"Were you in love with her?" I demanded. "For how long?"

"Forever. For always. But you were what she wanted, Q!" As much as I had been endeavoring to repress my rage, the blond-haired Q was making no such efforts. One could almost sense storm clouds gathering overhead in response to his building ire. "You were what she wanted. She trusted you to protect her, and you blew it, didn't you, Q?"

"I didn't . . ."

He wasn't going to let me get a word in. He kept right on going. "You stood by and let her and your son get sucked down into some pit, and you did nothing except rescue these two." He pointed angrily at Picard and Data.

"It wasn't as if I had a good deal of choice, Q," I said. "Believe me, if the choice had been between saving Picard or my spouse, Picard would have gone down the chute in a heartbeat, with Data right behind him."

"Thank you, your loyalty is heartwarming," Picard said.

"Oh, don't get sanctimonious with me, Picard. If both Data and I were being sucked into a black hole and you were faced with an either/or, you'd save Data— You'd save your toaster oven before you'd save me, and don't bother telling me you wouldn't. Look . . . Q." I turned my attention back to my associate. "If everything Picard has said is right . . . that you want me to take some sort of action to stop this, that you want me to get involved, that you want me to find the Lady Q . . . then get me out of this! You know you can do it. Release me. What have we to lose? If it's hopeless, then my departure means nothing. If it's not hopeless . . . then how can you stand by and let this happen? Do you think," and I turned the screws further, "that this is what *she* would have wanted?"

He glowered at me, and I could only guess how conflicted he was. We think we know each other, we Q, but I was starting to understand just how much we were deceiving ourselves. There was every possibility that we were just as capable of self-deception as humans are, and I, for one, found that a most disturbing possibility indeed.

"You," Q said to me, "are a screwup. That's the simple truth. Since virtually the beginning of time, you have screwed up one thing or another, including entire civilizations. I'm probably not in my right mind, but . . ."

He passed his hand in front of me, and I stumbled off the pedestal. Data caught me as I stood on unsteady legs, trying to fight the feeling of disorientation that was sweeping over me.

Q took a step toward me and continued his harangue. "In the past," he said, "your misjudgments have had negative consequences for you alone or the poor unsuspecting species with which you've meddled. But so help me, Q, if you botch this up . . ."

"You'll what? Kill me?" I asked, rubbing the back of my neck.

He shook his head and smiled sadly. "No. You will have killed us. The stakes are too high this time, Q. Do right by her, and don't make a mess of it, or—"

Suddenly there was a massive thunderbolt from on high. Q had just enough time to let out a shriek, and then . . . he was blown from existence. I shielded my eyes from the intensity of the flash, and when the light subsided, I ventured a look. There was nothing left of Q but a small pile of ashes.

I couldn't believe what I had just seen, and obviously neither could Data or Picard. I guess the Q on high were upset. It kind of makes you pause when one moment you're having a friendly conversation with someone and the next moment he's a pile of ashes. Data was checking to see if he had a specimen box on him to gather samples, when I suggested that it was probably best that we move on. The very air around us seemed charged with raw fury, and black thunderheads were converging on us. And these were not just any clouds. They had shaped themselves into a dark and fearsome face . . . the face of the Q we had met at HQ. He didn't look happy at all. I would even go so far as to say he looked pissed. And since he had just turned my buddy, my friend, my newly discovered coveter of my wife into a few flakes of carbon, it was really time to go.

Picard, who also recognized the cloud-faced Q, agreed. "Now," he said with characteristic understatement, "would be a superb time to be situated elsewhere."

A wiggle of my nose and we were gone. The last thing I heard was the roar of our leader, the great and all-powerful Q, raging, "You can't stop the End, Q! Nothing can!"

He'll get over it, I thought. As for me . . .

. . . I wasn't going down without a fight.

We went everywhere at once.

Humans can do that as well, except they do so on a much lower and more simplified level. They call it "dreaming." The human mind, were it capable of utilizing more than the meager ten percent or so that it currently does, would be able to project itself to all places simultaneously. The human mind would be able to conceive of a universe way beyond the paltry limitations it perceives. But humans are unwilling, or perhaps unable, to let their minds "journey," afraid of the responsibilities it would entail and the permanent change it might mean for them.

Going everywhere at once is fairly simple. The mind is the gateway, you see. The mind, each and every mind, is connected at a sort of matrix point to the rest of the universe. All one has to do in order to go everywhere at once is turn one's mind inside out and step through. It's quite elementary, really. A young Q is capable of such a thing within moments after its birth. A human, after a lifetime of study, might make a few halting steps in that direction, but inevitably stumbles. There are humans, a very small number of them, as I mentioned earlier, who look within themselves in self-reflection and introspection for year upon year, to the exclusion of all else. These few humans are the only ones who come close to obtaining the goal of becoming "one with everything." Humans contemplate themselves and ponder. I contemplate humans and laugh. Not very loudly; that would be distracting. I just snicker politely from behind my hand and wonder out loud what fools these mortals be.

So . . . I went everywhere. Stretched my consciousness throughout the universe and back, considered all the possibilities, and tried to determine just where we should go next. I had to do it on the Q.T. because the other Q were close on my heels. I could sense their collective disapproval. They had all been busy with their great End-of-the-universe party until I dropped in as the official party pooper. I wanted to put a stop to it, and therefore they wanted to put a stop to me.

Part of me couldn't blame them. Part of me would almost have considered it a mercy killing of sorts. If the only thing at stake had been the Q Continuum, I might very well have simply shrugged and said, "Fine. End it. The Q Continuum is so replete with humorless, cloddish dolts that we're just as well rid of the whole thing. Pack it in, tie up the entire Q Continuum in a large box with a bow, and toss it away. Anything to spare us the eternal, infernal whining of the Q about how blasted boring everything was."

But there was more at stake. There were, first and foremost, my mate and son, lost somewhere in the pit. I could not simply stride cheerfully and willingly into oblivion and let my last thoughts be those of confusion and uncertainty about their fate. I, who had spent my entire existence questioning, couldn't allow my life to end with that question.

And there were my own needs to consider as well. The ennui of the Q was not shared by me. I had said it quite succinctly to the head of the Q Continuum—I wasn't finished. Not yet.

But they would finish me off if they could catch me. No question about it. As I went everywhere, I could sense that they were doing the same: putting out feelers, trying to figure out where I would go next. And for what reason? To head me off. To stop me from stopping this great . . . whatever it was that faced us.

I kept ahead of them, but just barely. I extended my senses to the utmost, probing and detecting their presence before I committed myself to any one course of action. To the *Enterprise*, to Earth, to *Voyager*, to any one of a million different possibilities. But all those routes were closed to me; the Q Continuum was waiting for me like a lion in the high grass. I needed a safe place. . . .

And I found it.

It was the last place I had expected, but it should have been the first. I reached out and pulled Picard and Data with me, and a moment later we arrived, high on the precipice, poised on the edge . . . of the great abyss.

"What in the world—?" Picard managed to get out. He looked a little dizzy. The experience was quite unlike anything he'd encountered before. "Where . . . were we?" he demanded, trying to muster some of his old authority.

"Problem, Picard?"

"I felt . . . for a moment, I felt as if . . ."

"We were everywhere?" I asked.

He nodded. "It was an odd sensation . . . like . . ."

"Dreaming, yes, yes."

"Will you stop finishing my sentences, Q?"

"Then talk faster."

He looked at me a little perplexed. I continued to survey our surroundings. They were much as I remembered them. The great, gaping hole in the ocean's floor stretching out before us was just as I had left it. I fancied I could almost hear voices from deep within the crevice, crying out in torment, but I shrugged it off. For one such as I, to believe is to shape reality, and so the voices immediately ceased. Perhaps they had never been there, or perhaps they still were, and I simply didn't hear them. Either way, I didn't want to listen to them anymore.

"This is the area where you rescued us," Data observed. "Why have we returned here?"

"Do you have someplace you'd rather be?" I asked. Slowly I walked toward the crevice. The seabed had been wet and thick with mud, but now it was dried out and hard-caked. It was a vast and empty plain, with only this massive crack in the ground to give it any distinction. High above, the sky was a haze of purple, with shafts of red that conjured up the image of bleeding.

"Perhaps—"

"*Be quiet, Picard,*" I said, allowing the pressure of the moment to affect me for the first time. "You are here only at my sufferance. I have already saved your lives. You flatter yourselves to think you understand what is happening here, but you do not, you cannot!— The only thing standing between us and annihilation is my ability to concentrate and determine what we're going to do, and your constant prattling isn't contributing one shred of usefulness! This isn't the *Enterprise,* Picard, and believe it or not, there are some situations in this vast, wonderful universe imploding around us that you are simply not fit to handle. Have I made it plain enough for you? Have I spelled it out? Have I delivered it to you in sufficiently small enough, bite-sized pieces that you can digest it? Well? Have I?"

I was standing barely inches away from him.

And he slapped me.

He.

Slapped.

Me.

I couldn't quite believe it. Rage coursed through my entire

body, and Picard was a hairbreadth away from being transformed into a frog or a cloud of vapor, or simply having his atoms scattered in a billion different directions.

"You still . . . have no idea . . . what I could do to you," I stammered. "After all this time . . . all our encounters . . . perhaps your familiarity has bred contempt. Perhaps you think that I would hesitate to destroy you in the most painful way possible if it suited my fancy." I was now so close to him that there was barely any air between us, and my gaze bore straight into the back of his head. "I am the villain. That hasn't changed. Oh, we've had our fun with mariachi bands, and with Robin Hood and the like. But I'm still the bad guy. And any other bad guys you've faced since me . . . are nothing compared to me. The Borg? The Romulans? The Cardassians? I could have cracked apart their planets with a snap of my fingers. I could have sneezed and blown away their entire starfaring fleets. So whatever you think you are, Picard, and whatever you think your relationship with me might be, do not presume—for a moment— that anything less than a gulf the size of infinity separates you from me."

I thought it was a pretty good speech—a bit long perhaps but I was hoping Data got every word. While I was pondering whether the speech came under the heading of motivational or inspirational, that idiot actually raised his hand to me as if he were going to slap me again.

"Oh, do it, Picard. Make my day."

And he could tell, from my voice, from the look in my eyes, that this time I meant it.

He lowered his hand.

But he did not lower his gaze. Instead, to my surprise, it softened and I saw, of all things, sympathy.

"You're worried about them, aren't you?" he said. "The

End of the universe has less importance to you than finding your mate and your son."

He was right, of course. I knew he was right. And worse than that, he knew he was right, and he knew I knew it.

"They're going to be all right. We'll get them out," said Picard.

"Yes. Yes, we will," I responded. The use of the word "we" was generous on my part, since I was certain that I was going to be carrying the bulk of the workload.

Pretending that the last few moments hadn't taken place, I cheerfully tried to put us back on course.

"Picard," I said, "we have to get to the bottom of this." The two of them looked at me, waiting for the next shoe to drop. I didn't say anything.

"That's it? That's your plan?"

"Right! I mean, it makes sense, doesn't it? To find out what happening we need literally to get to the bottom of this. That's where we will find the answer."

"And if there is no answer?" asked Data.

"Oh, there's always an answer, Mr. Data. It may not always be one that we want to hear, or that we understand. But there is always an answer."

"Has there ever been an answer that you didn't understand, Q?" asked Picard.

I gave it a moment's thought, and then shrugged. "There's a first time for everything, I suppose."

"Let us hope this isn't it," Picard said.

"Indeed."

And with that we stepped boldly toward the crevice.

It was big. Grand Canyon big! And I wanted to observe it before plunging in. Was it steaming hot or freezing cold? I tried to get some sort of sensation from it, but nothing was forthcoming.

"So . . . how do we get down?" asked Picard. And then, because he'd never been much good at waiting around for others to plot strategies, he answered his own question. "It would seem climbing is the only option. Unless you can simply . . . materialize us down there."

"That, in fact, is my intention," I told him.

Relocation was the easiest trick I knew. It was no more difficult than moving mountains . . .

So, with an admittedly nonessential flourish, I caused us to disappear in a burst of light. Our next stop: the bottom of the abyss. Imagine my surprise when we reappeared and found ourselves right back where we started. I spun in place, so quickly did I look around, that I nearly tripped over my own feet. "Say what—?" I managed to get out, which certainly wasn't the brightest utterance I'd ever made.

"It would appear we have not moved," Data said.

"Thank you! Thank you for that brilliant evaluation, Data," I shot back. "Are there any other pithy comments you'd care to make?"

"What happened, Q?"

"I don't know what happened, Picard. All I know is that we should be down there, but instead we're still up here."

"Did something negate your power?"

"No. No." I was vamping. "It was as if we were . . . reflected . . . somehow. Bounced back."

"Something is capable of defying your abilities?"

I rolled my eyes. "Why don't you say it louder, Data? Why don't you walk around with a billboard and make a big fat announcement?"

"Calm down, Q. I know it's a bitter pill to swallow, but Data was just asking a question."

"One question too many! And while we're at it, let's get

something straight. I'm still Q. An infinity of options minus one is still an infinity of options."

There was a sudden flash, and three pairs of antigravity boots materialized on our feet. I smiled smugly and walked straight toward the crevice. "You see, Picard?" I said. "We shall float down, as gently and as noiselessly as hair follicles deserting your scalp."

I walked confidently over the edge, hovered there for a moment, the gravity boots working as expected . . .

. . . and then my stomach shot up into my mouth as I started to plummet.

The only thing that prevented my plunging straight into the void was the fact that I reached out and snagged an out-cropping as I fell. I held on with all my strength, trying to use the toes of the boots to push myself back up. No good. My fingers slipped.

I was clutching nothing except air. But in the instant before I started to fall, Data's golden hand grabbed my wrist and held me there. The strain on my shoulder felt tremendous. I thought my arm was going to rip right out of its socket. What was odd, of course, was that I was unaccustomed to feeling anything resembling pain, and why in the world I would experience such a sensation now, while dangling over the crevice, was a mystery to me.

"Your powers don't seem to function within the proximity of the crevice," Picard said.

"Oh, gee, Picard, you think so?" Masking my sarcasm had never been one of my strengths.

"So," said Picard, wisely not reacting to my annoyance, "do you have any other ideas."

"None spring readily to mind," I admitted, "but I'm working on it!"

"So noted," said Picard, as if everything that was occurring was going to be entered into his insufferable captain's log.

"I believe I can be of service in this matter," Data said. He walked straight to the edge of the abyss and looked down, contemplating it for a moment. Then he crouched and swung his legs over the drop, turned, and caught the edge with his fingers, all in one smooth motion.

"What are you doing?" asked Picard.

We heard the sound of chiseling. "Creating handholds, sir."

Indeed he was. We approached the edge and looked down to see. The bottom was not visible; for all we knew, we would descend and descend until our strength gave out, at which point we would fall and keep on falling forever. Then again, it was clear that nothing was going to be accomplished without some degree of risk. And Data was endeavoring to reduce at least one element of that risk. With the strength of his android arms and legs, he was punching and kicking holes in the rock face beneath us, which we could easily use as a means of descent. He moved like a monkey: a superstrong, gold-skinned monkey. Data continued to descend with remarkable efficiency and paused only occasionally to look up. He was already nearly out of sight. "Shall I continue, Captain?" he called out.

"By all means, Mr. Data," Picard answered back. "Good thinking."

"Thank you, sir. 'Good thinking' is what I am paid for." Data paused a moment, considered, then looked back up. "Am I technically still on salary, sir?"

"Data . . . keep working."

"Yes, sir."

He promptly continued his descent, and, a moment later, the darkness enveloped him completely. The only indication of his continuing descent was the sound of his hands punching into rock.

"After you, *mon capitain*," I said gallantly, bowing slightly and gesturing toward the edge of the crevice. Picard did not seem amused . . . but then, what else was new? Unlike Data with his flowing and seamless movements, Picard moved far more gingerly over the edge. I waited a few moments to give him a head start, and then I followed. The darkness was absolute, and for some reason I felt very alone. It was a long way down, and after a few tentative descending movements I began to wish I could pray.

We Q don't pray, you see. We never have. A prayer is, after all, an appeal to a greater source, a higher authority than we ourselves. That authority is created, defined, and deified by lesser beings: beings who attempt to put a label on that which they don't understand in hopes of grasping it.

The simple fact is that there is no such thing as god.

Oh, I've tweaked Picard with the notion of a god now and then. Made allusions and such. But the truth of the universe is not so easily quantifiable that any aspect of it—particularly something as wondrous and amazing as the creation of it—can be tagged and labeled as "god." I know, I know . . . there is more in heaven and Earth than is dreamt of in any philosophy, but the concept of one, single supreme being? No. No, it's too nonsensical even to contemplate. Yes, there are those things which one doesn't understand, and that is perfectly acceptable. There are things even I do not understand: The human fascination with the accordion, for instance. And coconut oil. Incomprehensible. Oh . . . and baseball. The only game more boring is found on Sraticon IV. It's called Frimble, and it consists of groups of sentient beings sitting around placing bets as to when a newly painted wall will dry. It's not bad enough that they sit and watch it dry; they spend their time commenting on it, as if it was a horse race! But baseball, in terms of boredom, comes a close second to Frimble. It makes me sad to think that the great coliseums of old, with all the pomp and circumstance, and the eating of the Christians, would be turned over to a sport as banal as hitting a little white ball around a field, all the time trying to catch it. It just goes to prove, certain things don't get better.

But, to return to the concept of god . . . I have been worshiped as a god, so I know about the mind-set that brings about these attitudes. It's all hogwash and nonsense. Gods exist for three reasons: (1) to explain that which cannot be understood at the time by the person who is asking; (2) to fulfill a spiritual longing; (3) to have someone to whine to about the unfairness of life when things go wrong. Obviously, none of the above apply to me.

How would one distinguish a god, anyway? Anything that might be attributed solely to a god's ability on an ordinary planet, we of the Q Continuum can accomplish with the snap of a finger (and even that much effort is required only if we're feeling overly dramatic). So how could we, or I, in turn, believe in something greater than ourselves? To explain the inexplicable? We've no need for that; to us, nothing is unexplained. Everything is clear, concise, and easily comprehensible.

The thought of breaking down and begging for help from some supreme, all-seeing, all knowing deity is nothing but absurd. After all, if you follow the logic, the alleged being allowed the predicament to occur in the first place. And it is from this same being you are asking for salvation. I just don't get it.

So, no. No prayers for me. If I were going to be introspective—it underscores the dichotomy of my existence. When I first encountered Picard, I presented myself as Q the questioner. And so I am: I probe, I dissect, I seek knowledge by testing lesser beings (of which there are a staggering number). But if I am truly omniscient, then what need is there for such interrogations? The results should be preordained and known to me, involving no more mystery than, say, an "experiment" involving an ice cube tossed on a skillet. My oh my, what will the poor ice cube's fate be, we wonder? Of course we don't wonder: the stupid thing is going to melt. What else is there to say?

Except . . . will it skid this way or that way on the skillet? Will it take five seconds to melt or six or seven? Will it scream? No ice cube in the entire history of the universe has let out a cry at such an ignominious fate, but . . . what if this is the first? Wouldn't that be interesting to witness?

You see what I'm getting at.

It's the equivalent of the human art form of pointillism. Omniscience enables you to see the big picture in ways that no one else can. But even if you are omniscient, you still have to squint to see the individual dots that make up the picture, the same as everyone else. So I spend my days studying dots, to see which color this or that one is, and how it fits in its particular place. In examining the minutiae, I find a way to spend eternity without going mad.

Sometimes . . .

Sometimes I wonder if I have truly succeeded.

How would I know if I were mad? Truly? There are mad creatures who believe that they have the power of the gods, or of the Q, if you will. Certainly their perceptions are as real to them as mine are to me. Q spoke to Picard earlier of how, if all units of measurement were shrinking proportionately, we could determine if the universe itself were shrinking. Well . . . if I were indeed insane . . . how would I know? I would have nothing to measure it against, particularly since my best anchors of reality—my mate and my son—were yanked so cruelly from me.

As I hung on the wall of the abyss, my hands tightly gripping the holes Data had created in the rock face, I couldn't help but wonder if I had indeed been seized by a sort of dementia. What if everyone else in the Q Continuum was right and proper and sane . . . and I had simply lost my mind, engaging in a crazy endeavor that any sane Q would have known to turn away from? Perhaps my abilities had been taken from me as a sort of fail-safe because I was on the verge of becoming a mad god.

To whom do mad gods pray? Englishmen?

I forced such thoughts from my mind, for that way lay . . . well . . . even more madness than I was dealing with already. I lowered myself down the rock face, grabbing cautiously onto each new handhold Data had carved. I heard the thudding beneath me as Data punched each new handhold, and as I listened, I began to realize what the problem was. It was, in fact, the big picture.

Remember, the big picture was routinely open and clear to me. But not this time. This time, I couldn't see the picture for the points. I was exploring completely uncharted territory, with no clue as to where I was going or what was going to occur when I got there. In a way, I sorely envied Picard. This was something to which he was quite accustomed. He ran headlong into things all the time without the slightest clue as to how it was going to turn out. I hated to admit it, but it was nice to have someone along who had no trouble boldly going where no one in his right mind had gone before.

And Data was along for comic relief.

"Data," came Picard's voice, distracting me from my reverie. "Data!" There was an urgency to his tone.

Immediately I realized why. Data's chipping away down

the rock face had been steady, almost rhythmic. The holes he had been creating had been perfectly consistent in their depth and frequency. Naturally one tended to expect machinelike precision when dealing with a machine. But the sound of his chipping had stopped with no warning. And if the sound had stopped, one didn't need to be omniscient to know that there weren't going to be any more toeholds.

I could see the rock wall because my face was right up against it, but otherwise it was as dark as a suicide's heart. I could not see Picard below me, and I certainly couldn't see Data. "Picard, what's going on with Data?" I called. "You're closer to him. Can you see him?"

"Not at all," Picard shouted back up to me. I wasn't sure why he was shouting. It was so quiet around us, the silence so absolute, that a whisper would have sounded like a cannon shot.

"Any thoughts as to our next move, *mon capitain?*" I asked.

And then I waited.

And waited.

"Picard, you're not remotely amusing," I told him, but I already knew that he wasn't there to hear it. "Picard," I said once more, and when still no reply came, I murmured, "Well, what a fine pickle *this* has turned out to be!"

That was when I heard the scream.

It was long, high-pitched, and distinctly female, and for a moment, just a moment, I was absolutely positive that it was my mate. I called out to her, trying to make myself heard over the howling . . .

. . . and suddenly the holes weren't there. I don't mean that my hands slipped out of them or that they closed up around my fingers. I mean that one moment I had a grip on the rock wall, and the next . . . nothing. And I hadn't even moved!

I slid down the wall, pinwheeling my arms helplessly.

The universe is dying, the words echoed in my head, *and I refuse . . . I refuse . . . to believe that it cannot be stopped. . . .*

And with the high-pitched scream cutting into my very soul, like the cry of a banshee ushering in the dead, I plunged into the depths.

The scream was earsplitting. After what seemed an awfully long time I began to realize it was not the shriek of a woman. It took me a moment to identify the sound as something I hadn't heard in ages. A train whistle? Yes, a train whistle!

At that same instant, someone kicked me in the stomach.

I shouldn't have felt anything. I should have been impervious to all pain. Instead it knocked the wind out of me. It also prompted me to open my eyes, which was a good thing because a foot was coming down on my face. I sat up quickly and the foot barely missed my head. The owner of the foot, a tall and somewhat panicked-looking man, hurried past without even the slightest acknowledgment that he had nearly left his footprint on my face, the face of a being who, if angered, could turn him into a flyspeck!

Except . . . given the present circumstances, I wasn't really sure if that were possible anymore, which prompted me to do a quick self-assessment. Was I bereft of my powers, as had happened once before? Thankfully, I quickly discovered that such was not the case. My powers and abilities were all intact; I could sense them. But there was a restraint, an impediment upon me, preventing me from utilizing them. In the final analysis, I suppose, it amounted to the same thing—I was powerless . . . The timing of such a loss could not have been more catastrophic. What was it about this crevice, this abyss, that robbed me of Me?

I looked around to get my bearings.

I was standing on the platform of an old train station. The wooden planking of the platform was rotted in places and generally covered with grime. There was a train in the station, and it let out another whistle. It sounded forlorn, like a child crying for its mother.

By this time my awareness of things was growing in stages, as if an artist somewhere were assembling a picture around me, layer upon layer, each layer becoming clear only after it was in place. It now occurred to me that I was also hearing, over the shrieking of the train whistle, voices . . . voices crying, pleading, shouting, begging—a cacophony of misery. Names were being called out, profanities hurled, but one sentiment was loudest of all, expressed over and over again: "This can't be happening. This isn't happening. This isn't real. We're all going to be fine, yessiree Bob." In spite of the fact that they were all being pushed and shoved and prodded like cattle, they held on to that sentiment as a drowning man holds on to a life preserver.

As for me, I was still occupied with keeping myself from being stepped on. It was a very unusual and disconcerting experience, having people crowd in on me. You have to understand: I am Q. I know I've said that, but it's comforting to repeat it. When people see me coming, they tend to keep their distance. Masses of people part like great waves when I arrive. I am quite accustomed, thank you very much, to having a sphere of untouchability around me. I like it that way— who wouldn't? It serves to remind others of who they are and who I am and the great expanse between us.

Do not begrudge me this, and certainly do not think me unique. After all, every god demands worshipers. No god is an island. Beings who are supposedly all-seeing, all-knowing, all-powerful nonetheless have an insatiable need to have worshipers reiterate their status, every day and twice on Sundays. Now me, I am no god, and I happen to know that no such beings exist; but even I like to have my fancy tickled every now and then. Hear me, fear me, steer clear of me, for I am Q, the alpha and the omega, the beginning and the end. It has a certain ring to it. A certain *"Je ne sais quoi!"*

So you can understand that being trampled didn't sit well with me at all. Unfortunately, there didn't seem to be a damned thing I could do about it.

It was then I spotted Data.

He was simply standing there, not moving at all. He was bolt still, which was somewhat entertaining to watch. It meant that if people bumped into him, they just bounced off. The irresistible force meets the immovable object, and this time the immovable object was winning hands down. What amused me was that Data kept apologizing. "I am sorry. Pardon me. Excuse me. I am most sorry." Over and over again, a steady stream of it. It was amazing!

I made my way toward him. He saw me coming and gave me that rather pathetic wave that only androids can muster— you know the one I mean . . . out of body, out of mind. I waved back, not wanting to disappoint him.

The station was teeming with all kinds of races. But no matter what their color or creed, be they blue, green, neon-yellow, aquamarine, or pink with purple polka dots, they all had the same expression on their faces: a look of incredulity that permeated every fiber of their being and rolled off them like blasts of heat from a desert dune; this can't be happening to me! *This can't be happening to me!*

Suddenly the mob parted, and I saw Data coming toward me. He was pushing people aside with a steady rhythm—so much for manners. His was a fairly studied pattern: shove, push, apologize, shove, push, apologize, all the way from one side of the platform to the other. Since he was doing such a good job of it, I decided to stay in place and have a look around till he arrived.

Aside from the train and the platform, there were no signs to indicate where we were or what was expected of us. There was a sky overhead, which I could not even begin to comprehend. If we were in some sort of crevice, could there possibly be a sky? But there it was, in all its glory, a most amazing shade of violet with a sun just descending below the horizon, the last rays filtering up into the night.

The train on the edge of the platform was . . . interesting . . . very interesting. A powerful steam locomotive with quite a number of cars attached—actually, they looked as though they stretched off into infinity. And they were not what would normally be considered passenger cars. They seemed more like cattle cars, designed for carrying freight or animals—not sentient beings.

But people were being herded into these boxcars by overseers who clearly were in charge and enjoying their job. I was not surprised to see that most of these overseers were from the more aggressive races. The Jem'Hadar, the Cardassians, the Kreel, on and on. The most warlike, the most predatory, and they were behaving in exactly the same way they always behaved.

They had whips and bludgeons; they had cattle prods; they had all the typical devices of torment that one associates with these events. And they used them with all the relish the average sadist typically employs.

I stopped one woman who stumbled past me, and I said, "Why are you all going along with this?"

"With what?" She was old, terribly old. Every difficulty she'd ever encountered, every year of her life, was etched into the wrinkles of her face. Her hair was white and stringy, and her eyes were empty. "What do you mean?"

"With this! Why are you going along with this?" I gestured to the herders who were shoving more and more bodies into the cars. "There are many more of you than there are of them. You could put a stop to it. Just resist."

"Resist what? Everything is going to be just fine."

"But . . ."

She then walked away or, more exactly, was swept away. Data arrived just at that moment. "Are you all right?" he inquired.

"Well, my powers aren't functioning, and I'm surrounded by zombielike oddballs who seem to have no grasp of what's happening to them. Other than that, I'm fine; how about a quick hand of pinochle?"

"These people do not seem to be thinking clearly. I have been listening to the conversations and the passing comments, and they appear not to believe that any of this is actually occurring."

"That's my impression too . . . ex*cuse* me!" I'd gotten an elbow in the face from a passing, shell-shocked Zendarian. "What do you think is happening, Data?"

"It is difficult to say. They do not seem inclined to discuss their opinions . . ."

Then we heard a familiar voice . . . the voice of Picard . . . from behind me. "Why are you standing there?" he said.

Data reacted with as close to open astonishment as he ever came. I turned to see what he was looking at, unsure why the android would be so stunned by the simple sight of his commanding officer.

Immediately, I understood.

It was Picard, all right . . . but he was clothed entirely in black. His left hand had been replaced by a conical blaster device. His face was deathly pale, and half of it was obscured by an elaborate visual mechanism that doubled as a means of tracking and regulating his every thought. He was, in short, no longer human. He was something rather frightening and very familiar. It was, however, most urgent that I keep in mind the amount of damage he could do us. Although my power was currently being denied me, this new version of Picard was very likely functioning at full, lethal capacity.

"We stand here," I said, carefully addressing this enhanced Picard, "because we don't wish to surrender to the herd instinct."

"Your wishes," said the being known as Locutus of Borg, "are irrelevant. You will enter the car."

"It is our desire," began Data, "to prevent the End of the universe. We are attempting—"

"Your attempts are irrelevant. Your desires are irrelevant." Locutus held up his weapon arm. "You . . . are irrelevant. Enter the train now . . . or you will be permanently irrelevant. . . ."

I made a move to walk past him, when Locutus of Borg swung his armored hand and struck me squarely across the face. I went down to one knee and felt blood welling up between my lips. I put my hand to my mouth, then looked at the blood in astonishment, hardly able to believe that it was mine. Locutus extended his arm. Data grabbed him by the wrist, twisting it and aiming the weapon straight up so that it discharged harmlessly into the air. For a long moment, Data and Locutus were face to face, almost nose to nose. Then Locutus said, quite calmly, "Data . . . do as I say. Now."

Data appeared to consider the situation a moment, and then he said to me, "Q . . . perhaps we should cooperate."

I didn't move except to touch my bleeding mouth. My thoughts were dark, very dark. "Cooperate with that . . . thing. That French canned ham? I'd rather die."

"You can be accommodated," Locutus informed me. And there was just enough of Picard in there to let me know that he'd enjoy it.

Data stepped closer to me, and said softly, "If you are dead, you will not be able to help your family. Furthermore, if your family is in fact on board the train, you will not be able to find them if you are here on the platform when it leaves."

I looked at him, feeling resigned to the inevitable. "Are you saying that resistance is futile?"

"I am afraid so, yes."

Slowly we moved toward the train. Locutus paced us, never wavering, never taking his attention from us. It was as if he were expecting us to pull some stunt, make some last-minute break for freedom. That concept became an impossibility as we were swept up in the crush of people around us. Even if we had wanted to resist, we would have been helpless to do so. The one benefit of the encounter with Locutus was that it had taken place in front of the train, and so by chance we were now being herded into the first boxcar. If I were going to make a car-to-car search, I would certainly want to start from one end and work my way to the other, although I had no idea yet how I would go about it. It was a most disconcerting feeling, not knowing things. Omniscient beings don't do well with improvising.

At that moment, I heard Picard's voice. "Data!" he shouted, but this time it was coming from a totally different direction. It had been my assumption until now that somehow, in this bizarre pit into which we had dropped, Picard had simply been transformed into his erstwhile Borg identity. Now, though, I realized that such was not the case. For there, big as life, was Jean-Luc Picard—the real one. He looked a bit the worse for wear, with some scratches and bruises, but otherwise he was hale, hardy, and as annoying as ever. He was caught up in a crush of people plowing in from the other direction, waving their arms over their heads as if they were swatting so many flies. Picard had spotted us and was shouting as loudly as he could, "Data! Q! I'm here!"

"Hello, Picard!" I called back and waved my fingers jovially. "Did you buy us anything?"

"What?" he shouted back. Grasping the fine points of sarcasm has never been Jean-Luc's forte.

Then the voice of Locutus of Borg rang out. It was the same voice, of course, but in the intonation, the delivery, the two could not have been more dissimilar.

"No talking. No fighting. Talking is irrelevant. Fighting is futile." Not a great conversationalist.

Locutus had taken up a position on the top of the foremost car. Smoke was billowing from the smokestack, obscuring him from time to time before the wind carried it away. He looked formidable from his perch, and clearly he was not about to tolerate anyone who gave him the least bit of difficulty.

Picard's head snapped around when he heard the voice. He couldn't believe what he was seeing. We were now in front of the open door of the foremost boxcar. The guards were working their magic, and within moments we were unceremoniously shoved into the car. The massive door slammed shut. Everything was dark. It took a few seconds for the eyes to adjust, during which time the reality of the situation struck home . . . we were imprisoned in a cattle car with a hundred other beings. Things looked bleak.

I called out, "Q, q!" But no one responded. No one said

anything. There was occasional sniffing and sobbing, and the smell . . .

Understand something: all beings give off aromas—which is a nice way of putting it. This is simply a fact of nature. Normally these aromas are checked by frequent ablutions, usually taking place once a day. However, if I had my wish, there are certain individuals who might consider attending to the problem every few hours! As you can imagine, this was an extremely stressful situation. Whatever scent control might have been in use was, under these circumstances, not working. It was a less than satisfactory olfactory experience, I can tell you.

After a few minutes my eyes adjusted.

We were a motley crew. Beings from every corner of the universe were packed in so tightly that everyone was forced to stand. Picard made his way to my side. He looked stunned, shaken to his core. "Did you see him?" he asked, and I could tell it was not a rhetorical question. He was genuinely open to the possibility that his senses had deceived him.

"Yes, Picard, we saw him," I said.

"Presuming," Data added formally, "that you are referring to Locutus."

"Of course I'm referring to Locutus, Data!" Picard snapped. Then, with obvious effort, he calmed himself. "I'm sorry, Data. I shouldn't have spoken like that." It was classic Picard. With the entire universe teetering on the brink, thrust into an alien situation, and faced with the flesh-and-blood ghost of one of the most horrific experiences of his past, Picard was still concerned about treating his pet android with tact. Manners: can't live with them, can't live without them!

"No apology necessary, Captain. I am not schooled in taking offense."

Under the circumstances, it was impressive that Picard

managed to smile at all. Then he grew serious. "How is it possible, Q? That Locutus could be here, as well as me?"

"Locutus is part of your past, Picard. Do you recall having been here before?"

"Certainly not."

"A cross-dimensional occurrence might be a possibility," Data noted.

"Yes, that would seem to answer it. Owh! Watch where you're going!" I snapped as someone stumbled into me. It was a large, beefy man. I pushed him back, hard.

"I think Data has put his finger on it," I continued. "We've been speaking thus far of the universe ending, but that's not really the case. It's the multiverse that's coming to an end . . . and as such, it would make sense that we might run into manifestations from other dimensions."

"So he . . ." Picard involuntarily glanced upward, assuming that the dreaded specter of his past was still prowling about on the roof of the car, "is from another dimension . . . a parallel universe . . . where I was never rescued . . . where I continue to be Locutus?"

At that moment the whistle screeched and the train lurched forward.

Picard spotted a Vulcan standing stoically in the corner. If one is looking for sound, logical thinking, a Vulcan is a good individual to go to. I must admit that even we Q find the Vulcans among the more impressive of races. Not on our level, of course. But of all the races I've encountered in my time, they certainly have the greatest potential not to make complete idiots of themselves.

The Vulcan was of medium age, his temples slightly graying. He appeared to be meditating. "Excuse me! Sir! You there!" Picard said. "Do you know where we are? Where we're going?"

He looked at Picard with quiet assessment, and then said, "We are not going anywhere."

"I beg your pardon?"

"We are in a circumstance that is clearly impossible," the Vulcan continued. "On the surface of it, we have been pulled from our homes, our lives, our livelihoods to this unknown place and crammed into a strange conveyance for no discernible reason. That cannot be. Such things simply do not happen. It is not logical."

"Yes, but . . . that is what's happening," Picard replied gently, feeling he needed to bring the Vulcan up to speed.

The Vulcan shook his head, looking ever so slightly amused. "That is circular reasoning, sir. The fact is that such things do not happen; therefore, this cannot be happening either."

Data, naturally, had to stick his golden nose into it. "That is also circular reasoning."

"Perhaps. But it is logical. The notion, however, that what I am currently experiencing has a basis in reality, is absurd at its core. It is far more reasonable to assume that this is a hallucination of some sort, or a dream. Perhaps a mind-meld gone wrong, or an illness which has befallen me that I do not comprehend. The simplest explanation is generally the correct one."

"Occam's Razor," said Data.

The Vulcan raised an eyebrow. "Sutak's Fifth Principle."

"Beethoven's Ninth," I chimed in, but no one found it amusing.

"It would appear that great minds think alike," Data observed. He was looking at the Vulcan instead of me when he said this . . . the little asswipe.

"This is a charming discourse, truly, and I would like to keep listening to it for seconds on end, but we have other things to attend to," I said. "My family isn't in this boxcar, so there's no reason for us to remain."

But Picard didn't seem quite so sanguine about leaving. He had decided to make it his personal challenge to convince everyone to attend to the situation. So, he assumed his "soapbox" voice and called out, "All of you . . . listen to me! You do not have to submit to this! We can commandeer the train! We can mobilize, we can defeat this thing, we can . . ."

"What are you saying?!?" someone screamed. "Nothing is wrong."

"Nothing is *wrong?* You've given over control of your lives to unknown oppressors who are shipping you to a place you don't know, for reasons that are equally murky. How can you say nothing is wrong?"

"There is no problem. Nothing is wrong. Everything is going to be fine."

Similar sentiments were expressed throughout the car. "It's fine. There's nothing wrong. Don't make trouble!"

To his credit, Picard continued the argument. "Listen to me!" he said. "This is a fact: as incredible as it may sound, some force, some entity is threatening the very fabric of the universe! We are, all of us, being subjected to an ordeal, the reasons for which we cannot comprehend. The only thing we can do is to rise against it and let whoever, or whatever, is behind this know that we will not tolerate it! That we are not cattle to be pushed and prodded about. We are people! Sentient beings with a right to control our own destinies! Now who is with me?"

I had to admit, it was a most stellar performance, and under ordinary circumstances, such rhetoric would have been sufficient to get even the most recalcitrant of individuals to bellow, "We're with you, Picard, and we will follow you into the very jaws of hell!"

Instead, the only response he got was blank stares and confused looks. And then the Vulcan, with the air of authority that only Vulcans can lend to a pronouncement, said, "There is nothing wrong. None of this . . . is happening." If Mary Baker Eddy had heard him, she would have risen from the grave and kissed that Vulcan on the lips.

"Why are you denying the obvious?" Picard shot back.

"The senses can be deceived . . . can they not?" said the Vulcan, and he looked me square in the eye. I was taken aback. I wasn't entirely sure why the Vulcan should be addressing me so specifically. After all, a little while earlier I had been musing on the very subject of how untrustworthy one's senses could be, particularly in a situation as totally alien as this one. I was beginning to feel that everybody was picking on me.

Then someone in the back of the boxcar called out, "It *is* most definitely happening, but everything is going to be fine. Just fine. Everything is going to be just as it was, and we're not in any danger whatsoever. Why . . . they're just taking us on a ride somewhere, and after that we'll be returned to our homes none the worse for wear." This Pollyannaish sentiment was getting huge nods of approval. What idiots!

"You are wrong. It is *not* happening," the Vulcan retorted. "None of us is here. But you are correct in your belief that no action need be taken. On that, we are mutually agreed; merely for different reasons."

I hope this exchange will give the reader some inkling of the absurdity of the situation. I felt as if I were in some "poor man's" philosophy class. A little hemlock at this juncture would have gone a long way.

Raising my hand as if I were a schoolboy, I said, "Picard, I've already stated that there is no reason for us to stay here, and given the banality of the conversation, can we get on with it? Can we continue searching the train?!"

I could not recall a time when I had seen Picard look so discouraged. "Yes," he said softly. "Yes . . . I see no reason for remaining here either. You're right, Q."

"My three favorite words," I said. "Now, any thoughts as to how we are going to get out of here?"

"Mr. Data—" said Picard, and then he motioned toward the far wall of the boxcar. At first, I thought that he was asking Data for suggestions. But then, as I saw Data nod, I understood that since the two of them had been working together for so long only a few words from Picard were necessary. All he needed to do to set the android into motion was nod.

I hate to admit it, but to some degree I envied them that relationship. For all the uncounted centuries that I've strode the galaxy, I had never really had anyone with whom I communicated on that level. Not even the Lady Q. Granted, we were able to communicate by sharing thoughts, as were all the Q in the Continuum. But there was a difference between that and not even *having* to think because the other person knows what you're thinking. That entailed a level of confidence and trust that was—remarkable as it may seem—outside of my experience.

Not that I would have said any of this to Picard, of course. So instead I simply said, "Yes, Data, get on with it . . . proceed. . . . Chop . . . chop!"

Without a moment's hesitation, Data made his way to the far end of the car and placed his hands flat against the wall. The Vulcan took a mild interest in what Data was up to; perhaps he thought the android was mind-melding with the boxcar. I, however, immediately understood what he was doing. He was silently testing the wall of the boxcar, placing pressure against it, sensing its give. Then, without any further hesitation, he drew back his fist and drove it right through the slats of wood. The boards splintered, and a gust of wind blew through the opening. Considering the stench within the car, it was most refreshing. In a moment Data had an opening large enough for a man to pass through.

Data turned and gestured for us to approach. We cleared away the remaining boards and got a good look at the situation. I couldn't say I liked what I saw. We were flying along the tracks at an incredible rate, the wheels clacking away like staccato thunder. The idea of hopping from car to car was quickly losing its luster. I had no idea just how much personal protection I had in this realm, but I was beginning to suspect that the answer was, very little. I had already felt muscular pain, cold, and discomfort. Based on that, I had to believe that tumbling to the ground at our present speed would have nothing but unfortunate consequences for me. Data, I suspected, could probably handle such a fall with minimal risk, but that wasn't going to do Picard or me one bit of good.

To make matters worse, the cars were attached by a coupling mechanism that was far narrower than I would have liked. Where were my powers when I needed them?!

Interestingly, Picard wasn't looking at the tracks; he was looking up at the roof of the car. "Looking for Locutus, are you, Picard?"

He nodded.

"Afraid of what he represents?"

Picard's brow furrowed. "Of course not! I am simply concerned about the security risk he presents. We don't need him shooting at us from overhead."

Picard had been so blasted smug since this business began, I was pleased to give him some of it back. "That's not it at all, Picard," I said, smirking. "I saw the way you looked at him when we were at the station. The very thought of him terrifies you, paralyzes you with fear."

"I've made my peace with that a long time ago, Q."

"One never makes peace with evil."

"You don't know my mind, Q."

"Well, that makes two of us."

Picard disdained to look at me after that crack, instead turning his focus to Data. "Data, can you get us through to the next car?"

"Yes, sir," Data said confidently. That was the useful thing with him: a human might answer such a question out of a misguided sense of bravado. He would then have to screw his courage to the sticking place and try to see through on the boast. Not Data. Clearly he had already analyzed the situation, considered it within the parameters of what he knew he could and could not accomplish, and concluded—based on all that information—that it was within his capabilities to accomplish the task at hand.

"Then make it so," said Picard. I love that expression! So typically Picard. Our hero couldn't settle for saying "Go ahead" or "Best of luck" or "Let's do it." No, he had to proclaim, "Make it so." Picard was someone who fancied himself master of his own destiny. No wonder he was so easily able to master the fundamental and underlying concepts of mindality in the Q Continuum. He was someone who routinely believed in shaping reality to his needs. "Make it so" basically translated to, "Make reality into what I wish it to be."

Damn the man. He would have made a passable Q, given different circumstances.

Data stepped out onto the coupling. Since he had decided that he could do it, there was no second-guessing or hesitation on his part. He simply did it. Rather commendable, really. With quick, sure steps he crossed the coupling, unconcerned for his personal safety, his uniform jacket and pants riffling in the wind, but his hair staying flat. I think he combed it with shellack. The adjacent car was only a few feet away, but for some, the distance might as well have been miles. Not Data. He might have just as easily been crossing the street to the bagel shop.

Data proceeded to punch through to the next car. I could only imagine the reaction of the people on the other side of the wall: standing about, squatting perhaps, when suddenly a golden fist comes crashing through the wall. Data was probably very sweet about it. He always said, "Excuse me." "Pardon me." "I hope I'm not interrupting."

Within seconds, Data had again cleared enough of an opening for us to step into the next car.

"After you, *mon capitain*," I said with a mock salute.

Taking a deep breath, Picard stepped out onto the coupling. He moved surely at first, but a sudden bump in the track sent him staggering. In a flash Data snagged Picard's wrist just as the captain started to lose his balance. With a little tug Data eased his commanding officer into the next car. He then turned to me and extended his hand. I thought I was at a debutante party. "Why, Data, I didn't know you cared," I intoned in my most coy voice.

I stepped onto the coupling and froze. All I could envision was me, tumbling onto the tracks—to my death. Actually, I'm being a little dramatic. Would I die?—of course not. I'm too grand to die. I might just . . . fade away, however, remembered by a few billion as a good friend and mentor. A happy-go-lucky soul . . . a bon vivant . . . a . . .

"Q! Come on!" shouted Picard. "Do you need me to help you?"

That was, of course, all I needed to hear to jar me out of my reverie. I set my jaw and stepped onto the coupling with a confidence that I couldn't begin to feel. The thing shook beneath me, but I paid it no heed. I took three quick steps, and started to trip, when Data grabbed me with the same assuredness he had used reeling in his captain. He pulled me through to the next car, and once more we were awash in the smell of confined beings in various states of fear, but this time the stench was almost welcome.

I anticipated great protestations from the assembled rabble but . . .

Nothing. Absolutely nothing. In this car, everyone was seated, and they were all staring in the same direction: toward the great sliding door. And every single person who was looking at the door was shaking his head.

It was almost as if they were practicing a strange religious ceremony. Back and forth, back and forth went the heads, in a slow and steady rhythm that was chilling to behold. "No," they droned, "no, no, no."

I called out, trying to find my family, but got no answer. They weren't there. Truthfully, it was hard to believe that even the people who were there were in fact there. They seemed so totally disconnected from their surroundings, even more profoundly than those in the car we had just left. No. No. No. No.

"Why are you all shaking your heads?" Picard demanded. The man was never capable of leaving well enough alone.

Naturally he received no answer. Why should he? How could he? If he were surrounded by people who were denying everything around them, how in the world could they be expected to acknowledge Picard's question, or even Picard himself?

"Leave them, Picard," I told him firmly. "There's no point."

"But—but—" Then he said nothing, realizing the truth of my words.

We pushed our way through the car to the far end, and once again Data worked his "magic." Fortunately when one is working with a being such as Data, concerns about his fatigue don't really factor in.

The next car was much like the last.

As was the next.

And the one after that, and the one after that.

Picard, his quixotic impulses in full bloom, every so often indulged them along with his budding messianic complex. He would make grand efforts to get the people worked up, to encourage them to take the situation into their own hands. But after a while even he gave up.

We continued on. Smash, step, "Excuse me." Smash, step, "Pardon me." From one car to the next. I began the search of the boxcars with high hopes that I would find my family, but that was not to be. The further we went, the more convinced I became that there was some grand purpose behind all this that required I go through a series of challenges before achieving my goal . . . the thought wasn't very original, but I had precious little else to hold on to.

As we passed through yet another car filled with people in different states of denial, Data announced, "It would appear that this is the second-to-last car."

Picard and I gave him that "Are you sure?" look, upon which Data poked his fist through the wall and we all climbed out onto the coupling. It was no small feat to get our heads round the corner of the boxcar so as to have a look for ourselves. He was right (surprise, surprise). We were almost at the end of the train.

On the one hand, this was good news. It meant that our immediate quest would be over. The good news, however, was quickly followed by the bad news. If the Lady Q and q were not in the next car, then I had absolutely no idea where to look for them. We might simply have to remain on the train, I thought, and ride it out to its ultimate destination.

But that was not someplace I wanted to go. My every instinct told me that the train's final destination was, literally, final. I had nothing upon which to base this conclusion beyond whatever vestiges of my omniscience remained. There just seemed to be such an air of . . . of doom. And to see this nightmare through to the end, I felt, would mean just that.

I looked to Picard, and I recognized he was thinking the same thoughts as I. The notion that Picard and I were of one mind was, I must admit, a bit horrifying.

"Let's get on with it, Data," he said firmly. "Let's see what's in the last car."

Data moved with the same confidence and surefootedness he'd displayed during this entire procedure. As I leaned out of the boxcar, I noticed mountains far in the distance. There was a rumbling of thunder, and every so often a flash of lightning. "Wonderful," I thought. "Rain. Just what we needed to make the adventure complete."

We quickly jumped the coupling. By that point, Picard and I had become nearly as adept as Data in crossing from one car to the other. The coupling still shook furiously beneath our feet, but we had become accustomed to "riding" the vibrations, like surfers making minute adjustments for changes in waves. I wasn't even glancing at the ground anymore, and the possibility of my tumbling off the train felt remote. Indeed, would that I had been a bit more hesitant in the final crossing, because when we climbed into the last car . . . it was bedlam.

I had no idea what prompted it, no clue as to why this car was significantly different from the others. The simple fact is: it was *very* different. It was borderline insanity. No, I take that back. It was south-of-the-border insanity—way south!

All around us, people were screaming at the top of their lungs: *"This isn't happening! Make it stop! They can't want me! They must want someone else! You! They want you, but not me! It's not time for me yet! It's not time!"*

The distasteful smell of alien body odor had been replaced by a uniform stench of panic, and I can assure you it made me nostalgic for the earlier fragrance. We tried to shout above the din, but we couldn't even begin to make ourselves heard. It seemed as if the people in this car believed that if they shouted their protests loudly enough and frequently enough, they might make the problem go away. Now, to their credit, I have tried that technique in the past, just as a child might scream repeatedly, "It's not time to go to bed." And, while it might work for omnipotent beings, lesser creatures usually learn that it's a behavior that gets you nowhere.

Finally—and I have to credit him for it—Picard managed to get his voice above the howling and called out, *"Stop it! Stop it! This is accomplishing nothing!* If you want to turn your energies to rectifying your situation, join us! Fight against those who are oppressing you! Stand up and be counted. All is not lost." It was the first time in quite a few cars that he had trotted out his rhetoric, and I found it quite stirring. I had a hint of "Crispin Crispian," "Once more into the breech" and all that rousing stuff.

And this time he certainly got a reaction. Not like in those other cars where they simply looked at us with vacant stares. Oh no. This time they took one good look at us and . . . attacked!

Several centuries ago, I was passing by a far-flung world and came upon a man steeped in misery. He was seated at the base of a cliff, staring off into space, and although he seemed lost in thought, it was clear that something quite tragic had happened to him.

He didn't see me or sense me, for I was hiding behind a bush. To my amusement, this man began to pray.

"Dear one," he moaned. "I am a dead man. I have committed an awful sin. My brother and I came to a disagreement over a female, and I struck him a fearsome blow. I did not mean to kill him, dear one, but I did. In our land, there is only one punishment for the slaying of another, and that is death. And so, I am a dead man. I am dead."

Deciding that I might provide some mild amusement for myself, I presented myself as a shaft of light from on high, and spoke to him. **"No,"** I intoned. **"You are not a dead man."**

He gasped and tried to clamber to his feet, but the strength had gone out of his legs. He put his hand to his chest. "I'm . . . I'm not?"

"No. You are not. Do you believe in me?"

His head bobbed so vigorously that I thought it might topple off his shoulders.

"Very well. Then I tell you that you are not a dead man, but you have done wrong. Do you see the fearsome

cliff high above you? You must climb to its very summit and stand upon the edge."

"Your will . . . is my command, dear one." He could barely get the words out, so breathless and stunned was he by this unexpected visitation. How many times, I wondered, had the poor sap poured out his heart to some alleged deity and received only silence for an answer. But now . . . now, god was speaking to *him*. Hope swelled in his heart as he verily flew up the side of the cliff. So quickly did he climb that he cut his hands against the sharp rocks and tore his clothes, but he did not care. All he knew was that he had been given a divine mission, and he had no intention of failing.

Finally he reached the top. The cliff extended to a narrow point in front of him. He steadied himself and made visible efforts to calm the racing of his heart. When he was finally able to control himself, he took a deep breath and walked with confidence to the very edge of the cliff, just as he had been instructed. There was not so much as the slightest bit of wind, nor the faintest sound from even the smallest of animals. Utter silence prevailed. He stood there, wondering what to do next.

Suddenly, the piece of ground he was standing on gave way. Which is not surprising, since it is rather stupid to stand at the very edge of a cliff. He waved his arms frantically, trying to defy gravity, but to no avail.

As he plummeted to the ground, my voice boomed from on high again, *"Now* you are a dead man." He landed with a splat, but I had already lost interest and was heading off to new worlds to accomplish more good deeds.

I know you think I was naughty, but in truth, I had done the man a favor. You don't believe me? You know as well as I that once his fellow beings had caught up with him, they would have dispatched him in a far more painful fashion.

The quality of mercy is not strained, but falls—like those who commit fratricide—from the heavens above.

The reason that any of the foregoing is remotely relevant is that, as the lunatics attacked us from all sides, I had an inkling of what that man must have felt in his final moments. The only difference was, I didn't have a supreme being to whom to turn and complain, because I was the closest thing I knew to a supreme being, and my presence wasn't doing me a damned bit of good.

I'm going to take this moment to admit that punch-ups are not exactly my strong suit. Willing an entire invading armada into the midst of an asteroid storm because I don't like how they've got their ships decorated . . . that I can do. But going *mano a mano* with crazed lunatics is outside of my field. The last time I attempted such a thing was when I endeavored to box with the commander of a space station. It had, I must admit, gone badly for me. He did not seem intimidated by my status. I got back at him, of course. But that is another story entirely, and one we need not pursue at this moment.

In this instance, however, crushed in as I was in the boxcar, I had no choice but to resort to fisticuffs. The madmen, voicing denial with a fervency and aggressiveness that would have given even the most steadfast lunatic pause, were tearing at me, pounding at me as if they hoped they could pummel me into the floor. I fought back as best I could. Picard was in the same situation, and having only marginally more success.

Data, on the other hand, had options open to him that we did not.

He leapt from the floor of the boxcar straight up to the ceiling, caught an overhead rafter, and punched through the roof. The wood splintered easily on impact, and without hesitation Data dropped back down into the morass of pushing and shoving bodies. He knocked people aside, tossing them this way and that, and the entire time his expression never changed. Indeed, he remained insufferably polite during the whole ordeal, murmuring, "Excuse me," "I am sorry," "Step to one side," "I hope I did not break your nose," and similar comments. It would have been almost enough to make me laugh, had I not been fighting for my life.

Data snagged Picard and threw him like a sack of potatoes onto the roof of the boxcar.

I then felt Data's hands grabbing me by the scruff of my neck. "I'd rather do it myself!" I started to say, but Data didn't care about my pride. In retrospect, considering that the people in the car were trying to bash my brains in, it was probably better that he acted in the manner he did. The next thing I knew I was airborne, and within seconds I was next to Picard on the roof of the boxcar. Data followed suit moments later, hauling himself up with alacrity.

If I had thought that our situation was precarious when we were gallivanting between cars, it was definitely worse now. The blasting of the wind was unbelievable, and we crouched low to avoid being blown off altogether.

I studied our options and realized that they were exceptionally limited. It was Data who observed, "I believe that we have made a tactical error."

"In what way?" asked Picard.

"We were previously at the front of the train. Instead of working our way towards the back, we might have made our way forward, initiating an attack on the locomotive. If we had managed to overwhelm the engine's personnel and bring the train to a halt, the task of inspecting the boxcars would have been far simpler and accomplished in a more leisurely fashion."

Picard and I stared at Data for a long moment, and then at

each other, and then back to Data once more. *"Now is when you bring this up?! Why didn't you say something earlier?!"* I said.

"My imperatives do not involve strategy. My skills instead lie in the analysis of scientific . . ."

"Oh, shut up, Data!" I shouted.

"Don't tell him to shut up! He's right! It should have occurred to me!" Picard snapped. "But it didn't. I don't know why."

"I can tell you why!" I shot back. "It's because it would have meant going head to head with Locutus!"

"That's not true!"

"Now who's in denial, Picard?"

Picard looked as if he were going to haul off and strike me. Instead he said to Data, "It's a plan we can still follow. On the roofs of the cars, if we watch our step, we should be able to make our way back to the front of the train."

I looked forward to the engine. It seemed to be several miles away. It was likely that the perception was an optical illusion, but it was an extremely convincing illusion. The alternative was either jumping off the train or making our way back through the boxcars—neither of which held much appeal.

Picard looked at me, and I nodded, indicating that I was along for the ride, no matter how harebrained the scheme sounded. Staying low, we began to make our way forward. The wind was overpowering and made progress slow.

Of course, I'm only describing how Picard and I were faring. Data, the mountain goat, took to the task as if he had been to the "manner" born. His positronic brain made a thousand tiny adjustments in his body movements to accommodate whatever was thrown his way, and as a result he didn't even need to crouch. He walked upright with a slow, steady swing of his arms. He was a one-android parade.

There was no small talk or chitchat between us as we made our way toward the locomotive. There didn't seem to be that much to say. We did, however, make significantly better time than if we had been crashing through the boxcars. And indeed, there may have been an optical illusion at play, because as we approached the locomotive, it continued to seem far, far off . . . and then, abruptly, it was only a few cars away. We were congratulating ourselves on our safe arrival when . . .

Locutus of Borg rose up from between two cars ahead of us. I'm not quite sure how he managed it. It was as if he were standing on some sort of elevator platform.

He simply stood there looking at us, his weaponed arm dangling at his side. Picard froze in his tracks. The color drained from Picard's face as he pondered the sight of his gone-but-not-forgotten alter ego. "Do not worry, Captain," Data said. "I shall attend to him."

"No." Picard's response was abrupt and harsh. "No, Data. I'll handle this."

"Captain, perhaps now is not the time—"

"Not the time for what, Data?" The edge in Picard's voice did not abate. As for Locutus, he had not moved. He was simply watching the exchange and calculating.

"This is not the time for a confrontation, Captain, that will assuage a deep-rooted psychological need to triumph over an inner turmoil, incarnated in a persona that you find daunting," Data said smoothly.

Heavens, I thought. Not only was he a walking calculator, he was a psychiatrist as well! What a bargain!

"Data," Picard replied slowly, "the End of the universe is approaching. Not only is this the right time . . . indeed, perhaps the perfect time . . . but it is becoming evident that it may very well be the *only* time. Step to one side, please."

"This is ridiculous," I said with obvious irritation. "If Data can dispatch Locutus, then he should do so. This is no time for you to make a grandstand play just to overcome a personal trauma."

"There's no personal trauma, dammit! I'm simply the best qualified to handle him!"

"More denial?"

He fired me a look that spoke volumes. Then he looked back to Data and said once more, "Stand aside, I said."

Data, of course, had no choice. Above all, he was obliged to obey his commanding officer.

It was quite a contrast. Locutus stood there, upright and arrogantly confident. Picard, on the other hand, approached with caution, in a semi-crouch. The mountains which had been so far in the distance earlier now seemed to be looming, and it became evident that we were heading toward a large valley.

Picard came within a few feet of Locutus and then stopped. They faced one another, each a distorted mirror image of the other. Every aspect of Picard's body language signaled that he was truly intimidated by the opposition. But then, to his credit, he squared his shoulders and faced Locutus unflinchingly.

"Get out of our way," Picard told him.

"No," replied Locutus.

"So much for negotiations," I said to Data.

Both Locutus and Picard said, "Quiet, Q." It was rather off-putting for an all-powerful being to be scolded by the same voice twice, simultaneously.

"I'm not afraid of you," Picard told him.

"Your fear is irrelevant."

There was that word again, "irrelevant." Didn't this guy know any other words?

"I want you to move."

"What you want is—"

"Irrelevant, yes, I know." Picard shook his head. "I can practically hear every response of yours before you even say it."

"If you know me so well . . . then you know how this engagement will end," Locutus said.

"I know how you think it will end. But you may be surprised."

"You cannot surprise me, Picard. You are me . . . only an early version." He actually smiled, but on his face it seemed a horrific thing, an obscenity. "You can no more stop me than an infant can stop an adult. You and your desires are irrelevant."

I knew if Locutus and I ever became friends, the first gift I'd give him would be a thesaurus.

I watched Picard lose his footing ever so slightly, but he kept talking. "Freedom is irrelevant, individuality is irrelevant; have you considered, Locutus, what will happen when you yourself become irrelevant?"

"Such considerations are likewise irrelevant," Locutus said calmly. And then he took a step toward Picard.

I was beginning to think they were going to talk each other to death.

"The universe is collapsing around us, Locutus. Your precious Borg collective is going to go the way of all flesh, unless we find a way to stop it. It is in your own interest to help. Why would you be in opposition to that? Who do you serve? Who is behind all of this?"

"I simply act as I must," said Locutus. "I understand my duty, Picard, with greater clarity than you possibly could." He took another step closer. "You pathetic creature. You were part of the perfect Borg collective, the most elegant accumulation of minds in the entire galaxy. How sad you must feel to be separated from that now. How adrift you must be."

"You know nothing of how I feel," Picard shot back. "Oh, but I . . . I know how you feel, Locutus. Because I was trapped within you, remember. To my mind, you are nothing but a bad dream, a faint whispering I'd rather forget. But within you there is me, crying to get out. Struggling against the oppression of the Borg collective, trying to obtain once more the freedom that is the god-given right of all creatures. I can hear myself within you, Locutus. That lone, human voice, crying out."

I couldn't believe they were still talking at each other. I really wished I had brought a box lunch. You have to understand, in my world if you don't get what you want in a few nanoseconds you blast the guy! "Get out of my way." "No?" Bam!!! But who am I to interfere in how other people do things? It's not in my nature. Live and let live, that's my motto.

Picard was still talking. I guess when you're talking to yourself you have a lot to say, and he was leaning very heavy on the psychological stuff. "You're trying to deny it, Locutus. I can tell. Trying to deny the voice in your head that demands either release . . . or an end to the living prison that's been fashioned around it. I know that voice, Locutus. It's mine. Crying out, hour after hour, day after day in soundless agony. Begging you to cease this obscenity, this travesty of an existence. You can fool others, Locutus. You can stalk around and talk about how one thing is irrelevant and another thing is futile. But you and I, we know the truth. We know that what you'd really rather do is put your own weapon to your own head and destroy yourself before allowing this monstrous nonlife of yours to continue one moment more. . . ."

In a low voice, I muttered to Data, "What does Picard think is going to happen here?"

"Perhaps he believes that Locutus will be so overcome by the captain's impassioned eloquence that he will take his own life rather than serve as an impediment to our cause."

"Great plan. And if that doesn't work, maybe the Easter Bunny will save the day."

Picard's voice was rising. "For all our sakes . . . possibly for the sake of the entire universe . . . throw off your programming! Give in to the voice within you that is begging for—"

Locutus lunged.

Picard didn't appear prepared for the charge, but he certainly adapted quickly. He deflected the Borg's weapon. Unfortunately, it wound up pointing in our general direction, and a blast sizzled the air just over my head.

The notions of psychological warfare had been shunted aside; now it was simply brute strength. The two of them went at each other "no holds barred." Data and I watched, mindful that if Locutus looked as if he were getting the upper hand we would quickly jump in to save Picard.

During this exchange the train was approaching a trestled bridge. Beyond the bridge, I saw something that made my heart stop: a tunnel. I also saw, just as quickly, that the clearance between the top of the tunnel and the top of the train wasn't going to be sufficient. And that wasn't the only problem. There was a light at the end of the tunnel . . . a flaming light! I could feel massive blasts of heat rolling from it. The tunnel was an entrance to an inferno that was going to incinerate the train and everyone aboard. The tunnel was clearly the end of the line!

We had to get off the train, but how? I didn't relish the idea of jumping, but there was little choice. It was either plunge into the river and hope the fall didn't kill us, or stay aboard and get incinerated. While I was calculating what to do . . .

Locutus delivered a tremendous blow to the side of Picard's head. Picard went down, and Locutus aimed his weapon to finish him off. Suddenly Data, who decided it was time to intervene, stepped forward and slammed his fist into the Borg's face. Locutus stumbled and fell off the roof onto the coupling below. Picard went after him.

For a brief moment they fought on the coupling, until Locutus managed to get up into the coal tender. Picard followed him there, but it was a move born of pride, not wisdom. Locutus quickly got the upper hand and hurled Picard effortlessly onto the boiler. Picard skidded and almost tumbled off, clinging like a gargoyle to avoid falling off.

We were running out of time, with the bridge and the tunnel coming up quickly. "We need to jump!" I shouted to Data. "Let's go!"

"We cannot leave the captain!" Data said with finality, and before I could answer, Data vaulted to the coal tender. He would have surprised Locutus had he not slipped on the treacherous coals. Locutus saw his advantage and gave Data a tremendous kick. Data stumbled and fell off the tender. The only thing that saved him from falling off the train altogether was that he managed to grab the injector pipes along the boiler. Picard, meantime, was trying to pull himself up to the steam whistle toward the front of the engine.

Locutus now had the upper hand. He stood on the coal tender, trying to decide which target he should go after first. He didn't seem to be paying any attention to me at all.

There wasn't much time left; we would be crossing the bridge within seconds. And then into the tunnel, and the flames.

Locutus made his decision; he went after Picard. Picard, unable to see where Data was, may very well have assumed that the android had fallen off and was lost. Certainly the poisonous look he gave Locutus indicated just that. But Locutus could not have cared less. He simply stood there, atop the locomotive, savoring the moment.

Picard turned, saw me on the roof of the freight car, and shouted, "*Q!* Help me!"

"Perfect," I muttered. "Now he wants help," and taking my heart solidly in my hands, I backed up and took a running leap.

I landed on top of the coal tender, and just as I did, we reached the bridge. I figured we had perhaps thirty seconds at most before the entrance of the tunnel. Locutus turned and fired his weapon at me. I ducked and couldn't help but think—for just the briefest of moments—that I had brought this all to some degree upon myself. It was, after all, I who had "introduced" the Borg to the Federation in the first place. If it hadn't been for me, Locutus of Borg might very well never have existed. In bringing the *Enterprise* into the sphere of the Borg, I had been trying to teach Picard a lesson. Now I was paying for that lesson. There was a disgusting amount of irony in that—and possibly another book: *Lessons Learned on the Way to Omnipotence.*

Apparently, deciding that I needed to be disposed of first, Locutus left the steam dome and Picard and went straight for me. I grabbed up several fistfuls of coal, and just as he got to me, I threw them in his face. Momentarily blinded, he missed his footing and started firing his weapon. He fired twice. One shot went harmlessly into the air; the other hit the coupling that attached the boxcars to the locomotive, severing the connection. Imagine our surprise, especially Locutus's, as we watched the boxcars slowly fall behind.

I would love to tell you that it was part of my master plan: that I had the welfare of all those people in the boxcars in mind all along; that I didn't want them sent hurtling into a fiery, flaming death; and that I had the entire strategy worked out and that Locutus had played into it perfectly. The simple truth of the matter was ... I ... I ... I did! Yes, I knew it all along! If Locutus thought he could dillydally with me, he was sorely mistaken. And if you, the reader, are wondering why I chose to intercede at this particular time, it's because ... I ... I ... felt like it. Superbeings have moods, you know, and I like to pick my time. I could have interceded at any time, mind you, but this particular time seemed the most dramatic. So ...

I took advantage of the Borg's momentary distraction to shove him to one side (with one hand, I might add), and I jumped off the coal tender, over the cab, and toward the main boiler where Picard was clutching onto the smoke stack.

Suddenly, Locutus was on top of me again—if I didn't know better, I would have thought he liked me. How he'd moved that quickly from the coal tender to boiler, I have no idea, but he was right there, and he hit me from behind. The impact knocked the wind out of me. He could have shot me, killed me right then and there, but instead, he aimed his weapon at Picard, his main "squeeze." Over the thundering of the wheels, the crackling of the flames ahead, and the howling of the whistle, he shouted, "Resistance ... is futile." What a rube!

Just then Data vaulted over the top of the locomotive. Like the commando I was, I grabbed Locutus's weapon arm, and shoved it into the space between the handrail and the boiler, wedging it in good and tight. Now this is the best part: the tunnel ... remember the tunnel? ... was less than fifty yards away!

Picard shouted, *"Jump!"* Data and I both leaped clear of the locomotive, and as I tumbled end over end, I managed to catch a glimpse of Locutus of Borg, atop the engine. He was struggling to disengage his weapon arm from the railing, but it was jammed in too tight—! Given a few more moments, he might well have been able to pull it clear, but they were moments he didn't have.

Because I was falling, I didn't actually see Locutus smash into the top of the tunnel. What I did see was a very large smear of red, black, and white over the upper section of the tunnel entrance, and Locutus's still-wedged arm . . . but no Locutus.

A moment later, there was an explosion so deafening that I thought I would never recover my hearing. I heard a very loud scream, and then realized with a sort of distant amusement that the sound was coming from my own throat.

Then, I hit the water.

It was not a good landing. The degree of difficulty was a 10 and I couldn't have scored higher then 2.6! I'm not good at sixty-foot free falls into water. It was a belly flop, I'm sure, and most of the air got knocked out of my lungs. When I hit the water, I sank like a stone! For a moment thoughts of my wife and son filled my head, and I was convinced that they were somewhere I would never find them and perhaps my drowning in this river was the best thing.

As I was having these dark thoughts, I watched a few precious air bubbles escape from my nose. I reasoned that they would be moving toward the surface and I decided, on the off chance that I could make it, to move in that direction as well. I scissored my arms and legs, pumping myself toward the top, and just when every muscle in my body was screaming for rest, my head broke the water's surface. I felt the cool air upon my face, but naturally there was nothing to grab onto, and I started to sink again. You see, I never learned to swim in Q camp. I didn't like the water. Of course, all the other Qs would blithely jump in and frolic about, squealing with excitement and uttering those imbecilities like, "You'll love it once you get used to it." But I didn't get used to it! However, this time, since I was close to drowning, I decided to give it a try. (The above, it should be noted, was intended as irony rather than literal truth. I do that sometimes. I'm mentioning it in case you're irony-impaired.)

The current of the river was strong, and I managed to keep my head just barely above water. I heard Picard shout, "Q!" and I angled myself around and spotted him. The bridge was already far in the distance, the boxcars resting on the track far from the conflagration which was still roaring in the tunnel. I had no idea if anyone within the cars would make it, or whether they would just sit there forever, or what passed for forever given the circumstances. But at least they had a chance and for that I was grateful. Our presence here had accomplished something.

Data was helping Picard. That did not surprise me. I was starting to believe that Data rivaled the Antarean slithering beetle and the earth cockroach in his ability to survive. He supported Picard with one arm around his chest. What with his flotation device abilities, I was half expecting Data to turn into a beach ball. While they swam toward me, I looked around. Our escape from the train, the fall from the bridge, and our subsequent survival was nothing short of miraculous.

I wasn't sure what Picard would say to me when he drew close. "Thanks for not abandoning us," was a possibility. "Q, you're more heroic than I would have thought possible," was another. "You freed the freight cars and saved those people. Congratulations, Q," was yet another option.

What I was not expecting was: "Do you hear a sort of roaring sound?"

Splashing about as I tried to keep my head above water, I didn't understand what he was talking about. I felt like saying, "Of course I hear a roaring sound! It's the sound of me trying to keep from drowning!" But I didn't say it because I had a mouthful of water at the time. And then I did hear a roar. It was a steady and loud roar and getting nearer with every second.

Of course I knew what it was. I had seen enough B-movies to know what it was.

It was a waterfall. A big waterfall.

We tried to swim against it, but it was useless. Even Data was helpless against it.

I suddenly felt a deep fury building within me. *The universe is dying . . . and I have managed to survive against impossible odds so far, and now I'm being dumped over a waterfall. It isn't right! It isn't fair! I hate this situation! I wish this weren't happening! I wish I weren't here! This is all unfair! I want to lash out to make someone pay for this ignominious situation.*

And then, we were swept over the edge.

My next recollection was of sitting up and coughing quite strenuously. I looked about and found myself lying against the riverbank. Apparently I had survived the waterfall and had been swept downriver. I stood and looked around to get my bearings.

Stretching out before me was a city, and the city was burning. Not all of it, just sections. The air was thick with smoke and sounds of misery. I took one deep breath and coughed violently.

Above me there was a small footbridge. I splashed over to it, noting that the grass on the bank was already thick with ash from the burning city.

I looked around and saw no one . . . at least, no one up close. In the distance, figures revealed themselves against the flickering of the flames for just a moment before disappearing down streets and alleyways. They moved with speed and stealth, and there was something about their posture that struck me as ominous. People moving in such a manner were doing so because they were concerned that someone else was going to spot them. I wasn't eager to find out who that "someone else" might be.

Nevertheless, they were far enough away to be of no immediate threat. My first concern was the whereabouts of Picard and Data.

I still had no real grasp of where I was, or what was happening. I was operating entirely on instinct. However, it was an instinct that had been formed by eons of omniscience, and whether I had access to my powers or not, that intuition was not to be discounted.

My instinct told me that from the moment we had entered the crevice we had been descending. I don't mean this to be as obvious as it sounds. This crevice was not a mere pit: it seemed to be an entrance to different levels of experience. But what brought one from one level to the next . . . I hadn't a clue.

Picard was nowhere to be seen, nor Data. Truth to tell, I didn't feel that I needed them. The business with the train had been a botched affair, and I felt that a continued association with them was going to divert me from my primary purpose—finding my family. Besides, Picard could truly be quite insufferable. He had this annoying habit of looking at me in judgment. Jean-Luc Picard, a paltry human, daring to judge me. Me! It was really rather intolerable. I had more knowledge than he could possibly accumulate in a hundred lifetimes, and he dared to sit in judgment upon me. Yes, quite insufferable indeed.

And while I'm at it, let's not forget Data. If nothing else he is a reminder of just how far short of its goal humanity will always fall. He is utterly efficient, totally unselfish, and willing to sacrifice himself on a moment's notice if it means the saving of others. Yet he wasn't human. He is an idealization of what a human could and should be. Humans fancy that their god made them in His own image, and a human in turn made Data in the image of man, yet Data exceeds the greatest capabilities that humans could possibly attain. If one were of a mind to speculate on theological notions—as time-wasting as that might be—one might wonder whether this were in fact part of a pattern. What if the hypothetical "god" had, in fact, fashioned a creation better than Himself. It would certainly explain His tendency to be vengeful, to find new and improved ways of wiping His creation off the face of the earth. He is resentful because they are greater than He would ever be, for all His power. Which means, if you follow my logic, that, sooner or later, humanity will turn upon Data and destroy him because he, the creation, had outstripped the creator. As annoying as I find Data to be, I do not envy him his eventual and inevitable fate at the hand of his masters—the humans.

No . . . I needed neither Picard nor Data. Bringing them along in the first place had been a mistake. I could do just fine on my own. Except for the fact that I was hungry and wanted lunch and someone to talk to. Which is probably why I cupped my hands around my mouth and shouted, *"Picard! Data!"* I called it several more times, my voice echoing in the distance.

My cries were met with phaser blasts. So I forgot about lunch and started running. There was a building nearby that was untouched by the fire. I made a beeline for it.

It was a tall brick structure, but the bricks were a bright red rather than blackened. Indeed, the entire structure had a look about it that was reminiscent of an old castle. And it was as yet untouched by the fire.

There was a brightly colored flag fluttering from a flagpole atop the building. For a simple piece of cloth, it seemed almost proudly defiant of the chaos that swirled around it. What was most curious was the emblem upon the flag. It was a striking, hissing serpent, its body coiled into the shape of the letter "M." Upon seeing that symbol, I couldn't help but feel a gnawing at the pit of my stomach. If it represented what I thought it did, then I might have even greater problems on hand than I previously thought. And considering the mess I was already in, that's a fairly powerful statement.

I heard gunfire. Whoever was shooting at me was getting closer. Suddenly, a blast blew me off my feet, and when I sat up again, I saw a sizable crater just a few yards away. A little more to the right, and I would have been Q-bits.

I was about to stand up and make my displeasure known when a blast blew yet another crater to my left. These guys weren't kidding! I had to get to that building and fast!

From around the corner came a group of heavily armed men. They were heading right for me, phasers slung under their arms—there was no point in my running. My only hope was to try to bluff. But it was going to be a hard "sell" convincing them I was omnipotent, with my clothes in disarray, my hair disheveled, and a fine layer of grime on my face. So, I just sat there. As I waited for them to reach me, I watched people bashing in the display window of a store. It occurred to me, as they were grabbing merchandise, that they might be exercising their political "voice," as in the days of old when commonfolk looted under the guise of "expressing" themselves.

As these protesters, for I have to give them the benefit of the doubt, ran off in one direction, the trio of armed individuals arrived. They were Romulans.

The biggest, and probably the dumbest, took a step forward and stared at me. I said nothing. In circumstances such as these, discretion is the better part of valor.

Everyone thinks Shakespeare made that up but who is Shakespeare? Certainly not the drunken sot I knew who couldn't spell his name the same way twice and willed his second-best bed to his wife in a document that is simplistic to the extreme. Truth be told, I made it up. Along with a bunch of other ditties like, "To thine own self be true"; "a rose by any other name"; "all the world's a stage"; and "let them eat cake," which that unwashed, uppity ingrate rejected on the assertion that the word "cake" should be changed to "fried dough"! What a jerk! I brought a plague upon his house and gave the line to someone else. Someone who had a head on her shoulders, for a while at least, and who understood its meaning and poetry. Don't talk to me about Shakespeare!

Now where was I . . . oh, I remember. The greasy Romulans.

"I know you," said the leader after scrutinizing me a moment. "There are . . . drawings of you in ancient Romulan texts . . . except you have ears like ours. You are the Laughing God."

Apparently my reputation had spread from Tervil IX. "So I am called," I said solemnly. This was going to be child's play.

"You do not appear godlike," he said. Oops! He was a Romulan who felt the clothes made the man.

"I appear however I wish," I replied archly.

One of the other Romulans—shorter and more pugnacious—said contemptuously, "He is no god. Look at him!"

"Stare into my eyes at your own peril," I said in as low and menacing a voice as I could muster.

Apparently it was neither low nor menacing enough, for the shorter Romulan abruptly brought his weapon up and aimed it squarely at my head. With a sneer, he said, "I will take that dare. If you are a god . . . strike me down . . . now!"

And then, as his finger started to tighten on the trigger, he suddenly lurched forward, his head snapping back, and just for a moment I was extremely impressed with myself because clearly my powers had returned.

He then sagged forward, blood trickling from his mouth, and directly behind him stood a gray and grizzled Klingon, his curved sword upraised in triumph, a large smear of blood running the length of the blade. He shouted one of those annoying Klingon battle cries that always sound like a cross between a belch and a hiccup, and he charged!

The Romulans brought their phasers up, but the Klingon was remarkably quick. With a single slice he cut off the big Romulan's hands at the wrists. The other Romulan was a little faster and managed to fire a shot that tagged the old Klingon squarely in the chest and knocked him off his feet. The Klingon hit the ground clutching his wound and growling. Klingons have this thing about not showing pain, which is kind of ridiculous since everyone else could see he had a hole in his chest the size of a grapefruit. So, while this big lug was writhing around on the ground trying to pretend nothing was wrong, the Romulan calmly stood over him and took aim to finish him off.

Out of nowhere, a blade cut squarely into the Romulan's throat, just above the collarbone. It was a surprise to us all, especially the Romulan. As the top of his uniform took on a dark green tint from the rapidly spreading blood, he grasped at the knife and tried to pull it out. But the edges of the blade were serrated, and the only way to remove it was to tear a huge, gaping hole in his neck. While the Romulan busily tried to decide what to do, he rather conveniently fell over and died. That left alive the other Romulan, who had lost both his hands. In an attempt to keep himself from bleeding to death he jammed his wrists under his armpits. He looked up at me, his face getting distinctly green. "Please . . ." he implored.

"Please?!" I said. "I don't think 'Please' is the magic word today; you'll have to try again. How about Swordfish?" He looked at me as if I had lost my mind. I looked at him as if he had lost his wrists and was making a big mess all over the place. "Go on," I said, "give it a try. It's not 'please' and it's not 'pretty please,' but I'll give you a hint . . . it's got 'My liege' in the sentence." He had no idea what I was talking about so, rather than continue the ordeal, he gave up the ghost. These guys are simply not party animals.

As I watched his soul slither down the street, I heard the sound of feet scuttling behind me and turned to see to whom they belonged. I was assuming that one of them would be the individual who had thrown the knife. Indeed it was. And she was a woman! She was accompanied by several more Klingons.

"Dax, isn't it?" I asked. "Jadzia Dax?"

She stared at me blankly for a moment, and then she recognized me. I could see it in her eyes. But she said nothing at first. Instead she knelt next to the fallen Klingon, and gently stroked his face. "Kor . . ." she whispered. "We should have been faster. . . . I'm sorry."

"Have I taught you nothing, Jadzia?" growled the old warrior. "No apologies . . ."

". . . no fear . . . no tomorrow," she finished the sentence, intoning it in a way that indicated she had heard it any number of times.

"No . . . tomorrow . . ." agreed the one called Kor . . . and then his eyes rolled up into the top of his head, and he was gone.

Dax and the others clustered around him for a moment . . . and then Dax suddenly pitched her head back and unleashed the most ear-splitting howl I'd ever heard. To make matters worse, the others took up the cry. There is nothing more embarrassing than standing on a street corner with a bunch of Klingons braying. It's so embarrassing! I looked at my feet, I looked up in the sky, and finally I just joined them. What the hell, a good cry is therapeutic and the way they were doing it was tantamount to a sonic colonic.

Don't get me wrong; it's not the most hideous sound in the universe. The most hideous sound in the universe is the mating call of the six-legged male *giz'nt,* one of the most short-lived species ever. The *giz'nt*'s call was so atrocious, so bloodcurdling, no one could stand to be within fifty feet of it, and that included female *giz'nts.* But male *giz'nts,* being notoriously chauvinistic, were unaware of this. Consequently their calls never managed to attract any females. They survived for a brief time by mating with females who happened to be sleeping, thus enabling the males to sneak up on them. In those instances, the mating call served more as a sort of paralyzing bellow that froze the female in her place so that— even once she was awake—she couldn't get away fast enough. Unfortunately, it was too little, too late, and the *giz'nt* died off within a few generations. Every so often, evolution simply makes mistakes.

I finally clapped my hands over my ears and shouted, *"Must you?!"*

They mercifully stopped, and Dax approached me slowly. Her hair was down, long, and somewhat ratty. She was not wearing a Starfleet uniform as she had been when I last saw her. Instead she was clad in Klingon battle garb. Upon closer inspection, I realized that one of her eyes was missing. How careless, I thought; it's one thing to lose your purse, quite another to lose your eye.

"Q," she said in a voice dripping with contempt. "I should have known you'd be behind all this."

"Then you would have known wrong," I told her. "I'm as much in the dark about all this as you. Maybe more."

"You expect me to believe you?"

"I don't have any expectations one way or the other. But let's say, for your sake, that I'm lying. Very well." I folded my arms. "Why would I be lying?"

She opened her mouth to reply, but clearly nothing readily occurred to her. She looked to the others, but they shrugged mutely. She looked back at me. "All right," she said, with a low growl that seemed to be a permanent part of her voice. "Let's say you're not. Tell me what you do know."

"The universe is coming to an End." Every time I said it I felt like Chicken Little, but it was the truth!

She considered for a moment, and then sighed heavily. "Figures."

"Makes everything else seem rather moot, doesn't it?"

"It does indeed. What about this place?" She took in the entirety of it with a nod. "Do you have any idea where this is?"

One of the Klingons rumbled, "We are in *Sto-Vo-Kor.*"

"Ah. Well, that certainly clears that up," I said.

Still, for all my sarcasm, it seemed as much an explanation as any other. *"Sto-Vo-Kor"* was the Klingon equivalent of warrior heaven and purgatory, all mixed into one. The charming part of the notion was that they were not acting under the watchful eye of any Klingon god, for as they were fond of saying, Klingons had killed their gods many centuries before.

"Yes, well, on the chance we might be somewhere else, I was hoping that Q might be able to provide us with some answers." She clearly didn't give much credence to this idea that we were in *Sto-Vo-Kor.*

"Would that I had some to provide. And not having answers is not my favorite position in life, I can assure you of that," I told her. "What about you? The last time I saw you was on Deep Space 9. What are you doing here, in the company of these . . . individuals?"

"Deep Space 9?" She raised a questioning eyebrow. "Haven't seen the place in several years. I am . . . I was," and she looked sadly at the fallen body of the grizzled Klingon, "the adopted sister of Kor. I saved his life during an expedition that went awry, we formed a tight bond, and he invited me into his family. I found I had a taste for battle, and I accepted the life he offered."

"I see." Truth to tell, I had paid little attention to Deep Space 9 and didn't know what she was talking about. For all I knew, this wasn't even the same Dax, but a Jadzia Dax from another reflection of the multiverse. After all, I had already encountered an alternate Picard. It had quickly become apparent to me that nothing in this place was what it seemed. "Have you spotted a woman and a child, by any chance? The woman is—"

Dax put up a hand to stop me. "I've seen more women and children than I can possibly count," she said. "No point in describing them to me. Every one I've seen has been a charred, burned corpse. It just . . ." Her eyes grew cold, and her fingers started to spasm as if she were anxious to throttle somebody. "What people are doing to each other . . . and it's all their fault . . . it makes me want to . . ." Her fury had come upon her so quickly that I was transfixed. She grabbed the hilt of the knife she had buried in the Romulan and yanked it out of his neck. It tore a hole the size of my fist. She bent over and wiped the blade clean on his pants leg before shoving it back into her scabbard, then snarled in a feral manner. "All their fault . . ." she continued.

"Who would 'they' be?" I asked.

"The Romulans!" said the ugliest of the Klingons, who was standing a few paces off. The other Klingons nodded in agreement.

I couldn't quite grasp what they were talking about. "The Romulans? You . . . can't seriously think that the Romulans are responsible for the End of the universe?"

"We don't care about that," Dax said tightly. "Do you see

all this?" She indicated again the vista of burning buildings, "This . . . this is a result of the battle between the Romulans and us."

"What battle?"

She looked at me askance. "For someone who's omniscient, you have a lot of questions."

"I'm new in town. What battle?" I asked again.

Another Klingon took a step forward and rumbled, "This place—there are a number of races here, but there are also many Romulans and many Klingons. That is how we know that this is *Sto-Vo-Kor.*"

"Because there are Romulans here?"

"Because we are being given a chance to settle old scores and we believe—as do many of the others—that this is . . ."

Suddenly phaser blasts shot over our heads. "We've been out in the open too long!" Dax snapped, apparently as angry at herself as she was at anyone else. "Karg, suppressing fire! Everyone else, fall back!"

"Klingons do not retreat!" one of them said angrily.

"You're not retreating!" I offered. "You're just advancing in the opposite direction! Do what she says!"

There was the briefest of pauses, but then they followed her, Karg lagging behind to fire a round of blasts for the purpose of driving back any pursuers. I could only assume that they were deferring to her status as adopted sibling to the late Kor, not that that was going to do Kor any good. There was obviously no time to pick up Kor's body and bring it along. I didn't even see where the Romulans were shooting from, but I knew if I had to throw my lot in with anyone, it might as well be the group who hadn't tried to kill me at first sight. So I followed Dax.

She was quite a woman. I wondered if she shaved. Maybe at a more quiet time I'd get a chance to ask her.

We ducked behind a burned-out building. The inside had been gutted, but the walls provided some degree of cover. We paused, catching our breaths, although I admit I seemed far more out of breath than anyone else. "You believe we are where!?" I asked Karg. He looked at me with a totally blank stare. I had to remind him that less than thirty seconds ago he had presented an idea about where he thought we were . . . *hello!* and while I didn't think he had a hope of being correct in whatever his theory was, I was open to any and all speculations. Now that his memory was jogged, he shared his idea with me.

"We are facing a final, ultimate test," said Karg. "The Romulans have always plagued us, tried to annihilate us. Now they are here, in *Sto-Vo-Kor* itself! No place is sacred! No place is beyond their defiling touch! This . . . this is the great Afterlife War that has been long predicted in Klingon scripture. The most valiant of Klingons to face their most despicable of enemies. Here, all the injustices shall be made right! And here, we will annihilate every last Romulan, and that will dictate which race lives and which dies! What we do here will have ripple effects to the land of the living, and beyond that! To—"

"Karg, are you stupid?!" bellowed Dax, and she turned and struck him. The blow rocked him and, although it didn't knock him over, he looked surprised. "How can this be the land of the dead!? Kor is dead! Others are dead! How do you die in the land of the dead? Do you get deader? Think! Think, you great Klingon oaf!"

She had a point, but I liked his story. I just needed: "Once upon a time . . ."

Karg's eyes glared with such fury that I thought they were about to leap from his head. "I do not care who you are or what your rank," he snarled, "you do not address me in that manner, and if you ever lay a hand on me again, I—"

"This is total foolishness," I said, trying to calm them both down. "What are you arguing about, anyway? It's moronic."

Karg turned his glare on me. "You . . . dare to insult me? You call me a moron?"

"No! . . . Yes . . . Well, not really. Do the math," I said.

"Dax," he said and stabbed a finger at her, "I shall deal with you later. But this one," and he suddenly pulled out his huge curved sword, "I will attend to right now!"

He was standing no more than three feet away. No one was going to be able to stop him from slicing me in half. And all I was doing was trying to help!

You know it always amazes me when I reflect upon the eons gone by, just how worked up some individuals get about what they know the least. Take Earth for instance: millions . . . no, billions of people cut down in the prime of life over arguments as silly as "what's on the other side of the mountain?" Mind you, no one has ever been to the other side of the mountain and come back to tell of it, but that fact has absolutely no bearing on the discussion at hand. Great "Cities of the Mind" spring up with accompanying "Maps of the Imagination" to guide you there. And hold on to your head if you don't go along with all this nonsense. Expressing even the modest sentiment that perhaps the proof is insufficient is enough to get you burned at the stake. Good thoughts are not enough; good deeds must be codified; individual expressions of charity must be brought into line. Why? To control. Give me a child to the age of twelve and I'll deliver back to you a superstitious savage for the rest of its life. This was precisely the circumstance I found myself in at that very moment.

And then fate lent a hand. Suddenly, the top floor of the burnt-out building exploded. Debris rained down, and the Romulans attacked from both sides. We were outnumbered.

Numbers, however, don't necessarily mean anything to a Klingon, for one of them can fight with the strength of ten.

"Wait!" I shouted. "This is fruitless! What point is there in carrying this hatred into oblivion? If—if . . ."

They were not interested in "ifs." They were not interested in talking, or reason, or anything except the blind fury that had clearly seized them. Even Jadzia Dax, her face twisted in anger, would have no dealings with the Romulans. Despite some of her high-flown rhetoric to the contrary, when faced with the enemy she was just as eager to throw herself into the fray as the rest of the Klingons.

The blasts of phasers scorched all around us, and the Romulans and Klingons attacked each other. Knives, short swords, daggers, everything was brought into play. There were the sounds of metal on metal, and grunts, and death rattles, and bodies falling to the ground.

I stood in the center of it, like a disinterested observer in the midst of chaos unleashed. Blood spattered about while curses filled the air. "What a bunch of yo-yos," I said, shaking my head.

There's a myth about where this behavior originated. Apparently in the distant past, sporting fans would get together in stadiums to cheer their respective teams. For some, the game was not exciting enough, and so the contest migrated into the stands. Hundreds of angry toughs would go about pummeling one another while the play continued on the field. Understandably, after the game was finished these toughs—high on adrenaline and whatever else—took their mayhem into the streets: breaking shop windows, overturning cars, lighting small fires to express their dissatisfaction that their team had lost the game. So far, so good. But what I found of peculiar interest is that these same toughs destroyed their city even when they won. It didn't matter! Pillage and mayhem if you lose; pillage and mayhem if you win. These people were called "fans," a derivation of the word "fanatics," and so, ever since, I've been very careful how I address fans—lest I get my head knocked off.

A Romulan spotted me and attacked. I was starting to develop a theory, and since I was too proud to run, this seemed as good a time as any to test it. So I didn't move. I simply stood there, picking my nose, making no effort to defend myself, instead concentrating on doing a little excavating.

The Romulan got within a few feet of me and leveled his phaser at me, and then an anvil fell on his head.

It had dropped out of absolutely nowhere. As the battle raged on around me, Klingons and Romulans shouted curses and racial epithets that went back thousands of years, but I paid them no mind. I simply strolled over to the fallen Romulan as if I had all the time in the world. The anvil had completely crushed his head and most of his upper torso. He was utterly flattened. I looked him over, and then saw the snake "M" symbol on the anvil, which was what I had expected to find. "Damn you, Q," I scolded myself, "can't you *ever* be wrong?"

I then turned and saw Dax with her hands at the throat of a blond female Romulan. The two of them were spitting and cursing, rolling about on the ground and doing everything they could to annihilate each other. It looked like mud wrestling with a vengeance. I gave them no more thought than Dax probably gave me, and I walked away without a backward glance.

However, Karg staggered toward me to somehow block my way. He had a gaping wound in his stomach that would have ruined most anyone's day, but not his. Somewhere he still found enough resentment, real or imagined, to want to get even with me; though by this point I was not the least bit interested, nor did I have reason to be concerned, as a curved Klingon sword sliced through the air with a high-pitched whistling sound and sent Karg's head tumbling from his shoulders. The Romulan who had thrown the sword took a step in my direction and was promptly consumed by a fireball that belched out of a nearby building. None of this concerned me as I walked with determination toward the one untouched building on the block. Things were beginning to come into focus.

In the distance I heard continued shouting, screeching, and cursing. I also saw that there were battles going on between others than just Klingons and Romulans, and many of those fights were divided along racial lines. Rage permeated the air. It was as if retribution was being sought for every wrong that was ever done against anyone.

What a bunch of fanatics! With the universe teetering on the brink, was this really the time for people to kill each other? It seemed everyone was seizing this final opportunity to obliterate anyone and everyone who really, truly annoyed them. Was that what the End of the universe was to be about in the final analysis? Last call for paybacks? It seemed uninspired and petty.

As I continued my walk toward the building, I was reasonably sure I was finally going to get some answers. The fact that I was still alive seemed to be an indication of that. That was my theory, you see.

By rights, I should have been dead. Several times they had me cold, and there was no way, simply no way, that I should still be alive. Someone was manipulating things. Someone, I thought, who had noticed my arrival and wanted to make sure I was still alive to face them. So they had taken it upon themselves to run interference. Someone who could do that had to be powerful. And if they were still powerful in this realm, they were also going to be very formidable indeed.

But I had no choice. I knew that the goal was to get me to come to the building that bore the flag. I could have delayed it, could have headed in the opposite direction, could have run . . . but what would have been the point? Sooner or later I was going to end up in there, and "sooner" made more sense to me than "later." My best gambit was to show them I was not the least bit intimidated. That should have been an easy enough task, because in the past, I hadn't been. But times change. We were not meeting as equals: She had the upper hand and she knew it.

But I was determined not to let her know that I knew it. Have I piqued your interest? Read on.

True story:

I once happened upon a man, a human, who was skydiving. His parachute failed to open. Once again, he was not aware of my presence.

And he cried out, "Oh God . . . why me!!"

And in as pontifical a voice as I could muster, I boomed, **"Because there's something about you that really pisses me off."**

Then, just because I was in a good mood, I made sure a haystack was under him so that he survived the fall. Every third bone in his body was broken, but he survived. He told people of his experience, and they all laughed at him; and soon his story entered popular culture and became a reasonably amusing joke that summarized quite neatly the feeling that someone is out to get them. Or, as the saying goes, just because you are paranoid doesn't mean that someone *isn't* out to get you.

What most people don't realize is that there is something of a universal constant about this. There is a symbol on earth known as yin and yang, which shows two semicircular designs wrapped around one another, complementing each other. It is supposed to symbolize the male and female counterparts. But there is another even more telling symbol on the world of Rimbar, which features the same designs, except they are clearly trying to strangle each other. It's all about point of view.

So, as I said, there are universal constants. The best-known one is, no matter how powerful you are, there's always someone who's more powerful.

Or no matter who you are, there are always people out there who simply aren't going to like you. Doesn't matter what you do, what you say, or for that matter, what you don't do or don't say. They're going to take one look at you and there's going to be something about you that just pisses them off.

Depending upon who is involved and just how far the grudge is allowed to get, this attitude can result in anything from personal feuds to homicide to genocide. Now no one likes to go to war against another race, unless there are some good reasons for it; like, they eat too much garlic, or they eat with their feet, or better yet, their skin looks different. All these reasons are good enough to really get behind and do some serious killing. If you can come up with some specific grievances that happened in the past, like, "My grandfather, fourteen generations removed, was spit on by your grandfather," it's even better. There is no statute of limitations on hatred. The more obscure the insult the better. And so groups spend years, even centuries, building up an abundance of grudges, like interest on a deposit. Sucking the marrow of the bone called hatred. Disputes over this person's land, or that person's third niece on her mother's side, or someone who made an obscene gesture once, and someone else who wore pants and a shirt that didn't match specifically because he knew it annoyed someone else, and so on and so forth. It's all very predictable and very silly, and quadrillions of sentient beings have been dispatched for some of the most inconsequential reasons you could possibly conceive of. The most outlandish, of course, is when two groups try to kill each other because they don't like each other's god. And the fact that both gods preach peace on the planet doesn't stand in their way for a moment. These groups are very clever in getting around such obstacles.

By now you must certainly realize that the Q Continuum consists of infinitely superior beings. You would think, then, that we would be above such things. Would that it were so! But the unfortunate thing about universal constants is that no one is spared.

And since we are infinitely superior beings, it should make a certain degree of sense that we would naturally have infinitely superior foes as well.

Not that our foes were really superior to us; at least, we liked to think that was not the case. They understood their place in the universe, as did we, and were able to coexist fairly well.

The enmity between us started this way:

We of the Q Continuum were—for lack of a better term—sitting around one day and minding our own business. Suddenly there was a brilliant flash of light, and we suddenly found ourselves facing beings who were utterly new to us.

These beings regarded us with the sort of distant and contemptuous attitude that we were quite accustomed to—in other words, they behaved like us. And they looked like us. That was really off-putting. Alien races slogging it out with each other, such as the Klingons and Romulans, are all well and good. But the true measure of a first-class enmity is when those who hate each other are indistinguishable from one another. That makes it all the more pointless, and the pointlessness is, in and of itself, the point. If you do not understand the foregoing, don't be concerned. You are not a superior being and are not expected to comprehend.

So . . . they sized us up, and we sized them up. "Hello," they said. They started out rather politely, considering they were going to be our bitter enemies. "We are of the M Continuum."

"Indeed," we replied. "And where, and what might the M Continuum be?"

"The M Continuum is where we live," came the reply. It was like talking to a Möbius strip. "And we, since you have asked, are your enemies."

"Enemies? Really? Why?"

"Because," they said, "there's something about you that really pisses us off."

And there it was, boiled down to the essentials, with all the trimmings and trappings neatly shunted aside. When you get down to it, it's hard to resent someone who puts forward such a bald-faced statement. Furthermore, it's difficult to begrudge them that right. They apparently looked us over and decided that they were put off by the way we strutted our stuff. We understood completely. Given the same circumstances, we might have felt the same way.

"You're here because of the universal constant," we said.

They considered that a moment, and then said, "Why . . . yes. Yes, it would appear so."

Another pause, and then we said, "So we understand one another."

"Yes. It would appear so. But you still piss us off, and we want to kill you."

"Interesting," we said. "But wouldn't it be best to develop a more eloquent reason?"

There was an awkward silence, and then one of them said, "That is always to be preferred."

They then went into a huddle. There was a lot of gesticulation and low mumbling that none of us Q could make out. Finally, one of the M was picked to deliver the "new, enhanced reason." He said, "You are aware, no doubt, that we preexist you."

"No, we weren't aware," we said and all looked at each other somewhat bewildered.

"You are merely a copy of us," M continued.

"Really?!"

"And since we preexist you and since you are a mere copy of us, we've crossed dimensions of space and time to annihilate you."

"Well, grease my monkey!" said one of the Q, but no one on either side seemed really upset. It just wasn't working! The reasons weren't pointless enough. Then, very much as an afterthought, one of the M blurted out, "Your mother!"

Well, that did it! That was all that was required. An insult like that was beyond the pale, and so we went to war!

War is a reason unto itself. Everything else is excuses. The fact that after the war no one could remember whose mother M had insulted, only makes the experience more quintessential. Think about it. What are two superior races supposed to squabble over? Territory? There's more than enough infinity for everyone. Property? Who needs it? No, we were simply enemies because . . . because . . . we were!

Although, truly, we were around first. And if any of us *had* had a mother, we would have been torqued on her behalf.

And so we went to war.

The Continuum war shook the entire fabric of reality to its very foundations. Most of the interstellar curiosities or paradoxes that no one quite understands originated with our initial battles. Black holes? Wormholes? Those were us. We drained energies of whole suns to fuel our struggles against one another and wound up creating portals that shredded entire sections of space.

And when the initial shock waves of the Continuum war ended, neither Continuum was able truly to claim victory, which meant naturally that both of us did. Every so often over the eons, skirmishes would break out. Curious as to what caused Earth's Ice Age? Wondering what formed the asteroid belt? Want to know how certain quasars came about? It's all in the QM chronicles. Read them and weep.

But we had not heard from the M Continuum for some time. Perhaps that was part of what precipitated the boredom and ennui that recently settled upon the Q Continuum. We bait them every so often, and they us, but the major disputes were long in our past. We did have one battle around the time of Earth's late twentieth century that caused a massive release of gamma energy that befuddled scientists on any number of worlds. Centuries before that, there was a skirmish which generated an explosion so massive that it was visible for light-years in all directions. Indeed, humans were so impressed by this shining star that they wound up celebrating its occurrence every year in midwinter from then on.

But recently, as I said, we had hardly heard from the M Continuum. And to tell you the truth, I was disappointed.

As I'm sure you've surmised by now, all of this is relevant because I had intuited—and indeed, had been correct in doing so—that a representative of the M Continuum was lurking around in one of the nearby buildings. I didn't know which of the M was behind all this, but I was hoping that it wasn't M. Anyone but M.

The flag fluttered in the same breeze that fanned the flames. Of course I had seen it when I first arrived, but sometimes the Q are slow. I'm admitting that only for dramatic effect. We still rate as AAA+ Superbeings.

I could sense a steady flow of power emanating from the building. I found it tremendously annoying that someone from the M Continuum was functioning at normal strength. Something was seriously out of joint, and it wasn't just my nose.

I heard voices from within, shouts of anger. Well, at least there was some degree of consistency in that. Then, abruptly the shouting ceased, and there was another voice, softer, reasoned, and firm. A female voice, and one that I knew all too well—it was M. I sighed softly. Just my luck. Of all the people, in all the crazy gin joints, in all the Multiverse, it had to be her.

I continued toward the building. In the street, surrounding the entrance was a phalanx of guards. It was impossible for me to discern their character, or what race or species they were a part of. They were heavily armored, their features obscured. I could sense, though, that they were powerful.

Sense. Yes, sense.

Slowly, as if waking from a heavy sleep, I became more and more "aware" of things around me. Some of the old "magic" was coming back. I could feel it in my fingertips. It was as if, in the great hurricane that engulfed this city, I was walking into the eye of the storm. The power of M radiated from every corner.

I scanned for Lady Q or q, but I detected nothing. Could it be they no longer existed? Could two of the many burned and charred corpses I had seen littering the landscape have been my wife and son?

I refused to accept that possibility. They were alive, I knew it! Or, at least, I believed it. And that was the one thing that kept me going.

I squared my shoulders, ignored the guards, and walked into the lobby of the hotel. A line of beings, single file, snaked around the lobby. Everyone was arguing with everyone else. The only things that kept them in order were the anonymous guards who walked the line, shutting people up with a menacing stare or a slap to the face.

I glanced at the end of the line and then proceeded to walk past.

"Hey!" shouted one of the beings in line—a Stentorian, with a loud booming voice. "Where do you think you're going?"

"To the head of the line," I replied.

"No cutting in! Wait for the Adjudicator like everyone else!"

I endeavored to move around him, but he stepped directly in my path, blocking my way. A guard stood watching but made no move, apparently interested in seeing how this was going to play out.

I was not up to full power, but I decided to attempt a simple display just to see what would happen. The Stentorian put his big fat face right up to mine with the expectation of bellowing his disapproval, when suddenly he discovered he was three feet shorter than he'd been an instant before. The others in line gasped. The Stentorian let out a cry, only this time it sounded more like a mouse. The next thing he knew he was two inches tall. "Size does count," I said and lifted my foot and allowed it to suspend over him. "Does anyone else have any problems with my cutting in line?"

Nobody said anything.

"Good," I said. I stepped around the Stentorian, giving him my heel by way of a parting gift.

Everyone was duly impressed, and I was feeling pretty good about myself. I now walked up to the guard, daring him to block my way.

He didn't budge.

I frowned and prepared to dispatch him as I had the Stentorian.

Nothing. I tried again. Still nothing. I pushed hard. Wrinkles were creasing my forehead, and beads of sweat were running down my face. The crowd began to notice something was up.

If this guard continued to stand in my way and I did nothing about it, I might very well be inviting problems I couldn't handle. The only thing preventing me from getting my head handed to me was that they thought me all-powerful. I had no desire to disillusion them. I was now trying to figure out how I was going to get myself out of this jam.

That was when I heard a voice from within. A female voice that I knew all too well.

"Q, I've been waiting for you."

"Yes, I'm sure you have," I said. The guard stepped aside and I entered the Presence.

It was a huge auditorium off the lobby, with a proscenium stage flanked by columns that rose to a glittering domed ceiling. The walls were festooned with murals, all depicting acts of violence. The oldest sins in the oldest kinds of way.

M was seated in the center of the stage, in one of the most lavish chairs I'd ever seen, with huge clawed feet, and a massive carved bird for a backrest representing justice rising from the ashes. She was not especially tall, but she had an annoyingly regal bearing, with close-cropped red hair, and a steely glimmer in her eyes. She was swathed in a great purple robe, and she wore her arrogance like a low-cut negligee. Suppliants lay at her feet attending to her every wish.

"Greetings, Q," she said. "It's been too long."

"Not long enough, M." My eyes narrowed. "Why do you need guards, oh powerful one?"

"Those? They're for display. Nothing more." Her voice sounded like it came from the bottom of a whiskey bottle.

"Really. I think they're here because your power is no longer infinite."

"That's a charming theory. And if you had any lead in your pencil you'd be able to test it. But, alas, you don't." She rose from her chair. "You know, I had hoped that if I wound up face to face with any of your insufferable Continuum, it would be you. Apparently things do work out for the best."

"What are you doing here, M?"

"Why, I'm the Adjudicator, Q. Surely you must have determined that for yourself. All around us is chaos. A frenzy of fire and destruction, fueled by hatred, nurtured by fury. It is my job to bring order to disorder."

"Is it now?" I folded my arms. "And how did you get this job? Did you answer a Help Wanted ad?"

She smiled with all the personal warmth of a spitting viper. "When I arrived here, it was simply the job that I had. It is my place within the grand order of things."

"How very humble of you, M. It's quite unlike you to know your place."

She rose from her chair and pointed at me in a preemptive fashion, her voice quite strident. "I disagree, Q. That has been not only my strength, but the strength of the entire M Continuum. We know and understand our place in the natural order of things. You—in particular—never have. It is you who are the incarnation of chaos and disorder. You do what you wish, when you wish, leaving nothing but anger and resentment in your wake. Your exploits are notorious. And now you have reaped the whirlwind." She adjusted her slip in a provocative way that suggested she had other things on her mind as well, and then she sat down.

I considered for a moment and then took a step toward her. "Are you saying you're not behind what's happening all around us?"

"I am but a player, Q, content with my part."

"And who *is* behind it, then?"

She shrugged. "That is not my part. I do not know, nor do I care. I sense the End of the universe and am satisfied that I have done right by that universe. My conscience is clear, my business in order. How is your conscience, Q?"

"I'm not concerned about my conscience just now, M, thank you," I said stiffly. "What I'm worried about are my wife and my son. Where are they?"

"How would I know, and why would I care?"

"I suspect you do know."

"You suspect wrong. Indeed, the fact that you're here without them should be sufficient proof to you. I sensed your presence the moment you arrived. So if other members of your pathetic Continuum had come as well, don't you think I would have brought them here?" She stroked her chin thoughtfully. "A son, you say. How very interesting. That is a new development, isn't it?"

"Yes, and no concern of yours," I said quickly, beginning to regret I'd brought them up at all.

"This is my place, Q. My concerns are what I say they are, not what you say they are. I am your host," she said and smiled. "You are here and still alive at my pleasure."

"I see."

She shrugged. "Everything here is as I wish it to be. It's not your place to judge me, but rather mine to judge you." Then she looked at me with open curiosity. "A son? A mate? Are those truly your priorities?"

"They are my immediate concerns, yes."

"Well, well . . . you *have* changed, Q. I'm not altogether certain it's for the better, but you have changed. I wouldn't have thought you capable of it."

"You said you don't know where they are. I believe you."

She laughed curtly at that. "Do you? How kind of you."

"And since you have no clearer idea than I as to who or what is behind this . . . this pit, this sinkhole in which we are all descending, then, if you'll allow me, I'll take my leave."

Immediately, two of the guards stood in my path.

"It's not that easy, Q," said M. "I've waited forever for this moment. You, who have sat in judgment on so many others, you are now going to have others sit in judgment upon you."

"I've had the pleasure of these proceedings already in my own Continuum," I told her.

"Ah, but that was a jury of your peers. Here, you are being tried," and she cocked an eyebrow smugly, "by your superior."

"In your dreams, M."

"That's right, Q. In my dreams. This is all my dream, one of my more pleasant fantasies. And you have had the abominable luck to be in the wrong fantasy at the wrong time."

Light suddenly flared, and I found myself standing in a courtroom dock. There was a railing around me that was waist high, certainly nowhere near high enough to contain me. However, I was sure the guards could adequately take care of that job.

I summoned my full strength, my carefully contained rage, and struck out against M. She could feel me, and she reacted to it. I could see her blink against the strain; she actually had to fight it off. But she tried to make it appear effortless, and she very nearly managed. There was a bead of sweat trickling down her brow, and she said, "A hit, a palpable hit, Q. But not remotely strong enough. Don't you understand what you are drawing strength from is not your own puissance, but mine? You have no more power than I allow you to have."

"You're certainly full of yourself tonight, M. But then, you always were, just as the rest of your kind. So what do you propose? A kangaroo court with yourself as judge?"

Two Tellarites were standing toward the front of the line, and one of them shouted, "Wait! Why is he being treated in a special manner? We've all been waiting here! We have rights! We came to you to adjudicate! He should be made to wait his turn!"

"Indeed?" said M coolly. "You have a dispute?"

"Yes!" said the Tellarite, and he pointed at the Tellarite standing next to him. "He stole my most precious . . ."

We never got to find out what the Tellarite had stolen. M snapped her fingers, and the head of the Tellarite imploded. It was very theatrical. He collapsed to the floor and was caught on the way down by one of the guards, who hauled him out. The only sound to be heard was the clanking of the guard's armored feet as he left the auditorium.

"Does anyone else mind waiting?" inquired M in that sulky voice of hers.

All the beings in the auditorium quickly and vigorously shook their heads "no."

"M," I said reasonably, "this isn't going to solve anything."

"Oh, isn't it?" It was the first flash of temper I'd seen from her, but once it started to roll there was no stopping it. "I disagree, Q. You insufferable prig. You think I haven't watched you and your activities? Witnessed your smugness, your self-satisfaction, acting as if you are better than anyone else. How dare you! How dare you behave in such a fashion, when you know that in truth we of the M Continuum are better than you?"

"You're ridiculous," I replied. "The reason I know you're ridiculous is because no one of the Q Continuum would bother with this . . . this . . . exercise of yours when so much is at stake. The End of Everything is nigh! What possible goal is going to be accomplished by subjecting me to some absurd trial?"

"The goal? The goal is to pay you back for the aggravation you've given both me and others in your lifetime, Q! And that's quite a long lifetime! The goal is to hurt you, to humiliate you, to make you feel my wrath!"

"Your wrath? *Your wrath?* Do you think I give a damn about your wrath?" There was no anger in my voice. If anything, I sounded tired, even patronizing. "Woman, your priorities are so far out of whack that it's literally not even worth discussing. That's always been the problem with your Continuum, M. You're so convinced that you are the center of everything. We clearly have problems beyond even our understanding—that should be enough to tell you that something is seriously wrong; but no, all you can do is bring it back to yourself. You may have the upper hand right now, but that doesn't mean you're playing it well. Time's running out for me as fast as it is for you."

"Shut up!" she snapped.

Understand, dear reader, that I am not easily given to fear. All right, it's true, I slept with the night-light on until I was thirteen, but after that I became fearless. And speaking from the position of a relatively fearless individual, I have to say that her rage at that point was truly frightening. I had made up my mind to stop arguing with her, but she beat me to it. A huge clamp sprang into existence and wrapped itself across my mouth. I pulled at it with all my might but was unable to yank it free.

M's face was now purple. She snarled, "I am tired of listening to you! This is my trial, and you have no say in the matter. You . . . you—!" For a moment it seemed as if her rage was going to consume her, and then—with obvious effort—she forced herself to calm down. She took several long, deep breaths before she managed to rein herself in. When she did, the fire was still in her eyes, but her voice had achieved a measure of calm. "I am not unreasonable," she said. One could have fooled me on that score, and I would have said as much, if I didn't have a verbal chastity belt around my mouth. "You will need someone to speak on your behalf, since you appear to have lost your voice." Better than losing my reason, I thought.

She nodded to two of the guards, and they exited the chamber. I was puzzled as to where they were going, but the question was quickly answered when I saw, of all people, Picard and Data escorted in. They looked filthy, but otherwise seemed none the worse for wear. It was not until I saw them that I realized I'd actually missed them. I then mentally chided myself. I certainly didn't want them to know that such sentiments were crossing my mind. That wouldn't do. One had to maintain some measure of decorum, after all.

Picard, for his part, took one look at my trussed-up mouth and promptly smiled. That figured. The universe collapsing around our ears, and he would find it funny that I had a large clamp across my mouth. His priorities were as out of sync as M's.

"We found these two wandering about," M said to me, sounding almost conversational, as if she expected me somehow to be able to reply. "They asked about you immediately. Curious how you didn't inquire as to their whereabouts. Why is that?"

Naturally I couldn't respond. To my surprise, Picard offered an explanation. "Obviously, considering the condition in which you're holding him, Q knew he was in a hostile environment. In such a situation, he likely thought it wise not to reveal our presence."

That sounded very convincing. I nodded my consent. It was, in fact, not remotely true, but any port in a storm, I say.

"Indeed," M said thoughtfully. "I wouldn't have thought Q to be so . . . aware." Boy, was she milking it! She also still wasn't showing any outward effects from the heat. Considering I was sweating, my clothing stuck to my body, I envied her relative "cool."

"Who are you?" demanded Picard.

M appeared amused at the stridency of his tone. "I am the one who holds your existence in my hands, little man. So I would be circumspect if I were you. You may call me . . . M." She tugged on her lower lip pensively. "On second thought . . . no. No, you may not. Do you know something, little man? I can't say that I like you. Hmm. No, no I can't. Sit down over there and be quiet." She then pointed to Data. "You shall serve in Q's defense."

"In what way does Q require defending?" asked Data.

"He needs all the defending he can get . . . and make it amusing! Now, take your place next to your client." She placed her hands serenely on the armrests of the great chair and waited for Data and Picard to take their prescribed positions.

Picard and Data regarded each other for a moment in mutual puzzlement, and then Picard—naturally taking command—indicated to Data with a nod of his head that he should do as M had instructed. Picard then turned to me and said softly, "Considering the circumstances in which we first met, I would think this to be a rather ironic turnaround, wouldn't you?"

I glared at him, making it clear I didn't find it remotely ironic. I couldn't believe what was going on . . . everyone had an ax to grind!

Data, to his credit, seemed perfectly capable of going

along with whatever M chose to toss at him. "Since we are put in the position of having to defend Q, may I ask what precisely are the charges against him?"

"Of course." M snapped her fingers and a lengthy list appeared in her hands. "Q is charged with not knowing his place. With excessive arrogance. With interfering in the lives of other beings. With being the living incarnation of death, destruction, and despair. But most of all, it is Q who is responsible for the End of the universe. This is all his doing."

I was chomping at the bit, literally, to give her a piece of my mind. But all I could do was stare at her bug-eyed in disbelief. She continued.

"I did not realize it before, because I had not given the matter adequate judicial consideration, but now I understand that Q's presence here is not mere happenstance. It was meant to be, because the ultimate purpose of this court is to find who is to blame for our current state, and to punish him accordingly. Q is the only one here who could possibly be to blame. Therefore, he must be guilty!!"

There was a cheer from the onlookers. It didn't matter to them whether what she said made sense or not. They were so consumed by a need to blame someone, to punish someone, that reason simply wasn't an issue.

I would have laughed out loud, had I been able to.

"Obviously," Data said smoothly, "all other considerations are insignificant compared to your final charge. It does appear, though, to be without foundation. What proof have you that that is the case?"

"What proof do I need?" said M. "I say it. Therefore, it is true."

"You are serving as both prosecutor and judge," Data pointed out. "That is not reasonable. A judge must be impartial. You cannot serve both functions and do an adequate job."

"My function will be what I desire it to be, not what you desire it to be!"

"That, madam, makes no sense. You are allowing your anger to cloud your judgment."

"My judgment and faculties are quite clear, thank you for your concern." She rose from her chair. "Let me put things into perspective. The Q Continuum, as well as the M Continuum, is one of the keystones of the universe. We hold everything together. That is our purpose, our reason for being, our place within the universe. But while the M Continuum has continued in its duties, the Q Continuum has abrogated its responsibilities. The Q simply sit about, consumed by boredom, caring for nothing, least of all their obligation for keeping the great universal machine running smoothly. And because of that, like a mechanism devoid of lubricant, the universe has broken down. And this Q is the worst of a bad lot!" She descended from her chair. "He struts! He preens! He boasts of his superiority when clearly the M are superior! He brings chaos wherever he goes. He is a black mark for all of us, and he has upset the universal balance!"

"The universal balance?" asked Data. "I am afraid that such a notion is not codified by any law that exists on any planet. You cannot try him based upon law that is being fabricated on the spot."

"Of course I can. Have you never heard of precedent, Data?" she said scornfully. "Someone has to set precedent. I shall explain the concept to you: everyone behaves improperly at some time or another. You, Picard, everyone," she said and gestured to the spectators, "even, on rare occasions, members of the M Continuum misbehave. Each of these improper actions has a small but definite ripple effect. These ripple effects are directly proportionate to the size of the being's importance in the grand scheme of things."

"Now when the Q Continuum abrogated its responsibility, or when members of its Continuum behaved in the abominable manner that Q has . . . that causes much greater ripples because they are more significant in the grand scheme of things. And the ripples that they have caused over time have brought us to the state that we are now in! Why, all this . . . all this misery . . . is a direct result of their actions! It's his fault! His fault! *His fault!*"

"I feel the need to—" Data began.

But he was drowned out. The audience was picking up the chant. "His fault! His fault!" It was beginning to feel rather hot in the great hall of justice. My shirt was soaked with perspiration. The onlookers had their hands raised in fists and were shaking them, rhythmically and angrily.

"Your Honor . . . it appears that . . ." Data tried to get a sentence out, but the rising din made it impossible. Finally he lapsed into silence, watching the fury building all around us. Picard was taking it all in, his concern growing with each passing moment.

And then, not only to my shock but to the surprise of Picard as well, Data shouted.

This was no ordinary shout, mind you. Data was a machine, remember, and he came with a volume control—ten being loudest, except I'm sure we cranked it to eleven. *"What are you people, stupid?!"* His amplified voice bounded and rebounded off the upper reaches of the dome.

I knew that Data carried within him an emotion chip. Although he was still quite reserved, I knew that he could access genuine human feelings when the mood suited him. But even I was surprised to see the android's face twisted in a paroxysm of fury.

"This is absurd!" he continued, not slacking off. The sheer volume of his voice was overpowering. **"You are let-**

ting your emotions completely carry you away! What she is saying makes no sense at all! She is playing upon your anger, your overwhelming need to tear down what you do not understand! And looking around at the bunch of you, I would have to say that what you do not understand would fill volumes!"

"Data—!" Picard said, dumbfounded.

Data wasn't slowing down. Instead, he advanced on M.

"Why are you doing this? Why are you looking to foist blame off on Q? You have no basis for anything that you have said! It satisfies no rules of evidence whatsoever . . . !"

And M lost whatever sense of self-possession she had. Her voice jumped over Data's in volume. **"The fact that I have said it makes it evidence, you stupid clod! My word is law here! I am the Adjudicator! This is my arena! And you—!"**

"And you are looking for someone to blame!" Data blasted right back, even louder than she. On his face was no semblance of the calm, discerning android that I had always known. He was a tiger. **"Why is that, I wonder? Why are you so determined to blame him?"** And he pointed at me. **"I will tell you why! I will tell all of you why!"** He turned and faced the masses, who seemed to have grown in number. Battered and ash-covered, they had congregated from all over everywhere to hear the exchange. The entire building seemed to be shaking.

"You will tell them nothing! You know nothing!" M shouted. I happened to look up when she was talking, and I noticed that the dome overhead was shaking.

"**I know more than you want me to know! I have figured out what you are trying to hide!**" Data faced the assemblage once more and, pointing at M, cried out, "**She ... she is responsible for it! She is the cause for the universe ending, and for all the suffering and turmoil that we are experiencing! She is causing it all, and she is seeking a scapegoat for her actions! She is the one! She is the reason for the End of Everything! Are you going to stand by and let her get away with this? Are you? Are you!? Look at you! Look at what she has done to you! Are you going to spend your last hours of life in fear, or are you going to take matters into your own hands and make a difference ... well, *are you?*"**

The crowd went berserk. What a performance!

With a unified roar, they surged forward. M turned to face them, her guards linked arms serving as a barrier. But the crowd would not be stopped. The guards staggered back and fell to the ground. The guards' armor shattered, and to everyone's surprise, there was no one inside. They were all empty shells.

The restraint on my mouth suddenly gave way and fell to the floor. The dome began to sway back and forth as dust and plaster rained down from overhead. The crowd let out a mighty cry and began to stampede the stage.

M was attacked from all sides. She fought viciously, but the mob swallowed her up. It was as if she had derived her strength from the anger directed at others; but when she herself was the target, it created a "bounceback" against which she had no defense.

"How dare you?!" she howled. "Stay away from me or I'll . . . I'll . . ." But they didn't heed her warnings.

The dome continued to shake, and huge chunks of stone fell to the floor. Cracks in the foundation were opening beneath my feet. I tried to get away, but they seemed to pursue me as if they had a life of their own.

I briefly glimpsed M tearing herself free of the mob. Her clothes were ripped, her hair disheveled, and when she saw me there was such hatred, such anger in her face that I laughed. But M was hardly sharing in my perception of the moment's more humorous aspects. There was fire in her eyes. I do not mean that metaphorically; I mean there was actual fire in her eyes. Whereas before she had managed to contain her anger, this time it consumed her. Her entire body erupted in flames. What a sight it was. To this day I shall never forget her screams. The death scream of one who could not die.

I wondered what my own screams would sound like and

realized that the day might be coming soon when I was going to find out.

There was a rending and tearing all around, as if the very structure of the building could no longer stand to hold together. It shredded itself, the noise deafening, as if the very environment itself was consumed with fury.

I looked up at the ceiling just as the great dome fell. I thought, *The universe is dying and I've accomplished nothing . . . my wife, my child, they counted on me, this isn't fair, this shouldn't be happening, I would do anything to stop it. . . .*

Suddenly the floor opened up at my feet and I plunged into darkness . . . but I didn't scream. I left such undignified behavior to M.

I had, at that point, no expectations. I had no clear idea what was going to happen, or where, if anywhere, I was going to land. In other words, I was open to anything.

Somehow, though, I wasn't expecting to land facedown in a pile of hay.

For a moment, the irony struck me, considering the stunt I had pulled on that parachutist all those centuries back. But then such thoughts fluttered away as I concentrated on other things, such as breathing. This was becoming a bit problematic, seeing as how I was facedown. The prospect of smothering to death in a stack of hay didn't seem especially attractive.

I struggled for a moment and quickly learned that it's difficult to get leverage when you're in a haystack. Every time I pushed my hand down for the purpose of raising myself up, all I did was sink down further. It was sort of a bristly quicksand. Eventually, though, I managed to flip myself over so that I was laying flat on my back, sucking in air that was refreshingly free of smoke. There was, however, the distinctive aroma of foul-smelling animals.

I started to sit up and then yelped in a most undignified fashion. Reaching behind me, I pulled a needle out of my rump.

"That figures," I muttered and tossed the needle back into the stack for the next unsuspecting fool.

I couldn't quite believe after everything that had happened to me that I was in a haystack. It seemed so pastoral. The sky was so bright I had to shield my eyes. Then I realized there was no sun, just brightness.

As I looked around I noticed I was in the midst of a vast outdoor marketplace lined with tents and small shops, each of them doing a fairly brisk business. I must confess, considering the last two places I had visited, it was a relief to be somewhere as benign as a bazaar. This marketplace was alive with spirit and excitement as people bargained enthusiastically over assorted knickknacks.

Naturally, I was waiting for the other shoe to drop. If anything seemed to be constant in this nightmare, it was that.

Something smelly, large, and warm bumped into the side of my face. I turned and saw a disgusting creature that looked like a cross between an earth camel and a Terwillian Dungoff. It stared at me with big brown eyes and then nudged me again. Apparently I was between it and its food.

I got up and watched as the creature stuck its nose into the haystack and found, not two inches from where my face had just been, a nest of grubs that it devoured with relish—I would have used mustard. As I stood watching, I heard a shout from the other side of the haystack, *"Merde!* Who put this damned needle here!"

"Picard!" I exclaimed, and sure enough, it was. He stepped from around the haystack, his bald head glistening in the light and, a moment later, Data emerged next to him. They looked as surprised as I.

"Q! You made it! How—?"

"I'm beginning to think, Picard, that the entire purpose of this adventure is to pile as many enigmas, mysteries, and confusions upon us as possible, to see how much we can stand," I said, looking around. Then I stared at Data a moment. He looked calm and levelheaded, not remotely approaching what he'd been a short time before. "Are you feeling a bit more composed now, Mr. Data?"

"I . . . 'feel' . . . perfectly fine, thank you," Data said calmly.

"It was a wonderful performance, Data, and I hope we will have no need to call upon you again," I said.

But Picard was at once both impressed and concerned with his android. "Yes, what happened to you back there, Data? I've never seen you in such a state."

"Nor have I, sir. Indeed, my decision to access my emotions as part of such histrionics dovetails with a theory that I am developing as to our present situation."

"I'm all ears," I said.

"Very well. In analyzing this odyssey upon which we have embarked, I am reminded of the studies of a twentieth-century doctor, one Doctor Kübler-Ross. She observed that in coping with the prospect of death, terminal patients went through five stages: disbelief or denial; anger; bargaining; despair; and finally, acceptance. We are faced with not only the imminent threat of our own demise, but the death of the entire universe—not a small issue. What we are experiencing as we progress on this journey is an actualization—a physical realization—of the steps a terminal patient experiences on his journey towards death. Each step or level or realization is defined by a different realm, and each realm is inhabited by those beings who are either passing through or are stuck therein.

I stared at him. "Wonderful. If I understand you correctly, we're trapped in a giant metaphor."

"I would not put it quite that simplistically, but to all intents and purposes, yes. That is correct."

"Data, that's absurd," I said.

Picard turned to look at me. "Do you have a better explanation?"

"Yes. The explanation is that the universe is insane, has always been insane, and in its death throes, its insanity is achieving new glorious heights of lunacy. But at this point, I don't care about where we are or why we're here. The only thing I care about is . . ."

Then I stopped. I felt something.

When someone loses a limb—an arm, a leg, whatever—oftentimes they can still feel it even after it's gone. Phantom pains, it's called. The lost arm feels itchy even though it's moldering in a trash can somewhere; the knee is cramping even though there's no leg to stand on. Phantom pains.

I felt it. An eerie sensation, a tingling, a sense that I could reach out and touch something that had been severed from me. And I felt it so strongly, so surely, that I knew it was more than a mere mental illusion.

"My son," I said. "He's here. My son, q, is here somewhere."

"Where?" asked Picard.

"What part of the word 'somewhere' don't you understand, Picard?" I snapped testily. "I don't know exactly where he is. He could be in a tent, he could be walking around, but he's somewhere here, at this level."

"And his mother?"

I shook my head. "No. No, she is not here, she is . . . elsewhere. And please don't ask me where elsewhere is. There's only so much obtuseness I should have to tolerate in a day . . . even in a place where days and nights are irrelevant."

"How do you know?" asked Data.

"Because . . . he's an itch. An itch I can almost scratch."

"Phantom pains," said Picard.

"Very good, Jean-Luc. It's like those times when you're found with an occasional urge to brush your hair."

Data was still pondering the hair joke when Picard asked, "Which direction do you suggest we go first?"

I looked around thoughtfully. "When one wants to get the most answers, the best place to go is where there are the most people."

I pointed to a spire a few hundred yards away. "My guess is that that spire is the heart of the marketplace; let's find out."

"As good a place as any," Picard agreed, and we immediately set out.

Along the way, people called to us from tents and storefronts, trying to get us to sample their wares. "Here! Over here!" they would bellow. "The best bargains in town! You won't be sorry!" We ignored them all, instead focusing our attention on the spire.

It wasn't long before we arrived. The spire was attached to a large, colorful tent. A line of beings from everywhere in the universe extended from the main door of the tent out into the marketplace. My inclination was to cut to the front of them.

"Where do you think you're going?" Picard asked.

"To the front."

"There are other people here."

"So?" I said impatiently.

Picard sighed. "Q . . . look around. There are a lot of people, and some of them are quite big, and their knuckles are dragging on the ground, which does not bode well. Do you think that perhaps, just for once, we might want to consider avoiding a fight? Because frankly, I'm getting a bit worn out."

I understood what he meant. It seemed a reasonable request, and furthermore, the line seemed to be moving quickly. Almost too quickly. At first I thought something strange was happening inside that tent, but then I noticed people exiting from the other end with big grins on their faces as if, somehow, a burden had been lifted from their souls.

"All right, Picard. Let's play it your way."

"Good. Let's queue up."

"Q up?" I said. "Up where?"

"To the queue."

"What Q?"

"That queue, Q," Picard said impatiently. "The line, Q. The queue line."

"If there's a line for Q's, let's stand on that one, instead."

Looking at me frostily, Picard said, "Stand . . . right . . . here." So we did.

Thankfully, the line began to move quickly.

When we entered the tent, it was dank and smelly; certainly no worse than any other aroma we'd encountered thus far, and better than some. There was a small room in the center where each person went for a private audience, the room fronted and backed by a curtain. Now that I had a chance to observe people more closely, I couldn't help but note the remarkable change that overcame them. They would enter the curtained area looking worried and ill at ease, but when they exited, they did so with a jaunty step and a total lack of concern. It was most intriguing.

It was our turn next and Picard whispered, "Well, Q . . . it appears that we're about to meet the man behind the curtain."

"Step right up!" a voice came from within.

We entered, and there was the single most shriveled Ferengi I had ever seen. He was cloaked in a large, elaborate robe that seemed five sizes too big on him. His lips were drawn back in the customary Ferengi sneer. He wasn't looking at us. Instead, he was sorting through a sizable pile of valuables that were to his left, which was only slightly smaller than the other sizable pile of valuables to his right. Now when I say "valuables" I use the word advisedly. Looking at his "treasures," I was reminded of the adage that one person's gold is another person's garbage. Gold-pressed latinum, diamonds, rubies, sand, hardened dung, pictures of Elvis, twigs, dried spittle . . . it didn't matter. If you thought it was valuable, he wanted it.

"Is there any form of payment you don't take?" I asked.

"Credit chips," he replied. "And out-of-galaxy two-party checks. Otherwise I'm wide"— he looked up at us, and then specifically at me, and finished—"open."

And then he let out a horrific shriek.

He tried to get up and run away, but that only resulted in his chair toppling backward with him in it. "Don't hurt me!" he bleated. "Don't hurt me, Q!"

I stared at this pathetic, twitching creature on the floor in front of me. "Now that's respect," I said to Picard. "It's good to see it from time to time. Learn from him, Picard."

Picard shrugged.

I turned back to the Ferengi. "Have we met?" I asked.

"No! But . . . but Quark . . . he circulated a picture of you to all Ferengi after you appeared at Deep Space 9! He said you were the most dangerous being in the entire cosmos!"

His whining was becoming quite grating, but I rather enjoyed his terror. "Ah, flattery," I sighed. "You'd be amazed how far that gets you."

He was now on his knees begging. It was a sight to see.

"Look . . . I'm sure we can work something out . . . you can take half my earnings . . . no . . . no, take all of them . . . in fact, you can have the whole business . . . just don't kill me with one of your thoughts. Quark said you could—"

"He cannot," Data said. "He has no power here. Not to any significant degree."

"Data!!!" I whispered between clenched teeth. "Keep your mouth shut!"

The Ferengi stopped trembling and looked wide-eyed at Data. "He doesn't? You don't?"

I glared at Data. "Thanks a lot."

Just like that, the little troll stopped quaking. As he dusted himself off and righted the chair, he said, "So . . . what business do you have before the grand nagus! Do you seek a dispensation?"

"The grand nagus." Picard looked a bit surprised and said to me, "The grand nagus is the head of the—"

"I know what he is. He's the top Ferengi. I know that, although I've never had the . . . 'pleasure' . . . of making his acquaintance."

"I know you, Q . . . but I don't know these two!" the nagus said impatiently. "Who are they?"

"This is Mr. Sherlock Holmes," I said, indicating Picard, and pointing to Data, I said, "And his 'big mouth,' associate is Doctor Watson."

"Actually," Data said, "I am usually Sherl—"

"Not now, Watson." I regarded the nagus with open curiosity. "Dispensation? What are you talking about?"

"It's my business! I give dispensations. In case you're unaware, in addition to being ruler of the entire Ferengi Alliance, I am also the central religious official."

"You have a religion?" said a surprised Picard. "I thought the only thing Ferengi worshiped was money."

The grand nagus stared at him blankly. "What's your point?"

"Nothing. None at all."

"Good. In any event, I," and he thumped his chest in a rather smug manner, "am the main—and only—religious figure in this entire bazaar. Fortunately, however, I am schooled in the religions of over three hundred thousand different races. And what I don't know, I make up."

"But what does that have to do with . . . dispensations?"

The nagus straightened his robes and then sat down again. "I absolve people of their sins. They come to me, one at a time or in small groups, and ask for absolution. It's most entertaining. And I look very serious, and hear their transgressions, and then I speak some mumbo-jumbo that erases all their sins. And they leave happy. A lot of them go out and sin again and then come right back for more dispensations. It's a great racket . . . I mean business."

"And each time, they pay you a fee." Picard laughed bitterly. "Nagus . . . haven't you ever heard that you can't take it with you?"

"Rule of Acquisition Number Ninety-seven: 'If you can't take it with you, don't go,' " the nagus replied.

"You have no choice," Data said. "The universe is ending."

At that, the nagus laughed. "I see what you're up to. You're hoping to intimidate me now with some huge lie."

"No. I am not."

"Another lie! A few more, told as convincingly, and you would make a passable Ferengi."

Data looked politely confused, but gamely said, "Thank you."

"So are you here for a dispensation?" He regarded me with interest. "I've never given dispensation to an omnipotent being—even a powerless one. I can't wait to look up the going price. What religion are you?"

"I worship stupidity, and you're my new god. I'm looking for my son, you posturing poseur."

"Your son? Why would I know anything about your son?"

"Because a lot of people come through your tent. They tell you a lot of things. Perhaps one of them has mentioned something." I gave the nagus a quick description of my boy. He listened thoughtfully, stroking his chin and nodding, taking it all in. When I finished, he said nothing. Just sat there like a stone. "Well?" I prompted impatiently.

"Actually," he said slowly, "it rings a bell. Not that I know for sure, you understand. But yes, it most definitely rings a bell."

"Would you be so kind as to tell us where he is?" I said in my most benevolent tone.

He rubbed his hands together. "What have you got?"

"Got?"

"Yes. Got."

I was about to launch myself across the table to wring that little twerp's neck when I felt Picard's hand restraining me.

"Go on . . ." I croaked.

"What do you have for payment? For trade? You can't possibly think," and he laughed derisively, "I'd tell you what you want for nothing, do you?"

"The thought had crossed my mind," I said.

"Well, uncross it. The very notion is insulting. To give you something for nothing? Absurd. I will require some sort of payment."

"I left my wallet in my other pants," I told him. "Look, I'm not in the mood to play these games. . . ."

"And I'm not in the mood to be trifled with!" Then he looked at Data and seemed to be considering something.

Finally he said, "Am I mistaken, or is he a machine of sorts?"

"Yes, I am. I am an android," said Data.

"What possible bearing does that have on—"

The nagus cut Picard off and said, "I'll take the android in trade. How's that? That sounds fair."

"Fine, take him."

"Q!" said Picard in annoyance. "We're not trading him!"

"I'm not leaving without the information. Time is ticking, Mr. Holmes."

"We don't leave him behind," Picard growled.

I blew air impatiently between my teeth, and then after a moment's consideration, I looked back at the Ferengi. "Are you interested in a challenge?"

"A challenge?" The nagus eyed me suspiciously. "What sort of challenge?"

"I think you'll find it rather intriguing. Forget the android. I'll put myself on the line. I, one of the most powerful beings in the galaxy, shall be your servant if you win the challenge."

"The 'former' most powerful being," he corrected me. "An intriguing proposition," he said, grinning in a fiendish manner. "And you have some sort of contest in mind? A battle of wits?"

"Simply put . . . yes. I will say a number that you are thinking of."

"Any number?"

"Yes."

"But you have no power. That's true, is it?"

"If I had power," I sighed, "wouldn't I simply turn you into a melting puddle of flesh and be done with you? If I had power, you toddy-faced throw-up, would I be coming to the likes of *you* for an answer to any question, least of all a question regarding my son's whereabouts?"

"Good point," admitted the Nagus. "I believe you. So, you will say a number that I'm thinking of?"

"That is correct."

"And if you cannot do so then you will be my servant. Forever."

"Also correct."

"Q," Picard said, clearly concerned. "Are you sure you know what you're doing?"

"Absolutely."

"All right," said the nagus after a moment's deliberation. "I've got it."

"Six," I said without hesitation.

"Haaaa haaa haa!" the nagus roared with laughter. "It was one million and three! You fool! You fell victim to one of the classic blunders! The best known, of course, is never get involved in a land war on Vulcan. But only slightly less well known is this: Never go up against a Ferengi when money is on the line!"

And he continued to laugh very loudly until I said calmly, "One million and three. Now where's my son?"

That stopped him. He frowned and said, "What?"

"One million and three. Did I not make myself heard? Are you thinking of that number right now?"

"Well . . . yes." There was clear confusion on his face. "Because we're talking about it now, yes, but . . ."

"I did what I said I would."

"No, you didn't!" His voice went up an octave. "You were supposed to guess!"

"I never said that." I turned to Data and asked, "How did the conversation with the nagus and me go, precisely? Word for word?"

Completely in his element, Data said crisply, "You said, 'I will say a number that you are thinking of.' The nagus said, 'Any number?' You said, 'Yes.' He said, 'But you have—' ' "

"I know what I said!" raged the nagus. He had been trembling earlier with fear; now it was with anger. "But what challenge is there if you just say the number after I've already told you what it is?"

"I never said I would say the number before you said it. I'm not responsible for your incorrect inferences. Besides, I'm not looking for a challenge. I'm looking for my son. We had a wager; you lost. Now tell me what you know on the subject."

"No!" The nagus petulantly folded his arms. "I'll tell you nothing! You cheated! The bet is over, and so is this audience!"

Now Picard took a step forward. He smiled, and there was something about the smile that was distinctly unpleasant. "Nagus . . ."

"Grand Nagus!"

"Grand Nagus," Picard said with a shrug, "you must certainly have wondered about the circumstances that brought you here?"

"Yes, of course I have. My ship was jumping to warp, and suddenly then I wound up here. No others are certain how they wound up here either." For a moment, just a moment, it seemed to disturb him, but then he obviously shook it off. "It doesn't matter, though. I've managed to prosper, to profit. And that is all that matters."

"Indeed. Well, let me make some things clear to you. We were telling you the truth. The universe is coming to an End. If you believe it or not, it doesn't matter. Furthermore, we are trying to find a way to stop it. Whether you believe that is also beside the point. But here is something that I strongly suggest you consider." Picard leaned forward, closing the distance between himself and the nagus. His expression hardened, and there was a significant threat in his tone. "If we succeed in our venture, the universe will be restored to the way it was. If that happens, Q will once again be omnipotent. I've known him for a long time, Grand Nagus, and I can promise you this: he never forgets an offense, even a trivial one. And an offense involving both welshing on a bet and lack of cooperation in finding his son, why, that's not trivial at all." Picard's voice became quieter and quieter, and in doing so the menace grew exponentially. "And the things he will do to you . . . you can't even begin to imagine. But you will. Whether you're here another day, a week, a year, or eternity, you'll spend all that time imagining just what shape his revenge will take. And no matter what you come up with . . . it will pale compared to the reality, I assure you. Now, we may very well fail. The odds are against us. But we just might succeed. Are you interested in playing those odds?"

The nagus was quiet for quite a long time. So long, in fact, that someone in line outside the tent shouted, "What's taking so long in there?"

"Shut up!" the nagus shouted back, and there was a quaver in his voice. Then he said, "The directions are complicated."

"I will remember," Data said.

"Yes. You would, wouldn't you?" the nagus said, annoyed. He proceeded to rattle off what was indeed a very complicated set of directions. "Once you get there," he said, "the master of that place should be able to help you. He has a young lad in his service, I hear. He sounds like he may be your son."

"Thank you," Picard said.

The nagus was shaking his head. "I, the nagus, outwitted. Inconceivable."

"I do not think that word means what you think it does," said Data.

I stepped closer to Picard and murmured, "My admiration, Picard. That was quite deft."

"Elementary, my dear Q." Then he turned to the nagus as we were leaving. "The 'master' of that place . . . does he have a name?"

"Yes," replied the nagus. "He calls himself god. Didn't mention a last name."

God's house was something of a fixer-upper.

It was not only the largest tent at the bazaar, it was the largest tent anywhere. It stretched so far that I couldn't quite see where it curved off. Furthermore, it was the skyscraper of all tents, the poles stretching so high that they literally disappeared into the clouds.

But as I said, the tent was not in the greatest shape. The edges were frayed and threadbare, and there were many holes, some of which had been patched, others left torn.

Picard, Data, and I stood outside, trying to find a way in. There may be things more frustrating than circling a tent looking for an opening, but at that point in time, I couldn't think of one.

The walk had taken us forever, and it was a good thing that Data was along to reiterate the directions. There was absolutely no question in my mind that we would have become hopelessly lost, had we been left to our own devices. I toyed with the idea of crawling under the tent, but the edges were so tight to the ground that it was impossible. That left us with no option other than to circumnavigate the tent again.

I thought back on our conversation with the nagus. I remember he said, as we were leaving his tent, "You don't believe me, do you?"

"Not especially. But if it's where my son is, that's all I

care about. And if it's not . . . then sooner or later I'll get back to you, and it won't be pleasant."

"It's that God fellow, I tell you!" the nagus said. "We chatted when I first got here! He's the one who suggested my new business of dispensations and absolutions! I believe in Him because He believes in profit and in me! You better watch out; if He doesn't like it you He'll smite you!"

"He smite. Or He smite not," I had replied, not wanting to continue the conversation with this low-life.

We were walking single file around the tent. Picard was walking in front of me. He was deep in thought. "What's on your mind, Picard?"

"How do we know that 'God' is in this tent?" he asked. "What does God need with a tent?"

"What does He need with a church or a synagogue? What does He need with angels?"

"That's true," said Picard. "But a tent?"

"Picard, we're seeking to learn who or what is responsible for the End of the universe."

"I agree," said Picard. "And the existence of some anchetypal 'God' might go a long way to explain who or what is responsible for this calamity. Might it not be a reasonable leap to think that this calamity and this 'God' are one and the same?"

"A leap of faith?" I shook my head. "Picard, every time I think there's some modicum of hope for you, you disappoint me. One step forward, two steps back. It's becoming the story of your life. Listen, Picard, I know that a situation such as what we're facing is almost incomprehensible to you, and to me, for that matter. But your instinct is to go running back to the mind-sets of your most primitive ancestors to seek solace and explanation. As in the words of the ancients, 'Since I don't know what it is, it must be god.' It's simple—lazy but simple. 'Lightning comes from the gods, right? Rain is the tears of the gods, so forth and so on.' The universe simply isn't made like that, and the sooner you come to realize that, the sooner your kind has a shot at true advancement."

"You're saying that the only way to move forward is to leave behind faith, and a belief in something greater than ourselves?"

"Exactly. Do you think the Q got to where we are by believing that there's anything greater than ourselves? Of course not. We assumed the responsibility of being the greatest force in the universe, and lo and behold, we are. We make our own reality, Picard. It's not shaped for us by some vast, unknown, and unknowable being."

"If you are the greatest force in the universe, Q," Picard said quietly, "why is it you can't even get into this damned tent?"

Unfortunately, I had no immediate answer for that. However, as luck would have it, a section of the tent abruptly flapped open, providing us with an entrance that had not been there a moment before.

"Right on cue," I said and, noting the pun, added, "How appropriate." "After you, *mon capitain.*"

" 'After me' when we're heading into an unknown situation. I'm not certain whether this is courtesy or whether I'm cannon fodder."

"You can send Data in first. If we hear a growl and his head comes rolling out, we can take that as a hint that this isn't the right tent."

Picard sighed. He tended to do that a good deal when he was around me, I'd noticed. Then without another word, he walked through the entrance of the tent, followed by Data. I cheerily took up the rear.

It was extremely dark. God had obviously not paid his

electric bill. There was a faint glow, coming from a source that I couldn't identify, giving us just enough light to see one another but not much more. However, there was one thing I could see, or more appropriately, sense. Power.

I couldn't tap into it, couldn't draw from it. But it was there, just the same, and Picard noticed something as well. He looked at me.

"Power. All around," I said to him in a low voice.

"Power?"

There was something in his tone. "Picard, let's not go through this again. There was power in the stronghold of M as well, and she was hardly divine."

"But you don't know, for sure."

"No, Picard, I don't," I said, becoming more and more exasperated by the moment. "But unlike you, I don't fall back on fairy tales to deal with what I don't know. I assure you of one thing. I have personal knowledge of, and experience with, every being that exists on the sort of power level we're discussing. In short, I know all of my peers and all of my near-peers. So if any of them are here, we'll be able to chat it up nicely and I'll be sure to introduce you."

"Why, though," Data piped up, "would others have power in this realm and you do not?"

"Perhaps," I speculated, "the longer one remains down here, the more power one acquires. In fact . . ."

"In fact what?" prompted Picard.

"Perhaps one acquires power by resigning oneself to remaining in one area. We've moved from one place to the next so quickly, refusing to stay put, that we haven't had an opportunity to find out. Because of that, I may be 'deprived.' "

"How long would we have to stay at one level, do you think?"

"I've no idea," I admitted. "Time in this place isn't measured in the same way, and doesn't flow in the same manner, as in the outside world. Besides, we're faced with a deadline. The universe is going down the drain, and for all we know, we've only minutes or perhaps seconds left. We can't afford delays."

He nodded.

And at that moment, the lights suddenly came up. Picard and I flinched, shielding our eyes against the brightness. Perhaps god's electric company had a change of heart.

I turned and saw myself standing next to myself. An infinite number of me's, a virtual army of Q. And they were all thinning in the hair department.

But for an instant, I actually took heart. The notion of an army of me's, rallying to the cause, was quite uplifting. But, alas, it was only an instant, because that was how long it took me to realize that I was simply looking at a mirror. But such a mistake was no reflection on me (ba DUM bum).

I backed up and noticed that Picard was likewise captivated by an endless array of himself. Data tilted his head slightly and I knew, I just knew, that he was likely counting them. I couldn't resist: "How many, Data?" I asked.

"One billion, seven hundred million . . ."

"Thank you . . ." I said, shutting him up.

It was like being in a "fun house," except this wasn't fun. The hallway twisted and turned ahead of us. The floor was solid black beneath us, mirrors were all around us, and I still had no idea where the light was coming from.

"The light . . . is from me."

I looked around. None of us had spoken. And it was disturbing to have a question answered when it hadn't been voiced.

"Come forward. I await you. You may enter my presence."

Picard and Data looked at me. "Sound familiar?" asked Picard.

"Vaguely," I said, and it did sound vaguely familiar. I couldn't place it, but I was reasonably sure I had heard it before. "There are several possibilities as to who it might be. The only way we're going to know for sure is to keep walking."

We made our way forward. I watched the mirrors carefully and noticed the images shifting the further we went along. My "army" went from vast to nonexistent, to fat, to thin, to grossly distorted. Each distortion was more horrific than the one before. It wasn't the simple stretching that one expects from fun house mirrors and such. These mirrors twisted my features in such a way that they made me look positively evil. I looked over to Picard and Data, and their reflections were completely unchanged. Indeed, they were so unremarkable that Data and Picard weren't even giving them any notice. This was getting ominous.

The floor beneath our feet began to feel gravelly. We turned a corner, and the mirrors disappeared . . .

. . . and so did the tent.

Before us lay a vast plain, craggy and windswept. There was not a hint of vegetation anywhere. In the distance was a small hill, and on that hill . . . there sat someone. It was too far to make him out clearly, but he was seated in a fairly relaxed fashion and appeared to be looking in our direction.

"Data," Picard said softly, "are we in another level . . . another place?"

"If we are following the Kübler-Ross pattern, this would be the land of despair," Data observed.

"I don't feel particularly despairing," said Picard.

"Nor do I," Data said, "although I have far less experience in such matters than you."

"No, we're right where we were when we first arrived at the bazaar," I said. "We haven't gone anywhere. Our surroundings have . . . but not us."

"How do you know?"

"Because I still sense my son is around here. Somewhere. Somewhere, he's . . ."

And I looked at the figure sitting alone on the darkling plain . . . and I understood.

"It's him," I whispered.

"What?" Picard didn't quite understand. "What is him? Who—?" But then he got it. He pointed at the solitary figure and said, "That . . . is your son?"

I didn't stop to reply. I was already in motion, running across the plain. I stumbled several times, and once fell flat, tearing my knee badly. I didn't care; I barely even felt it. I just kept going. Picard lagged behind me. Data naturally pulled up alongside as if he considered it bad form to take the lead.

The figure never moved. He could have been carved from marble or ivory. But when I drew within range, he finally spoke. His tone was tinged with a hint of condescension as he said, "Slow down, Father. You'll live longer."

I came to a halt at the base of the hill and stared at him. I could scarcely believe it. Picard caught up with me. "Is that . . . ?"

I nodded.

"I was under the impression that your son was a child," he said.

"So was I," I told him.

The confusion were understandable; the being that sat before us was not remotely a child. Yet he was my son, definitely. It was q. I knew that as surely as I knew my own letter. But he was a child no longer.

His features were a perfect synthesis of his mother's and mine. His black hair came to about his shoulders; his eyes were dark, smoldering with intensity. His lips looked cruel and harsh and when he spoke, his voice was deep and had a biting edge.

"Welcome to my home. I regret I haven't done much with it."

I could scarcely believe it. Since this odyssey began, it had been my overwhelming desire to find my wife and my son. It was for their sake, even more than the sake of the rest of the universe, that I had driven myself so. Yet now that I was here, that he was here . . . I didn't know what to say. It was like looking into the face of a stranger.

No. No, worse than that. It was like looking at someone who . . . who despised you.

"Well?" he said, not moving from his spot. "Aren't you going to say hello?"

I could barely trust myself to speak. "Hello, q," I managed to get out.

He shook his head. "Not anymore. I'm Q now. I'd appreciate it if you would address me in that manner."

So cold he was. So flat. Parents often say how it seems as if just yesterday their child was a bundle of energy, a loving creature who looked at them with adoration.

But for me, it really was just yesterday.

"All right . . . Q . . ." I said. "Son . . . it's . . . it's good to see you."

Understand . . . I am not a touchy-feely being. I don't hug or kiss or drape an arm around one's shoulder in a friendly, "Hi how are ya?" fashion. But even I, the distant and remote individual that I am, I still felt an urge to step forward, my arms wide, to embrace him.

"That's far enough," he said. I froze in place.

"Son, what's happened to you? How did you come here? Don't you know I've been . . . we've been . . . looking for you?"

"And looking ever so hard, Father." Slowly he rose to his feet and looked down at us as if we were bugs. "What's the old joke? That something is always in the last place you look . . . except where's the sense in that, because who keeps looking after they've found something?"

"Scientists keep looking; it is their nature," Data said without hesitation.

My son took one look at Data, and Data exploded into a thousand pieces.

The move was so quick, so staggering, that I didn't see it coming. Picard was stunned. Where Data had been, there was now a scorched hole in the ground. Pieces of the android rained down, but bits so small as to be unidentifiable. The only thing remaining were Data's boots, both standing upright and smoking. Then the boots fell over.

"It was a rhetorical question," Q said to the space that had been occupied by Data moments before.

"What have you done?" demanded Picard, finding his voice at last.

My son stared malevolently at Picard and replied, "The very same thing I can do to you . . . if you annoy me."

Picard took a step forward. "Your father," he said, "has moved heaven and earth to find you. Why are you acting in this manner?"

"And how many other things did he find to occupy his time while he did it?" replied Q. He was addressing Picard, but he was looking right at me. "I arrived here as a child, nowhere to go, no one to turn to. Completely on my own, and powerless. And I waited for you to come and find me . . . waited and waited and waited, but in vain."

"In vain? What do you mean, in vain? I'm here, aren't I? All I've thought about was finding you, and your mother. With the universe on the edge of destruction, my priority was you and your mother."

"The universe can go hang. You can, too, for all I care," he added. "I didn't need a universe. Just you. You and mother. You have no idea how long I waited for you. An eternity. And you were nowhere to be found. And now here you are, gallivanting about with humans . . . well, human. Picard! It would be Picard. Face it, Father," and his voice dropped to such an angry whisper that I could barely hear him, "they were always more important to you than I was."

"That's ridiculous!" I told him. "Don't you see that there are time distortions of all manner here? To me, you disappeared a short time ago, but for you, a great deal of time has passed, I'm sorry about that. But I'm not responsible for this perception, I'm—"

But Q wasn't listening. Instead he had descended from his hill and was walking back and forth in front of us. "I found someone else. When I waited and waited and you didn't come, another did. God came to me, Father. God."

"Nonsense!"

He stabbed a finger at the charred place where Data had been standing. "You call that nonsense, Father? I don't see you flashing your powers about! Go ahead! Display your might for me, I dare you!"

"You're telling me," I said slowly, trying to grasp what he was saying, "that you derive your power . . . from this 'god.' From the 'creator of the universe.' From the 'almighty.' "

He nodded. "That is correct. All that I am . . . comes from Him."

"Where is He now?" I asked. "I'd like to speak with 'Him.' "

"He does not wish to speak with you."

"Perhaps 'He's' too afraid to," I said.

"Perhaps He does not care what you think," replied my son, but his eyes flashed in warning. Clearly he did not like having his new mentor spoken of in such a disrespectful fashion.

"Where is 'He,' then?"

"He is here," my son said and spread wide his arms to take in the entire firmament. "He is in the ground . . . and the skies. His power is everywhere . . . and I only feel sorry for you that you cannot feel Him."

"And 'He' speaks directly to you," I said.

"And I to Him."

This was sickening to me. I had seen this before. This, "I am the prophet of the Lord, bow before me, scrape before me, give me your money, your trust, your life in HIS service." It made my teeth hurt. There had to be a way to reach him.

I draped my hands behind my back. "All right," I said after a moment's thought. "You tell this god of yours . . ."

"He's yours as well."

". . . your 'god,' " I continued, "that I am not leaving without my son. So He might as well let you go right now, because I have gone through too much to leave without you. Furthermore, tell Him that I haven't given up . . . that I am going to save the universe. I don't care about entropy, or the grand, divine scheme. He's no mysterious, unknowable entity to me. I will stop Him, somehow, no matter who or what He is."

"You can't."

"I will. And you will, too, because you're going to come with me."

"I'm going nowhere, Father. I'm needed here."

I reached out, grabbed him by the wrist. "Why? Why are

you needed? What does a god need with a deluded young boy?"

"I'm neither a boy nor young, and the only one deluded here is you!" he snapped at me and yanked his hand away. "I am here to rejoice in His power. I'm here to worship Him. . . ."

"Worship!" I threw my hands up in disgust. "What sort of superior being has a need for inferior creatures to worship Him?"

"What sort? How about yourself, Father? How about a being who is not content to simply reside with his fellow superior beings, but instead has to seek out new lives and new civilizations so that they might worship his presence."

"I seek knowledge, not worshipers."

"Delude yourself if you must, Father, but do not for a moment seek to delude me! Admit it! You cannot be truly content unless there are poor, powerless beings who are terrified by your presence. That's why you've found such creatures as Picard and Janeway so irresistible. They stand up to you. And you keep coming back to them, time after time, not out of curiosity, not out of a need to explore, but because you keep hoping that sooner or later you're going to be able to batter them into submission and force them to worship at your altar."

Picard stepped forward and said, "No. You are wrong. I hardly would consider your father an exemplary instance of the proper use of power. But he has more genuine human emotion within him than you credit him for. Than I think he would credit himself."

"I'm not sure you're helping here, Picard," I said under my breath.

"And," continued Picard, "being worshiped is not what your father is about."

Q turned away and looked to the skies. "I made a bargain

with Him, Father. A most excellent bargain. I promised to serve Him, to worship Him . . . and in return, He not only gave me power . . . but He promised that He would never, ever leave me alone. You can sense Him, Father, if you try. That much, I think, you are capable of. Sense Him. Feel Him. Let Him into you, and you too will understand, or at least begin to."

He was right. I did sense another presence there. Free-floating, powerful . . .

. . . and malevolent. A malignant, festering thing. If it had a name, it would be a name that would be called out in terror, not blessed with reverence. And I sensed its power as well. . . .

"No," I said softly.

"No what, Father?" Q regarded me with mild curiosity.

Picard turned to me and said, "Are you . . . perceiving something?"

I nodded. "There is something there, all right . . . but the power it exudes . . . it's not . . ."

"Not what?"

"Not . . . its own."

Dark clouds were starting to gather, and I heard a distant rumbling. I did not like the sound of it, not one bit.

"What are you talking about, Father?" There was cold derision in his tone.

"What I'm talking about," I said, "is that there is a being here, yes . . . some sort of entity. But, son . . . you don't need it."

"Of course I do. He—"

"No." I shook my head. "It needs you. You don't understand what's happening. You don't comprehend because you were too young when you first arrived in this place, but I fathom it."

"Fathom what?" He was clearly becoming impatient and a little addled. "What are you going on about—?"

"The longer you stayed here . . . the more comfortable you became with it . . . the greater your powers became. And the creature that lives here . . . it's drawing that power from you. The only power it has is its ability to derive strength from that which worships it. When you sense power, all you sense is a reflection of yourself."

Lightning cracked overhead.

"That's a lie, Father!" Q shouted, his finger trembling as he pointed at me accusingly. "That's all you know . . . lies! You promised! You promised you would never leave me alone! But you did! You did! And now you'll pay for it! Beg me, Father! Beg me for your life! Make your best offer, and maybe I'll take you up on it and maybe I won't. Maybe I'll just leave you alone, like you left me—"

I should have been compassionate, I suppose. Sympathetic. I should have spoken warm words to him, letting him know how much he meant to me.

Instead I said sharply, "Stop it! Stop that bleating. Mewling like a child . . . it's unbecoming! You're a Q now! Stand up straight! Stop whining!"

His face whitened. I'm not surprised that it did. I had never raised my voice to him, not ever. The lightning overhead was deafening now, and I shouted above it.

"Have I taught you nothing? Have you no pride in who and what you are? You are Q! You are of the Continuum, with all the responsibility and pride that accompanies that! You are better than this—better than He is," and I gestured to the sky. "And you are certainly better than this whining brat I see before me! And what if I don't beg and bargain, what then? You'll kill me? Go ahead! I'd rather be wiped from existence—I'd rather never have existed at all—than know that

I wound up fathering a pathetic creature like you! Well? Come on." I gestured impatiently. "Annihilate me!" He seemed frozen, unable to put together a coherent thought. "Come on, then! Get on with it! Destroy your father! That's what that *thing* up there wants you to do! But remember, it also wants you to worship it, and in so doing it saps your strength and sucks from you the very 'you' that makes you 'you'! I fought all this way to you to keep my promise, to not leave you alone, and I did it with no powers and I wasn't daunted, and you know why? Because I held you and your mother's love in my heart, and that is what got me through! If that's not good enough for you and the divine 'monkey on your back,' then fine. I wash my hands of you! Stay here with your god and both of you be damned! Come along, Picard!" And with that, I turned on my heel and started back in the direction I'd come. After only a moment's hesitation, Picard was at my side.

"Stop! *Stop!*" The rage of my son was beyond measure, and lightning bolts crashed to the ground all around us. The smell of ozone was suffocating. I ignored it and kept walking. Picard, for once, followed my lead without comment. We kept moving. . . .

And then I didn't know what happened. One moment I was walking, the next I was hurtling through the air, unable to hear anything, and it was only just before I landed that I realized I'd been struck by lightning. When I hit the ground everything went black.

It might have remained so if I hadn't been startled back to consciousness by the slamming of a fist against my chest. I looked up, and there was Picard leaning over me, and he struck my chest again. I coughed then, and he saw that my eyes were open. He looked at me, a mute query as to my health, and I forced a nod. I sat up, every joint in my body

209

aching. I reached up and felt my hair. It was standing on end. And one of my eyebrows had been seared off. There was a smoldering hole in my shirt from where the lightning had hit. I ignored it and forced myself to stand. I wouldn't have made it if Picard hadn't helped me to my feet. The weather was still incredibly foul, the sky almost solid black, lightning cascading about. My son hadn't moved from where he'd been standing. There was an expression on his face that was an odd combination of defiance and fear.

I licked my cracked lips, tried to speak and got nothing but a dry rattle. I cleared my throat and then called out over the wind. I wanted to make a lengthy speech; I wanted to say something long and memorable and pithy. Ultimately, all I was able to get out was three words. But they were enough to summarize my sentiments on the matter.

"I love you." And then I turn away once more, knowing in my heart that if another lightning bolt struck me it would be the end.

And then I heard his voice, crying out above the storm, crying out as if calling from the abyss.

"Father! Don't go! Don't leave me." He started to run. His arms and legs pumped furiously as he charged across the plain, and incredibly, with each step he took toward me, he shrank a little, as if he were running across the years. The pain, the anger, the anguish evaporating with his every step. And when he leaped into my arms he was the child I remembered, and he was sobbing so violently that it convulsed his little body. "I'm sorry, I'm sorry, I'm sorry, don't go, don't go, I want to stay with you, please, don't go," a torrent of words that I could barely separate one from the other.

I couldn't calm him, and I didn't even try. All I did was hold him tightly, far more tightly than I ever had, and I kept whispering to him over and over that everything would be all right, that everything would work itself out.

"Q, look up!" shouted Picard, and he pointed to the sky.

A massive column of flame was coming toward us, like a tornado of fire. It moved quickly across the plains and bore down on us, and from within came a howling such as I had never heard.

"Sodom and Gomorrah," I heard Picard say.

Was it possible? Was it possible that we were facing something that had once walked the earth and formed the basis of an entire religion? Or were we seeing some imitator who was copying the essence of another, greater being? There were so many possibilities. However, not a single one of them was pertinent to the immediate concern, which should have focused not on theology, but on another, preeminent consideration.

"We've got to get out of here!" I shouted.

"No argument there!" Picard returned, and he was already in motion. I grabbed q, slung him under my arm, and we ran.

Whatever, and his ball of fire, came right after us, voicing its fury. **"You have broken the bargain! Now feel My wrath!"** it howled in biblical fashion.

We reached the tent and the hall of mirrors. I glanced at the reflections. There was nothing. That didn't seem to bode well either.

"Maybe he won't follow us!" q said.

"We can't take that chance," Picard told him.

"That's right, we can't!"

We dashed out the front of the tent and ran as far as our legs could carry us. I risked a glance behind me and saw the tent shaking, quivering wildly. Tears in the fabric were ripping through the upper reaches of the structure. Wind and flames blasted out of the top of the tent, and I knew then that we had a serious problem brewing.

"Keep going!" I shouted.

"Where?"

"Anywhere. Just away from the tent!"

"Where's Mother?" called q. "Maybe she could—?"

"I don't know! I wish I did, but I don't!"

We kept running right through the bazaar, knocking over stands and crashing into people. People already knew something was wrong. Many were on their hands and knees praying in assorted languages, and pointing in the direction of the great tent.

And then the top of the tent blew open, and a fireball leaped heavenward. It paused a moment above the tent, as if looking for its prey, and then started moving . . . toward us.

We ran, and kept on running. All around us was panic, people stampeding this way and that, blocking our path.

"We need someone to push through!" shouted Picard. "I'd give anything to have Data right now!"

"All right," q said, and he snapped his fingers. To the shock of not only Picard but myself, Data appeared in a flash of light. He looked around, a bit confused.

I turned q around and said, "You have your powers?!"

"Sure," he nodded. "You said it yourself . . . the longer you're in a place, the—"

"Get us out of here!" I told him.

The ground began to shake. The fireball bore down on us.

"Hurry up!" I said.

"I'm trying! I'm trying, but it's not working!" he cried out, and he pointed at the fireball. "He's blocking it! He's really mad at me, Father!"

"I think I've figured that out."

I grabbed q and we started moving again, knowing that we were only buying seconds at most. The column of "divine fury" smashed toward us, destroying everything in its path.

The ground was trembling so violently we could barely stand up. Tents, items, people were all yanked heavenward, tumbling about helplessly. I had a brief glimpse of the nagus being hauled into the air, shouting, "Wait! Wait! Let's make a deal!" And suddenly we were at a dead end. A wall of fire as high as a mountain blocked our way. The god had won. I had no cards left to play.

The universe is dying, I thought. *I have my son in my arms, but my wife is still missing. I did everything I could, and it wasn't enough . . . I give up . . . I give up . . . I give up . . .*

And then we were suddenly sliding into the void, the ground melting under us. "Father, don't let go!" shouted q, and I didn't.

And all was blackness.

My next thought was that I was buried alive.

There was dirt everywhere: in my eyes, in my ears, in my mouth, everywhere. I flailed about, trying to pull myself up, and was struck by how soft the dirt was.

Next, I felt a hand clasped firmly onto the back of my shirt, and I was extricated from my shallow grave. It was Data who pulled me out. I was forced to the conclusion that he was a handy fellow to have around. He was covered with dirt too; obviously he'd been in the same situation, but had managed to liberate himself from it far more quickly.

"Have you got him?" I heard Picard say.

"Yes," replied Data. I lay there, on the ground, my heart racing. Then q ran up to me and embraced me, and this time I didn't hesitate to return the embrace, patting him on the back and whispering to him how happy I was to see him.

"Where are we, Father?" asked q.

As was becoming the case far too often, I had absolutely no idea.

It was muggy, though; that was for sure. The air was thick with the humidity. It seemed as if once there had been a jungle here, but the trees had been cut down, and now there was nothing but mud everywhere.

Picard and q were filthy. Apparently Data had been the first to extricate himself before helping the others. I turned to my son and said, "q? Can you clean us off? Can you make us clean?"

He concentrated a moment and then looked rather surprised. "No! I . . . I can't. What's happened, Father? What am I doing wrong? Why can't I . . . ?"

I put a calming hand on his shoulder. "It's nothing you're doing wrong. It happens. It's happened to me ever since I climbed into the crevice. You were fortunate . . . for a time. But I guess your luck has run out." I looked around, feeling a creeping apprehension. "I just hope it hasn't run out for all of us."

"Did you hear that?" Data said suddenly, peering off into the distance.

"Hear what?" I asked, concentrating. And then I heard it as well. It was a distant moaning.

What was even more disturbing was that the moaning had no emotion attached to it, as if it served no purpose except to remind the moaners that they were still alive.

"Father," q said slowly, "I . . . don't think I want to be here."

"Your mother's there," I said.

And q nodded slowly. "I know . . . I feel it too . . . that's why . . ." His voice began to choke up.

". . . Why what, son?"

"That's why I don't want to be here."

I couldn't believe he would say such a thing. I dropped to one knee and looked him in the eye. "What are you saying, q? Are you saying you don't want to help her?"

"No one can help her," he whispered, and he was trembling. "And I . . . I don't want to see her like that."

"Of course we can help her; by just being with her we can help her," I said firmly. "Are we not Q?"

"Are you sure she's here?" asked Picard.

I nodded.

And so we set out to find her.

Considering everything that we had been through, it was a remarkably easy trip. No one tried to attack us or kill us. In fact, we didn't encounter another living soul. There was just the bleak surroundings that might very well have been lovely, once upon a time. But now the vegetation was dead and rotting.

"You know what it's like?" Picard said after a time.

"No, Picard, what's it like?"

"It's as if . . . it's as if all the plant life around here . . . gave up."

"I agree," I said. "But is such a thing possible?"

He shrugged and we continued walking.

As we were drawing closer to the moans, the sounds became less pronounced. Had some people simply stopped moaning? Or had they died?

We then saw a cluster of huts just ahead of us. They were small and wretched, and some of them appeared on the verge of falling over.

People were scattered about on the ground.

They looked desperately ill.

Some of them were huddled together. Others were sitting by themselves, staring off into space. I saw one woman with her legs curled up under her chin, rocking back and forth and singing softly to herself.

Every last one of them was emaciated. They looked like skeletons with aspirations of life. Their clothes were for the most part in shreds. A good number of them were naked, and that was the most horrifying of all. Their eyes were sunken, their skin sallow. A number of them were making the moaning sounds that we'd heard before. Others were silent.

Picard was trying to keep his composure, but he was unable to hide the revulsion that he obviously felt. And Data . . .

Data began to sob.

There were no tears. But the emotions were there, his chest heaving, his eyes closing against the despair he saw all around him. Picard put a firm hand on his shoulder and said, "Steady, Data, steady," but Picard was having a hard time hold himself together as well.

I knew exactly how he felt.

We had come through obstacle after obstacle, challenge after challenge expressly designed to beat us down, to sway us from our course. We'd been battered, bruised, and blown up, and all along the way I had kept hoping that somehow it would get better. That we would find answers. That we would find improvement. But it didn't seem to be so; if anything, it was getting worse.

And this was most definitely the worst yet. The silence was punctuated only by the occasional whimper. The misery that surrounded us was almost too much to take.

"We've hit bottom," whispered Picard, and I knew he was right. This was it. It couldn't get any worse. That wasn't self-delusion; that was just the truth.

I picked a man at random, a man who was just sitting there. An Orion. If anyone had fight in them, it was Orions. He was easily the most scrawny Orion I had ever seen, but Orions were among the most savage of races. Only Klingons surpassed them for sheer nastiness. "You," I said, approaching him kindly. "We need answers. Who's behind this? How long have you been here? How did you come to . . . ?"

He fell over. He wasn't dead; he just fell over. It was simply as if he had run out of whatever meager energy was required to keep him upright, a puppet with his frayed strings cut. And then he looked up at me . . . just looked at me, and then through me. I don't know if he even understood that I had just been talking to him.

And then the ground turned liquid beneath him, like quicksand, and he began to sink. He offered no protest, gave no struggle to free himself. He just sank!

"Get him!" Picard shouted, and Data started forward, but I waved him off. It was too late; what was the point anyway?

The Orion let out one final moan, but it wasn't one of pain; it was relief. He then disappeared beneath the surface without so much as a ripple. I knelt down and touched the place where the Orion had just been, but the ground had firmed up again.

"Madness," I whispered. "Madness."

"Q . . . we have to leave this place," Picard said urgently.

"And go where? You said it yourself, Picard. We've hit bottom. There's nowhere else to go."

"We still have a mission. We still have to—"

"Father!"

My son had spotted something. I looked where he was pointing, and I almost choked.

It was the Lady Q, looking as forlorn as the others. Her hair, long and stringy, covering her nakedness. And her eyes . . .

. . . they had crystallized. She was blind.

"Look away," I whispered to q, but he didn't. Instead he stared, transfixed.

"Is that her?" Picard spoke barely above a hush. I nodded, unable to find words. "My god," said Picard.

I turned and glared at him. "Your god? Your god. Don't talk to me about your god, Picard, because if He should happen to show his face, we're going to have words."

"Mother . . . ?" q called to her. There was no response. "Mother . . . ?" he said again.

Nothing.

"Stay here," I cautioned him, and this time he obeyed. It wasn't that difficult for him to obey, really. I knew that he was terrified by the sight of her. I couldn't blame him. So was I.

Slowly I approached her. I walked carefully, stepping over the bodies of some of the moaning creatures that might once have been considered sentient beings. In the distance, I saw a light begin to shine, but I couldn't make out exactly what it was.

I knelt down next to her. "Q?" I said.

To my surprise—indeed, to my uplifting hope—there was the faintest hint of a smile.

I spoke her name again, and this time she said ever so faintly, "I knew you'd come. I knew, sooner or later I'd hear your voice. Tell me I'm not dreaming."

"You're not dreaming. It's me."

"No, it can't be true," she said. "We're dead. All of us. You're not here. You can't be here."

"I am." I made a move to take her hands in mine but she remained out of reach.

I moved closer, and closer still, and still she seemed just as far as she had before. I felt as if I were caught in Zeno's paradox, halving the distance between us constantly and still never arriving at my destination.

"I am dead. We're all dead," she continued. "It's over. It doesn't matter. None of it matters anymore." And she closed her blind eyes and whispered, "There's just no point."

"Come back to me," I said. "Come back to us. Our son is here . . . I found him. I've been searching for him, just as I've been searching for you. This isn't what you think it is. It's a challenge of wills, ours pitted against whatever sadistic creature has put it all together. But you can overcome it. You have more will than . . ."

The Lady Q pitched forward, sprawling onto the ground . . . and the ground began to dissolve under her, just as it had with the Orion.

I could hear the shriek from q behind me, but it was drowned out by my own cry as I leaped forward, trying to cover the distance between us with one desperate lunge. But it was no use. I hit the ground just short of the edge of the liquefied dirt. I stretched my arm out and shouted, "Here! Reach toward my voice! I'm here! I'm right here! I'm right here!"

She said the worst thing she could possibly say . . . which was nothing, and she continued to sink, faster and faster into the ground. Her legs disappeared beneath the surface. She was making no effort at all.

"Don't you do it!" I howled at her. "Don't you give up on me! On us! I don't care what you're feeling down here, you can overcome it! You can still beat it! I can help you beat it!"

She then spoke, "Nothing . . . I have nothing to live for . . . nothing—"

"That's not true! I love you!" My voice was cracking. I could hear the sobs of my son, begging me to do something. I inched forward on my belly, stretching as far as I could, trying to get to her. I had to get a grip on her, to pull her out. And I said three words that were anathema: *"Picard, help me!"*

But Picard was already in motion, as was Data. They looked hideously far away, though, as far away as I must have been. I pushed my body further forward, so that the entire upper portion was suspended over the grave. I was dangerously overbalanced; if I did manage to snag her, I wouldn't be able to pull her back. I didn't care, though. I was desperate.

I shouted, "Q! I love you! I do! Come back to me! Don't leave me! Don't leave us! Don't! *Don't!*"

The back of her head had already sunk out of sight. Only her face was visible, her face and the hair which framed it. She stared at nothing, and then let out that terrible, rattling moan . . .

. . . and she was gone.

The ground closed up around her and hardened. I had lost her.

A shriek of pain such as I had never voiced rose from my throat, and then I started to claw like a madman at the dirt. Picard and Data were next to me, and q was there as well, and we all ripped away at the soil. We dug for the longest time, until our fingers were caked with filth, our faces, every visible inch of skin was encrusted with grime. But we found nothing. The ground had swallowed her up without a trace. . . .

"Q," Picard said in a subdued voice.

"Not now, Picard! I—"

"Q," and he put a hand on my arm and said firmly, "look around."

I did.

I was just in time to see the last of the poor souls sink beneath the dirt. Sinking into utter despair. The ground closed up behind then . . . and we were alone.

I looked down at the hole that we had dug. It was already deep enough for me to stand in. My son looked at me and began to weep. Even Data was stunned, since the grief around him was beyond his comprehension.

"Q . . . I'm sorry," Picard said.

A hundred responses came to my mind. Almost all of them would have allowed me to give voice to the anger and bitterness that I felt, but the only words that seemed appropriate were . . .

"Thank you, Jean-Luc."

I then held out a hand to my son, who took it firmly. I said nothing. There was nothing left to say.

We stood there for a while, deep in our thoughts, until Picard broke the silence.

"That light over there . . ."

"I saw it."

"Perhaps it . . ."

"Perhaps it what, Jean-Luc?" I asked wearily. "Perhaps it leads to somewhere else, somewhere we can feel more helpless and watch more people die?"

"That is right, yes," said Picard. He cocked an eyebrow. "Why? Do you have a better idea?"

I uttered a laugh tinged with the misery I felt. "No. No, I suppose I don't have a better idea, and I certainly don't want to stay here any longer."

We walked in the direction of the light, and I wondered as we walked along if we were going to encounter the same problem that I had had with trying to touch my Lady Q. But that was not to be the case. We covered the distance with no difficulty. It was almost as if we were meant to get to the source of the light.

Strangely I began to feel my age, and when one has lived for as long as I have, that's a lot of age to feel. It was subtle at first, but after a while every step was harder than the one before. My feet seemed leaden, and I found I literally had to command my legs to operate as I trudged along. I glanced at q and saw how tired and worn he looked. But he was remarkably stoic and didn't complain. I stopped to lift him up with the intention of carrying him the rest of the way, but q squirmed out of my grasp and stood up straight as if he had found new strength. It was quite endearing.

"That's all right, Father," he said firmly. "I can manage on my own."

I had never been more proud of him than I was at that moment. I caught Picard's eye, and he was smiling. For some reason, I was pleased Picard liked my son.

We drew ever closer to the light. However, I found myself caring less and less what we would find when we got there or what we would do when we found it. All I could picture, over and over again, was Lady Q sinking beneath the dirt, embracing oblivion without caring one bit for life. I kept berating myself with "what if's." What if I had gotten there sooner, even by minutes? What if I had convinced her that I was truly alive. What if . . . ?

What if . . . she was right? What if I weren't alive?

I pushed the thought away, but it came roaring back at me no matter how much I tried to keep it at bay.

"I see it," Data said.

"What do you see?"

"A house, Captain. A small house with a white picket fence."

"I see it as well," said Picard, as he squinted into the light.

I could see the house too. A charming little house with a white picket fence and a brick path that led up to the front door.

And then my heart stopped, or leaped out of my chest, or got stuck in my throat, or any other expression of surprise that doesn't begin to do justice at moments like this.

There, standing in the front door of the house was the Lady Q, waving. "Do you see her?" I whispered to q.

"Yes," he said amazed. "She's very pretty. Who is she?"

"Who—?" I didn't understand. "That's . . . that's your mother . . ."

"No, it's not Mother." q was shaking his head. "It's someone else . . . a pretty lady . . . with long black hair . . . she's smiling at me. . . ."

224

Impossible. Perhaps the strain was getting to him as well, poor little guy. "Picard," I said, "do you see her?"

"Vash," murmured Picard.

"What?" I turned to him. "What do you mean? Where?"

"There! Right there!" Picard pointed at the house. This was amazing. I was seeing the Lady Q, my son was seeing some woman he didn't know, and Picard was seeing Vash! I hesitated to think what Data was seeing.

"Vash," he said, "I'm . . . I'm so sorry . . . I'm sorry I wasn't here for you . . . do you see her Q?"

"No. I don't. Apparently I don't need to." I tore my gaze away from the flickering form of Lady Q. "And you don't need to see her either, Picard. She was a victim of this place, just like my wife. At least you were spared the sight of her sinking into her grave. Consider yourself fortunate."

"Fortunate?" Picard looked at me with incredulity. "Fortunate? How can you say that? If I had been here—"

"Nothing would have changed. Nothing would have been any different. I see that now. Nothing we've done has made any difference. It's all been one endless exercise in futility."

"But . . . but that's not true, Father," q said. "What about me? You found me! You . . ."

"Yes, I've found you and that's wonderful, but, honestly, son, I don't think we'll ever get out of here. We're doomed."

"No, we aren't!" q said with fierce determination. "You'll find a way. I know you will. You're Q. You can do anything."

The childlike innocence. The naïveté. Once I would have found it charming, invigorating. Now it simply seemed yet another burden for me to bear, another expectation I could not live up to. I looked back to Lady Q and saw that she was no longer standing in the doorway. She had vanished, and I could tell from Picard's expression that Vash had likewise disappeared.

"Come," I said. "Let's see this farce through to the end, shall we?"

I walked up the brick pathway leading to the front door of the house. When I placed my hand on the doorknob, I paused and wondered what new trap we were walking into and whether I even cared.

I swung open the door.

The room was empty . . . except for four chairs. Four simple metal chairs. There was a door at the far end of the room and I moved toward it. As I walked, I continued to wonder: Is it now? Is it the end? Will I know when it happens? Will I know after it's happened. Will q suffer? Except for him, I really didn't care.

The only thing I wanted was for the end to come quickly.

I made it to the door at the far end and turned the handle— It was locked.

"Data," Picard said, and pointed to the front door.

Data crossed quickly, but not quickly enough. The front door slammed shut. No manner of pushing or prodding would budge it. "It's locked, Captain, and I cannot budge it," he said.

"Very well," said Picard after a moment's thought. "All the door would do is just lead us back outside anyway. I think we . . ."

And he stopped talking. I turned to see what could possibly have caused the loquacious Picard to clam up, and I immediately saw the problem: the front door was gone. We were now in a house with one locked door and one vanishing front door. The situation was not improving.

"Now what?" asked q.

I looked around the room and said, "It doesn't matter."

And I sat down in one of the chairs. I had no strength left in me at all.

Picard walked up to me. "So . . . that's it?" he asked skeptically.

"Yes, Picard," I told him. "That's it. We're done."

"We are not done," Data said. "There is much yet to do. There is . . ."

"No." I shook my head. "There's no point."

"There's your son," Picard said angrily, pointing at q. "He's enough of a point for trying to continue, don't you think?"

I didn't say anything.

"You know, Q, you're fortunate. I have no son . . . no family. In this entire universe, I'm alone. At least you have a son to fight for. I know the loss of Lady Q was a crushing blow . . . but that doesn't mean you have to let yourself be crushed by it."

"Fine, Picard. Whatever you say."

My reply clearly surprised him.

"What do you mean by that?" he said.

"I mean I'm tired of arguing with you. I'm tired of fighting through one pointless obstruction to the next only to find things getting worse and worse."

"That doesn't mean we quit."

"Well, you know what, Picard? Let's say that it does. Let's say that maybe, just maybe, I've lived far more lifetimes than you could possibly conceive. And let's say that maybe, just maybe, I know a bit more about the situation than you do. Picard . . . it's hopeless. All right? Do I need to spell it out for you? You said it yourself, we've hit bottom. And here's a thought: what if we haven't? What if there's worse beyond this? Eh? What if whatever we encounter next makes this . . . this horror seem like a family vacation by comparison? If that's so, I'm not interested in finding out. There's no point, all right? No point at all."

"We need to find out who's behind all this . . ."

"You see, q?" I said to my son as if Picard hadn't spoken. "That's the amazing thing about humans. Their lifetimes are so pathetically short—barely the time it takes for you or me to blow our noses—and yet they will do anything, deny anything, rather than accept when it's over. But fortunately . . . I do. I'm saving us time, aggravation, misery, and more misery."

"In exchange for what?" demanded Picard. "For sitting here? For waiting?"

"Picard . . . one of two things is happening," I said. "Either the universe is ending through entropy . . . or it's ending at the behest of some being or force. In either case, I accept it. All right?" I raised my voice and shouted to the heavens. "I accept it!! Do you hear me? I accept it!" I looked back to Picard. "I refuse to keep running around like a rat in a maze. It's an exhausting and pointless way to spend one's last moments. And I'm just not going to do it."

My voice faltered. It was as if that final speech of mine had drained all the energy from me. I put my face in my hands. I couldn't even stand to look at Picard anymore. I felt q next to me, putting his arms around my leg, and then he hugged my leg tightly—partly out of compassion, I think, and partly out of fear for what was to come.

"Q . . ."

"What?"

"I was thinking . . ."

"Oh joy, oh rapture."

"You are in the depths of despair," Picard said with that annoying degree of authority he always seemed to carry. "If there is another level, it may very well be acceptance. If that is the case . . ."

"Picard . . . I don't care. I just . . . don't care."

And then I stopped talking.

Picard tried to get through to me. He encouraged, he cajoled, he threatened, he stormed . . . he ran the entire gamut of human persuasive techniques, but I simply had nothing left within me with which to respond. I just didn't give a damn. My son knelt mutely next to me, apparently content to watch the back-and-forth . . . except it wasn't really much back-and-forth. Picard would yammer, I would sit, and that was the extent of the discourse.

Finally, even Picard gave up. Data stayed out of it. He was smart.

It took me a while to realize no one had said anything for a while. Picard had dropped into the chair across from mine, apparently exhausted by his efforts. He merely stared at me, shaking his head. He had the air of a man who had given his all and come up short. Seated in the other chair was q. He was watching me rather intently, but there was a look of hopelessness in his eyes as well. Data stood directly behind Picard, as if waiting for further instructions.

"Run out of things to say, Picard?" I inquired.

"There's nothing else to say," he replied.

"Good."

More silence. More of a creeping sense of hopelessness.

There was light within the room, although I had no idea where it was coming from, for there were no windows and no apparent means of illumination. But now the light was slowly starting to fade. Before long, we would be sitting in the dark. Fine. That was fine, too. It didn't really matter. Nothing mattered. More silence.

Then Data spoke up. What he said, however, was not designed to prompt anyone's heart to swell with joy.

"The far wall is 2.343 centimeters closer than it was before."

The three of us looked. Data was right. The wall was getting closer.

"That's not good," said Picard.

The wall continued to move. It did so in utter silence. There was no scraping, no sounds of gears turning; it was all very quiet.

It did not take long for us to realize that if this continued we would soon be crushed.

"We have to do something!" Picard said.

"Why?" I asked.

Picard looked at me with poison in his glare. "I'm a mere human, Q. I don't have the option of simply throwing up my hands and giving in."

"Maybe you're just too stupid, Picard," I said, but I was on my feet as well. I had no idea what the purpose of fighting back was. We were in a clearly hopeless situation, and nothing that we were going to do, no last-ditch effort to combat it, was going to improve it. But I was on my feet anyway!

The wall continued to move toward us. Picard put his hands up against the wall and began to push. Data did the same. It was pointless. It was as much of an exercise in futility as anything else we had encountered. That did not deter Picard and Data in the slightest from pushing against it even harder. If I hadn't held their efforts in so much contempt, I might actually have joined them.

"Q, damn you, get over here!" shouted Picard.

My son looked to me and said nothing. Clearly he was waiting for me to take the initiative. With a sigh I stepped to the center of the wall, and q immediately followed me. I placed my hands against it; then with all my might I pushed.

No luck. My feet kept sliding out from underneath me. I continued to shove back as hard as I could, but I knew in my heart that it was all in vain.

Picard was panting from the exertion, a thin film of sweat covering his head, the dirt caked on his face starting to trickle down in filthy rivulets. "Don't give up!" he shouted. The wall was closer; only a few feet now stood between the back wall and the front. "We can do this!"

"Picard . . . you're an idiot!" I grunted. "It's hopeless! This is it! Don't you understand anything, you foolish human? This is it!"

"You want to know . . . what I understand?" shot back Picard, never slacking in his efforts. "I understand . . . humanity . . . Q! You . . . with all your claims of omniscience . . . you don't understand us today . . . any better than you did . . . when you first met us! I'm human . . . I never stop fighting . . ."

"You will when you're dead," I said as I continued pushing. We were close, so close now to being crushed between the walls.

"Not even then," shot back Picard. "I won't surrender—"

"You surrendered your ship the first time you met me, Picard! So don't get high and mighty on me!"

"I surrendered when I thought there was something to be gained . . . lives to be saved."

The opposite wall was right behind us. We turned, braced our back against the wall, and brought our feet up in a last, pointless endeavor to halt the movement. Data did the same.

And during all this the man was still talking . . . still talking. "But there's . . . no point in surrendering now! Nothing to be gained! No point—!"

"Perhaps," I said. "But sometimes there's nothing to be gained by fighting. And this . . . is one of those times. . . ."

"Q—!"

We were right up against it now—the wall and the locked door. We were being crushed to death. I took q in my arms and tried to protect him. "I'm sorry, Picard . . . I guess you'll just never understand."

I then kissed my boy, closed my eyes, and surrendered to my fate.

And that was when the door sprang open.

We tumbled through, q and I, even as I heard the horrific slam of the two walls together and a nauseating crunch of flesh and bone. We had gotten out. Picard and Data had not been as fortunate. And I . . . I, who should have been relieved to be free of his yammering . . . I felt as if I'd just lost my best friend.

q and I fell forward . . . into a puddle. A pothole, actually, and all around us were shouts and cheers, and the deafening noise of people counting. "Ten . . ." they cried, "nine . . . eight . . ."

There was the honking of horns and a general air of cele-bration.

I looked around in confusion.

We were back in Times Square. Back in the Q Continuum. Back where we had started.

And Q, the blond Q who had aided me in my escape, the one who had been blown out of existence by a bolt of power from above, drove up in his taxi and grinned lopsidedly. "Nice to see you finally accepted the inevitable, Q. You're just in time . . ." He pointed at the huge black ball at the top of the building which was starting to drop, ". . . for the big finale."

Think of the letter "Q." The symbol of our Continuum.

You start at the lower right, and you proceed around it counterclockwise. You travel around and eventually you wind up right back where you started . . . at which point you simply tail off.

I understood. Our letter was a symbol, a very potent symbol. It was a prophetic way of preparing all of us, and me in particular, for this day. This final day. I understood everything now.

"You let me go," I said to the blond Q, "with the full knowledge and understanding of the others. You did it to keep me busy. You were the ones who created that rift . . . and everything in it . . . just to occupy me so that I wouldn't be able to get in the way . . . get in the way of the End, right?"

The chanting was increasing, the other members of the continuum packed in so tightly together that no one could move. "Seven . . . six . . ."

"Perhaps," said Q. "Or perhaps you're giving us too much credit. Perhaps we're really as much in the dark about this as you are. Perhaps in the final analysis . . . there are some things we're simply not meant to understand. We learned long ago to accept that fact, Q. You never did. But perhaps now, finally . . . at the End . . . you have." He shook his head, and there was a hint of sadness on his face. "Accept, Q . . . as

233

we have. She would have wanted you to be an example to your son, to q. Show him. Show him that a truly omniscient being knows where he stands within the universe. It may be the single greatest gift you can give him. It will most certainly be the last."

"Five . . . four . . . three . . ." The ball of a black hole was descending, steadily, unstoppable.

"Is it . . . time, Father?" asked q.

"I . . . I . . ."

I looked around at the joyous faces of the other Q, individuals had known for eternity. They were at peace and I envied them. I looked back at q. "I . . . think so, son. Yes."

"Two . . . one . . . Happy Endings!" everyone screamed.

The black hole erupted. It expanded in a flash, and all of reality began to twist and distort. Through the explosion I could see something at the center of the hole. It was . . . it was . . . the crevice, the pit, the void . . . the drain! The giant "drain" that the universe was flushing down. Everything was turning, slowly at first and then faster and faster.

The Q Continuum began to split apart, and it wasn't just us, it was everything, everywhere, in every corner of the universe. Those who understood what was happening and those who didn't, those who were attuned to the cosmos and those who had been simply going about their business, were swept away. It was the End, no mistaking it this time. The End of Everything!

My son held on to me as the Q Continuum broke apart around us. We watched the buildings of Times Square dissolve and swirl away into the drain. I saw members of the Continuum happily hurtling themselves into oblivion. Everything around us was being torn asunder. But still we held our ground. It was as if it we were being saved for last.

My son looked up at me. "Father," he said, and though he

spoke softly, I could still hear him perfectly. "Father . . . I am very afraid. I . . . do not want to accept. But if you say I should . . . if you say it's all right . . . then I will. Tell me what to do, Father. I need to know."

I looked into his eyes and could see reflections of the Continuum spiraling away, as reality itself from every edge of the universe began to fold in upon itself.

I have no recollections of my own beginnings, not really. I feel as if I have always been. So, in a strange way my sense of self was not really personal. However, when I stared into the face of my son, I saw myself as if for the first time. I felt a beginning, a first, a personal me start to emerge. This was my universe too, I felt. I helped create it. And this is not the way I want it to End. Oh, I knew everyone else wanted me to lie down and give up . . . and I had tried to, but that's not me! Whatever was doing this, for whatever reason it was happening, I wanted to make sure at least someone objected. Someone stood up proud and said . . .

"No!!!" "No!!!" "No!!!"

"No!" To the great swirling maelstrom above.

"No!" To the abyss.

"No!" To the capriciousness of it all.

"No!" To everything I had ever believed. For I had been certain that we of the Q were the ultimate power. That we were alone in the universe. But now, staring into the void, I found I could no longer subscribe to that belief. Because it just made no sense, no sense at all, to believe that this was completely, utterly random. It had to be the work of some great mad being. Mad with grief, just as I. Mad at the death of my wife. Mad at the death of Picard and Data. Mad that my son would never see another day. Mad at the hideous fate the held us in its grip.

"I will never accept!" I howled into the storm. **"Denial,**

anger, bargaining, despair, all of these I've know and experienced, but acceptance? Never! I will never go quietly into that good night! I will rage, rage against the coming of the End, I will howl against oblivion, I will spit into the face of the void with the last bit of strength I have!" I held my son close to my chest. "You want me? Come and get me! Show me your face! Come and get me, and expect a fight in the bargain! Whoever and wherever and whatever you are, I will never give up! Never! From the pits of oblivion I will rise up and strike at you. I will never accept! I am Q, I am forever!"

I stretched out my hand and a bottle appeared . . . a bottle . . . with this manuscript tucked inside. A testimony to all I had been through, and what we have suffered.

"These! These are my terms! Read them and weep, and know you that I, Q, am the trickster. I, Q, am the lord of chaos. I, Q, defy you to the last, and if you think you can stop me just by ending the universe, then I'm here to tell you that you're going to have to do better than that!"

And as the howling enveloped us from all sides, I drew my arm back and hurled the bottle with all my strength into the mouth of the abyss. At that second my son q was torn from my grasp, and the bottle tumbled, end over end and into the heart of maelst

John de Lancie and Peter David

Heh

Heh heh . . .

Heeee heh heh heh . . .

She realized it had been ages since she had laughed. It was good. It was good to laugh. It made her forget herself for a moment; it made her feel light and fun and . . . attractive.

"I should have known, though," she said, beginning to enjoy the sound of her voice after all this time. "I should have known . . . if anyone could move me to laughter . . . it would be you, trickster."

She rose from her place on the beach, where the waters lapped against her legs, and stretched. In one hand she held the bottle, and in the other the manuscript. She started to walk. Where? She knew where because, naturally . . . she knew everything. She knew what she would find. She knew who would be waiting. So she just walked, enjoying the feel of the water running between her toes.

And sure enough, after a time, she found him there. The boy lying on the beach, washed ashore like a piece of driftwood. He was unconscious, but breathing. She clothed herself in sea foam because it pleased her. She had been naked for so long, but she felt it somehow suited the moment. She knelt next to the boy and shook him.

He coughed several times, opened his eyes, and then looked up wearily. "You . . ." he managed to say.

"Give yourself time to gain your strength," she said calmly.

He took her advice and slowly pulled himself into a sitting

position at her feet. "I saw you . . . in that last place . . . outside the little house . . . you smiled at me. . . ."

"Yes," she said.

"Why were you there?"

"It pleased me to be there."

"You're very pretty. You have very nice eyes. They're very blue."

"Thank you." She tilted her head, regarded him thoughtfully. "You have much of your father about you. Some of your mother, too, but . . . mostly your father."

"You know my parents? My father?"

"Oh yes. I've had my eye on your father for quite some time now. We met once, face to face, although he didn't understand the significance of the meeting. He didn't know who I was. He thinks he knows so much. He knows so little."

"He knows everything," the boy said, challenging her to refute him.

"I believe you." She smiled.

They sat silently for a time. "Now what?" said the boy.

"Do you know," she told him after giving the matter some thought, "that if only one decent man had been found, Sodom and Gomorrah would have been saved?"

"Who are they?"

"They were cities."

"Oh." He eyed her curiously. "Are you saying my father is a decent man?"

"My, my. You're quick to grasp, aren't you? Clever boy." She ruffled his hair affectionately. Then she said, "It's not quite that simple. Decent, perhaps . . . but also stubborn and irritating. What pride! Fighting to the last . . . and in the end . . . he acknowledged. He even . . . prayed, after a fashion. A rather belligerent prayer, I'll grant you that, but a prayer nonetheless. That wasn't easy for him. And . . . he made me laugh. I had forgotten what that felt like. I think I have forgotten . . . a great many things, more than I would have thought possible. I think I shall live for another day."

"I don't understand."

"Good lad. Remarkable lad. That's the eternal and internal conflict about omniscience, you see. Only those who know they don't know can truly know."

"I still don't think I understand."

"That's all right. Neither do I. And I've been at it longer than you."

She took the last page of the manuscript, produced a pen, and wrote four words on the back of the page. Then she rolled it up and put it back into the bottle, sealing it in with the cork.

"My father made that," he said. "He threw it—"

"I know. And I'm throwing it back. And you too, I'm afraid. Selfishly, I wouldn't mind keeping you with me. But I'll have to settle for keeping you," and she tapped her chest, "locked up in here . . . safe and sound."

She then scooped up sand, hardened it, and fashioned a small boat the size of the boy. Remarkably, it floated. She then handed the bottle to the boy and said, "Here. Get in. Take this and be off with you."

"But—"

"No buts." And she kissed him lightly on the forehead and helped him onto the boat. "Tell your father . . ." She stopped to think.

The boat was already drifting out to sea.

"Tell him what?" called the boy. But he was beginning to feel sleepy, although he had no idea why. He had felt so awake just a moment ago. "What should I tell him?" he called languidly.

"Tell him . . . that Melony says hello." And she blew him a

kiss. He fell asleep immediately and she watched him until he was gone. Then she laughed once more and enjoyed the sound of herself laughing. Enjoyed . . . herself.

She thought it extremely ironic, and amusing, that her prayers had been answered. Especially when she didn't even know that she'd been praying.

She laughed once more, allowed her dress to dissolve back into sea foam, and walked away . . .

. . . and vanished into the universe.

The deck of the *Hornblower* bobbed up and down slowly as Picard raised his head and looked around in confusion. The sea was as smooth and blue as it had been at the beginning of their fishing trip. The sky was cloudless. Nothing seemed amiss.

He looked down at himself. His skin was clean, with no cuts, bruises, or gashes. He was, as near as he could tell, perfectly fine.

"Data, Data . . . ?"

"I am down here, Captain." Data's voice came from belowdecks. "I think you should see this, sir."

Picard rose on shaky legs and made his way below. Data was pointing toward the back of the cabin. There, on the floor, was me . . . and the Lady Q. Picard thought we were dead. Then again, until moments ago, he had thought himself dead as well. "Q," he said.

I blinked and slowly sat up. I put a hand to my chest as if checking in disbelief that I was there. I propped myself up on one elbow and looked around the cabin. When I saw Lady Q lying beside him, I cried out.

She sat up, and we embraced with such ferocity that it moved Picard to tears. Finally he said in a very low voice, "Q . . ."

"Yes?" we said in unison.

"What happened? The last thing I remember . . ."

"We all have different last things that we remember," I said. "Where are we?"

"On the holodeck of the *Enterprise* . . . at least I believe so," Picard said.

"Where's my son?"

"I have not seen him," Data said. "But I have not searched the entirety of—"

"Then what are we waiting for?" said Lady Q. "Now! Right now!"

Under ordinary circumstances, Picard would have taken issue, but these were hardly ordinary circumstances. They searched the ship from stem to stern but found nothing.

Nothing.

The Lady Q collapsed on the railing; I stood behind her, holding her by the shoulders, comforting her . . . and then suddenly I spotted something. "There!" I cried out, pointing. "Out there!"

Everyone looked, and sure enough, floating on the water was a small boat, and on it was q. He was asleep on his back, and he was clutching something to his chest.

"Data! Hard to port! Bring us . . . Oh, *to hell with it, end program!*" This time the holodeck obediently disengaged. The water, the *Hornblower,* all of it vanished, leaving me, the Lady Q, Picard, and Data on the glowing holodeck floor.

And q was there as well. But incredibly, he was still in the little boat, and the bottle was still in his hand. Why they hadn't vanished, Picard couldn't even begin to guess. Then again, nothing had made any sense, so why should this be any different?

My wife and I ran to the boy, and Lady Q scooped him up into her arms. He opened his eyes wearily, not quite understanding who he was looking at, at first. When he did, he squeezed her tightly around the neck. The bottle fell to the floor with a thud but did not break.

"What happened, Father?" whispered q. "What did it all mean?"

"I don't know," I said. "And I don't know if we ever will." I picked up the bottle and stared at it. "There's a piece of paper in this bottle."

"It's a note. The lady wrote a note."

"Lady?" I said. "What lady . . . ?"

"She said . . . she knew you. That her name was Melony."

Picard had never seen me look as stunned as I did at that moment. "Is the name familiar to you, Q?"

"From centuries ago . . . Times Square . . . but she . . ."

I stared at the bottle once more . . . and then turned to Picard. "Here. You open it, Picard."

"Why me?"

"Picard," I said slowly, "I've spent my entire existence looking for answers. I think . . . there's an answer in this bottle . . . and I'm not certain I'm quite ready to receive it."

Picard didn't pretend to understand. Instead he uncorked the bottle and pulled out the paper. He unrolled it and read what was written on it. Four words. Just four little words.

Picard smiled.

"Actually, Q . . ." he said gently, "I think you should read it. It may be the only answer you'll ever get." He handed the note to me. I took it and read the message.

"Let there be light."

Look for STAR TREK fiction from Pocket Books

Star Trek®: The Original Series

Star Trek: The Next Generation®

Novelizations

Star Trek: Deep Space Nine®

Star Trek: Voyager®

Star Trek®: New Frontier

Star Trek®: Invasion!

Star Trek®: Day of Honor

#1 • *Ancient Blood* • Diane Carey
#2 • *Armageddon Sky* • L.A. Graf
#3 • *Her Klingon Soul* • Michael Jan Friedman
#4 • *Treaty's Law* • Dean Wesley Smith & Kristine Kathryn Rusch
The Television Episode • Michael Jan Friedman
Day of Honor Omnibus • various

Star Trek®: The Captain's Table

#1 • *War Dragons* • L.A. Graf
#2 • *Dujonian's Hoard* • Michael Jan Friedman
#3 • *The Mist* • Dean Wesley Smith & Kristine Kathryn Rusch
#4 • *Fire Ship* • Diane Carey
#5 • *Once Burned* • Peter David
#6 • *Where Sea Meets Sky* • Jerry Oltion
The Captain's Table Omnibus • various

Star Trek®: The Dominion War

#1 • *Behind Enemy Lines* • John Vornholt
#2 • *Call to Arms...* • Diane Carey
#3 • *Tunnel Through the Stars* • John Vornholt
#4 • *...Sacrifice of Angels* • Diane Carey

Star Trek®: The Badlands

#1 • Susan Wright
#2 • Susan Wright

Star Trek® Books available in Trade Paperback

Omnibus Editions
　　Invasion! Omnibus • various
　　Day of Honor Omnibus • various
　　The Captain's Table Omnibus • various
　　Star Trek: Odyssey • William Shatner with Judith and Garfield
　　　Reeves-Stevens

Other Books

STAR TREK
THE EXPERIENCE
LAS VEGAS HILTON

Be a part of the most exciting deep space adventure in the galaxy as you beam aboard the U.S.S. Enterprise. Explore the evolution of Star Trek® from television to movies in the "History of the Future Museum," the planet's largest collection of authentic Star Trek memorabilia. Then, visit distant galaxies on the "Voyage Through Space." This 22-minute action packed adventure will capture your senses with the latest in motion simulator technology. After your mission, shop in the Deep Space Nine Promenade and enjoy 24th Century cuisine in Quark's Bar & Restaurant.

- -

Save up to $30

Present this coupon at the STAR TREK: The Experience ticket office at the Las Vegas Hilton and save $6 off each attraction admission (limit 5).

Not valid in conjunction with any other offer or promotional discount. Management reserves all rights. No cash value.
For more information, call 1-888-GOBOLDLY
or visit www.startrekexp.com.
Private Parties Available.

CODE:1007a   EXPIRES 12/31/00

HAPPY HOLIDAYS
FROM NEELIX AND

Cream the butter and brown sugar and beat in the whole egg, flour, vanilla, cinnamon, and salt. Roll the dough and chill in your refrigerator for about 15 minutes while you preheat your oven to 375 degrees. When the dough has been chilled, break off individual 1-inch pieces and roll into small balls. Lightly beat egg white in a small bowl until it's slightly frothy, not membranous. Next, fill a small bowl with granulated sugar. Coat the balls in the egg white and then roll them in sugar to coat them. Now arrange them on a flat greased baking sheet and make a slight impression in each with your finger—or you can use the broad end of a chopstick or even a thimble. Drop a small amount of raspberry or strawberry jelly or preserves into each depression and close over the depression with the cookie dough. Bake at 375 degrees for about 10 minutes. Allow to cool before serving.

These make incredible Christmas and holiday gifts and can become a holiday tradition. Wrap them in fancy paper and bows for friends and neighbors. Yields two dozen cookies.

THE STAR TREK® COOKBOOK
Star Trek cuisine for the earthbound chef!

HAPPY HOLIDAYS
FROM NEELIX AND

KOMAR COOKIES *from the* STAR TREK COOKBOOK

When I was courting Kes, I was a lot leaner—in fact I spent a few years as a swimsuit model on Talax—but now I've filled out, and why not? I always say, "Beware the skinny cook." One of the reasons I've gained a little weight is this dish created by the Komar. They live in a nebula and feed off the neural energy of other species. They're not real nice, but they make a great cookie. They don't bake theirs—they zap the dough with a magnetodynamic TL 5 solar-photox blast, but you don't have to do that, unless you know how. The dough is made from rattle fern caviar, Turian stardust, and Betelgeuse butter. The Komar also add wineworm blood, but I think this detracts from the already intense taste.
ADAPTED FOR 20th CENTURY KITCHENS

1 cup all purpose flour
1/2 cup (1 stick) of butter
1/2 cup light brown sugar
1 egg

1 egg white
1 tsp. cinnamon
1/2 tsp. vanilla extract
1/4 tsp. salt

granulated sugar, as needed for coating
raspberry or strawberry jelly or preserves

THE STAR TREK® COOKBOOK
The official cookbook from <u>Star Trek</u>'s first chef!